# *What We May Be*
## *The New Hope Series, Book II*

Also by Gretchen Craig

**NOVELS**

*Here Will I Remain*
(The *New Hope* Series, Book I)

*Always & Forever*
(The Plantation Series, Book I)
*Ever My Love: A Saga of Slavery and Deliverance*
(The Plantation Series, Book II)
*Evermore: A Saga of Slavery and Deliverance*
(The Plantation Series, Book III)
*Elysium: A Saga of Slavery and Deliverance*
(The Plantation Series, Book IV)

*Tansy*
*Crimson Sky*
*Theena's Landing*
*The Lion's Teeth*
*Livy: A Love Story*

**SHORT STORY COLLECTIONS**
*The Color of the Rose*
*Bayou Stories: Tales of Troubled Souls*
*Lookin' for Luv: Five Short Stories*

# What We May Be

*The New Hope Series, Book II*

Gretchen Craig

# What We May Be
*The New Hope Series, Book II*

# Characters
# in the *New Hope* Series

*What We May Be, Book II*

**Sister Joelle**, a novice
**Sister Bernadette**, an older nun
**Father Xavier**, a priest at Fort Louis
**Giles Travert**, a settler; his children, **Rosalie, Isabel,** and **Felix**; wife **Bella** is deceased
**Seraphina**, one of the new brides
Other women sent to the New World to marry colonists: **Rachel, Simone, Nicole, Harriet, Emmeline, Cecile, Miranda, Sarah**

*Characters who also appear in*
*Here Will I Remain, Book I*

**Catherine de Villeroy,** granddaughter of a powerful nobleman. Catherine's greedy cousin drugged, kidnapped, and shipped her to the New World where she married **Jean Paul Dupre.**
**Jean Paul Dupre**, a former musketeer. He was unjustly accused of murder and fled France.
**Agnes,** a bookseller's daughter. Her father sold her into prostitution to pay his debts. In the New World, she married **Valery Villiers.**
**Valery Villiers**, a former musketeer who got into trouble for sleeping with the wrong man's wife and so fled France.
**Marie Claude,** a country girl disappointed in her hope to become a Parisian seamstress. She chose prostitution over starvation, and married a hateful man, **Leopold Joubert.**
**Thomas, Simon and Remy**, slaves of **Leopold Joubert**
**Laurent Laroux**, in love with **Fleur**, a Biloxi native.
**Akecheta**, chief of the Biloxi tribe
**Mato**, son of the chief
**Fleur**, Mato's sister
**Colonel Blaise**, commander of Fort Louis

# Historical Note

Imagine an old map of North America divided into three territories, British in the east, Spanish in the west, and French in a huge swath in the middle. By 1682, New France stretched from the Great Lakes to the Gulf of Mexico and from the Appalachians to the Rockies. Because Louis XIV was on the throne, the French named this territory *la Louisiane française*: Louisiana.

*What We May Be* is the story of French settlers in the lower reaches of Louisiana, on what is now the Mississippi Gulf Coast. Biloxi natives already inhabited the area and had an intricate civilization established long before the French arrived, but to the newcomers, Louisiana was a wilderness to be tamed and exploited. These hardy souls braved an unfamiliar climate, exotic beasts, and thick jungle in order to clear the land and make their fortunes.

As you might expect, the first colonists were nearly all men. Lonely men. The Church at times disapproved of liaisons with native women, at other times allowed it, but at last the French court decided what the French settlers needed was French women.

Over a few decades in the early 1700s, a number of French ships delivered wives-to-be to the colonies both in the far North (Quebec) and in the lower Mississippi valley. These women are best-known as casket-girls after the small chests they carried into their new lives. Many of today's Canadian and Louisianan families proudly trace their ancestry back to a casket girl sent over from France.

Book One of the *New Hope Series, Here Will I Remain,* was the story of the women who were taken from the prisons and asylums and sent to Louisiana.

Book Two, *What We May Be,* continues their story. In addition, a second voyage of the *New Hope* brings young women from convents and orphanages to join their fallen sisters in building a new world in Louisiana.

# Prologue

*Spring 1721*
*A convent outside Paris*

Idly stroking Jasper's fur, Joelle leaned on the windowsill to gaze down on the lane below the convent. Over the years, she had named everyone on Rue des Boulangers. The laundress, for instance, was Madame Laramie, and here she came, sailing down the lane with a basket of linens on her head. Oh, no. That gang of ragamuffin boys was bearing down on her, dashing and weaving around carts and people. If they bumped Madame Laramie . . . oh! down goes the basket, all those white linens spilled into the mud.

"Sister Joelle!"

She startled and whirled around with guilt surely written all over her face.

"Whatever do you see out that window to make you forget your duties?" Sister Bernadette scolded. "Are those stockings darned? They are not, I am quite sure."

"No, Sister. Not all of them."

"Well, put them aside for now. Mother Superior wants to see us."

"Mother Superior?"

"That's what I said. Hurry now."

Why would Mother Superior want to see her? She hadn't even taken her vows yet. Had she heard about the mittens she tossed down to the rag man last winter? She shouldn't have done it, she supposed, the mittens having been knitted for Sister Agnes. But the rag man was so poor and he looked so cold that morning.

"Is it because of the mittens?" Joelle asked in a low voice.

"Mittens? What mittens? Oh, gracious child, it has nothing to do with mittens."

"Then what?"

1

"You will pester me to death, Sister. I don't know what she wants, do I?"

Sister Bernadette knocked, waited for the muted "Come," and Joelle followed close behind her into Mother's office. Father Anton stood with hands behind his back, looking like a haughty raven with his black robe, his beady eyes and sharp nose.

The priest had never spoken to Joelle before, but now she had been called before Mother Superior *and* Father Anton. If it weren't about the mittens, Joelle wondered, what else could she have done? Standing before Mother Superior's desk, Sister Bernadette folded her hands at her waist so Joelle did the same.

No one spoke as the priest looked each of them over, wimple to shoes. Joelle twisted her fingers hidden in the long sleeves and felt the guilt rising in her even though she could think of nothing she had done more sinful than the mittens.

"The older one," he said. "Heavy, isn't she? The heavy ones don't do so well in the heat, you know. And gray-haired under the cap, no doubt."

"Sister Bernadette is quite fit, I assure you, Father. She works in the gardens and she runs up and down these stone stairs all day long seeing to the novitiates and her other duties."

"Hm," he said. His eyes turned to Joelle. "How old is the young one?"

"Nineteen."

"Why hasn't she taken her vows yet? She's been here since she was, what, five? Is something wrong with her?"

Joelle flushed. Maybe something was wrong with her. Sister Marguerite and Sister Abigail had both become nuns more than a year ago, but Sister Bernadette had told Mother Superior that Joelle wasn't ready. She'd cried into her thin pillow for days, but one did not argue with Sister Bernadette.

"There is nothing wrong with her, Father. I simply have no wish to hurry the girls. It is a life-time commitment, and some novitiates need maturity to find their calling."

"And these are the two you have chosen, Mother?" Father Anton's gaze raked them over once more, clearly not impressed with either of them.

"Yes, Father," Mother said, her jaw firming. "Sister Bernadette has years of experience guiding young women here at the convent and will do well ministering to your brides-to-be.

Sister Joelle, well . . . she has been a great help to Sister Bernadette in this past year, has she not, Sister?"

Sister Bernadette blinked, and Joelle wondered if she knew what she'd been asked.

"Yes, Mother. Of course," she finally answered.

Father Anton blew out a sigh. "The young one is evidently of little use here, and I suppose she can take her vows over there. Very well. I'll leave it to you to make the arrangements, Mother. Have them ready in one hour." With that, Father Anton swept out, his black robe swirling around his ankles.

There seemed to be more air in the room now that he was gone. Joelle breathed in, but kept her eyes dutifully lowered. And waited. She dared a glimpse up at Mother and found her studying her.

"Sister Joelle. Sister Bernadette. You have been chosen for a great duty."

Sister Bernadette drew in a sharp breath. Was that a happy breath, or the opposite?

"You are aware France has a colony in Louisiana? We have claimed a vast territory, and to hold it, French men must build homes and towns, farms and . . . families."

Joelle had never heard of Louisiana. In fact, all she knew of the world beyond the convent walls was what she could see outside her window.

"Therefore," Mother continued, "our young king's ministers have decreed the men settling the new territory need wives. A ship, the *New Hope*, will be taking twenty young women, some from the orphanage, some from here at the convent, to Louisiana. These girls are not nuns, of course, nor are they meant to be, but they will need the guidance and protection of Holy Sisters on so long a voyage, and no doubt once they have arrived as well. The two of you will accompany them."

"But isn't that in . . . ?"

"Yes, Sister Bernadette. It's in the New World."

"But we will return to France, yes?"

Joelle heard the tremble in Sister Bernadette's voice and felt the fear leap into her own heart.

"No, Sister." Mother Superior's voice was firm. "Father Xavier is alone there and he needs assistance. You will make a home for him and for yourselves and will continue to see to the young women you escort across the ocean." Mother leaned back in her chair. "Later in the year, perhaps we will send more young women, and perhaps the two novices you have just begun to work with. It is an honor, you understand, to serve God and your king in this way." Mother stood up, ending the interview. "You may go gather your things."

Joelle followed Sister Bernadette into the hallway. All she could think was what about Jasper? Who would sneak him a saucer of milk if she were not here to do it? Who would ever seek out her touch if Jasper never pushed his head under her hand to be petted? Joelle swallowed. These were unworthy thoughts. If Mother Superior chose her to --

Sister Bernadette threw her apron over her face and burst into sobs.

Alarmed, Joelle put a hand on her sleeve. "Sister?"

"I have not set foot outside this convent in nearly forty years," she said as she struggled to control herself. "How am I to sail all the way across an ocean?"

Joelle blinked and then stared at this woman who had been a stalwart guide and companion all her life. If even Sister Bernadette was overcome . . . Joelle beat down a surge of anxiety. How was she to leave all her friends on Rue de Boulanger, well, not friends, of course, but all the familiar faces she watched from her window?

Sister Bernadette wiped her eyes. "Excuse me, Sister. I must ask God's forgiveness for these selfish thoughts. I will find you in ten minutes. See if you can get one more stocking darned before I come for you. Then we will collect our things."

Nearly numb with the enormity of what was happening, Joelle returned to her window in the work room, the stockings forgotten. She leaned out the window to see Rue des Boulangers one last time. The butcher's son, a kind boy, stopped a moment to pet the puppies and laugh with the baker's two little girls. What a fine man he would make, and maybe one of these girls would fall in love with him someday and bear him many children. With a pang, she wished she could see which girl he would choose for his own.

She raised her hand as if to wave goodbye, but of course the people in Rue des Boulangers did not know her, didn't even know she watched them from this window. No one knew her but the sisters here in the convent.

As she gazed on the scene below, Joelle experienced something she hardly recognized -- a tingle of excitement. She was leaving these safe walls. She would meet new people, new faces. Perhaps she would live among people instead of watching, always watching, from far away.

# French Louisiana

*The Gulf Coast*
*June 1721*

# Chapter One

*Daisy Shopping*
*First Sunday*

Giles Travert was neither short nor tall, neither handsome nor plain. What made him remarkable was that three little children followed in his wake as if they were his ducklings.

Rosalie, the eldest, held a string in her hand which was tied to her little sister Isabel's wrist and then to her little brother Felix's wrist. Giles was quite satisfied that thus trussed, his offspring would not wander off while he was about his business.

That business this particular Sunday was to have a look at the wives-to-be recently arrived from France aboard the *New Hope*. It was time he found a mother for his children.

"Papa," Rosalie said with her queenly eight year old impatience. "Papa, you must take smaller steps. Felix can't keep up."

Giles turned and looked with dismay at his youngest picking himself up from the dirt. "Ah, Felix. I beg your pardon, young man." With deft fingers, he released Felix from the string, handed Rosalie his straw hat, and to Felix's great glee, swung the boy to his shoulders. Felix immediately placed his grimy hands on Giles's forehead and suggested, "Go faster, faster, Papa."

"Son, there are times when a man's dignity is more important than a romp. See all the pretty ladies?"

Felix looked.

Rosalie and Isabel looked.

1

"I want the prettiest one," Isabel said.

"If you tripped and skinned your knee, who would you want to bandage it? The prettiest lady or the kindest?"

"The prettiest," Isabel said.

Giles laughed. "We'll see."

The young women were plainly dressed, but even so they seemed like daisies to Giles. Twenty ladies, he'd heard, had come over on the second voyage of the *New Hope* bearing girls of good character. Gentlemen from up and down the bayous around Fort Louis had this Sunday and three more to get to know the daisies and hope one of them would choose him to wed.

Giles had no great confidence he could entice a young woman to choose not only an ordinary man like himself but also three small children. Still, he needed a wife, and the children needed a mother. For now, with the colony still struggling to establish itself in Louisiana, these were the only women available. And so he would try.

Several dozen men and the lovely ladies they came to peruse, and be perused by, occupied the acre or two of open ground around the fort. Most of the women stood in groups of four or five, far more comfortable for them, Giles was sure. It could not be easy for girls who had grown up sheltered in convents and church-run orphanages to be surrounded by all these men.

Here and there a woman had abandoned her companions to stand alone, invariably surrounded by admirers. Giles wondered if he would like a woman who was so bold. At any rate, these stout-hearted mademoiselles deserved a look.

The first solo female was listening closely to Jacques Anton as if he had a lick of sense. The man reeked of bear grease which he swore kept the mosquitoes from biting. Did she have no sense of smell? Her eyes flickered over him, his girls, and Felix on his shoulders and moved back to Jacques. Apparently not interested in children.

Giles was content to mosey around the grounds for an overall view of the ladies, and he might as well acknowledge it, his competition. There was Beau Gervais, handsome devil. He would have no trouble attracting a bride. And Marc Blaine, not handsome, but graced with fine manners. He must be one of the gentry's third or fourth sons to find himself here in this wilderness.

2

Well, Giles had neither looks nor grace, but he did have a loving heart and a strong back. And three fine children. He stifled a sigh. Why would a very young woman, and none of these daisies seemed more than twenty, choose him?

He led his children past another singleton girl entertaining three gentlemen. Pretty girl. She seemed to enjoy flirting with the men. Seemed quite good at it, in fact. Not what he was looking for.

The suitors were not the only men in evidence. During the week, everyone toiled from dawn to sunset trying to push the wilderness back and create a farmstead, but on Sundays, Fort Louis hummed with settlers who'd come in to attend mass, to trade, to socialize. Under an ancient oak, Giles's friends Laurent Laroux and Jean Paul Dupre stood watching the marriage mart.

"Bonjour," Laroux said. "Come to find a bride, have you, Giles?"

"I have."

"And a mama for us," Isabel said, taking Laroux's hand and swinging his arm. His youngest girl had from the first time she saw Laurent Laroux decided he was the most wonderful of men. Giles suspected it had something to do with his curly black hair and handsome face as well as the obvious enjoyment he took in her.

Laroux touched the tip of her nose. "What a lucky lady, to become your mama."

Jean Paul nodded at the young women scattered around the yard. "Does one lady in particular catch your fancy, Giles?"

Giles cast his eye over the women and sighed. "I haven't spoken to any of them yet. What we need is a kind woman, do we not, Rosalie?"

"And a pretty one, too," Isabel said.

With a smile, Giles shook his head and nodded toward the wives gathering under the pine trees. "Is Catherine over there?"

Jean Paul's eyes lit when he found the tall blonde talking animatedly with the other women. He was a changed man since he married. Morose and secretive and unsociable, that's how Giles would have described him a year ago, but his bride had penetrated the reserve that had walled him in. Somehow, against the odds, Jean Paul had fallen in love with his wife, and she with him.

Giles hated the pang of envy he felt to see Jean Paul's eyes on Catherine. He and Bella had been in love like this. Sometimes, when the children were asleep, he ached with loneliness. But, he reminded himself, he had their children, his and Bella's, to love and care for. That was the Lord's blessing if anything ever was.

"Catherine and the others have a school of sorts. To teach each other what they've learned. Today," Jean Paul said with evident pride, "Catherine will show them how to make shampoo from berries."

What a mixed up world it was, Giles thought. If the stories were true, that Catherine was the granddaughter of the great comte de Villeroy, then it was a fine irony that she was here, showing her friends from the streets and prisons of Paris how to make shampoo.

Next to her stood Madame Joubert, tall as a man, probably taller than Giles himself. Rumor was that she'd killed her husband only a few weeks ago. Hadn't she been seen with the marks of a severe beating about that time? Giles didn't suppose the rumors were true, but he had met Monsieur Joubert, and if she had killed him, he likely had it coming.

"And what of you?" Giles asked Laroux. "Do you not need a wife for yourself?"

Ah, that was a tactless question. Giles had seen Laroux with the young Biloxi woman, showing every sign of being smitten. But when Laroux eventually went back to France, as he planned, he could hardly take a native wife with him.

"Not me, Giles. I will, however," Laroux said with a grin, "be glad to help you choose yours."

Giles laughed. "I already have three to please besides myself."

Rosalie tugged at his sleeve. "Papa, can we have a drink?" She pointed to a table set up under the pines where the younger of the two nuns stood with water bucket and ladles.

"Of course." Giles nodded to his friends and let Rosalie lead him to the table.

"Sister," he said in greeting. He'd talked with Sister Bernadette last week, an older, rather stern nun. He couldn't remember this sister's name. "I have a thirsty crew here."

He lifted Felix from his shoulders and helped him drink. Isabel eased around the table and leaned into the nun's skirts. Poor little thing was starved for a woman in her life.

Giles wracked his brain to remember the nun's name. Something to do with Christmas. Noelle! No, Sister Joelle. "Isabel, don't crowd the sister."

"Oh." The young nun turned a shining face to him. "She is not crowding me." She looked at all three children. "I saw you in mass last Sunday. You were sitting very quietly. That is not easy to do, is it?"

"Papa said if we made a fuss he would feed us to the alligators," Rosalie said, as if that were a perfectly reasonable consequence of fidgeting in church.

Giles rolled his eyes. Oh, good. Now the sister would think he was a monster. But no, she laughed. This young woman wasn't like the nuns Giles remembered from his youth, full of starch, frowns, and scolds.

Isabel stretched up to whisper in the nun's ear. "Will you be our maman?"

Giles was sure anyone within twenty feet could hear that whisper.

"Oh," the sister said, flustered. "I can't."

She probably flushed easily with that fair skin, Giles thought.

"I'm sorry, Sister. My children had not seen a nun before you and Sister Bernadette arrived. I will explain to them. Thank you for the water." He held out his hand for Felix and Isabel to come to him. Felix came, but Isabel did not.

"Please, Papa?"

He didn't understand her. "Please what, Isabel?"

She came closer and whispered again, very loudly. "Can't we have this one for our maman?"

She stuck out her stubborn chin and Giles feared she would start one of her *why not* arguments.

He bit his lip and looked to the young woman for help. She came around the table and knelt to Isabel. "I can't be your maman, Isabel. I am to be a bride of Christ."

"There you have it, Isabel. Say good bye to Sister Joelle and we'll go meet some ladies."

Giles let out a silent breath, relieved Isabel for once didn't argue.

On the other side of the yard were several young ladies who, at least for the moment, were not surrounded by potential husbands. The brunette had pretty hair, he thought as he led his brood toward them.

Isabel swung his arm. "She was pretty, wasn't she, Papa?"

"Who, sweetheart?"

"The lady with the water."

Giles hadn't noticed. He supposed a woman in nun's garb became invisible in a way. One saw nun, that's all. "She was very nice."

"We could marry her, then."

He laughed. "Isabel, she told you. A nun is already married to her Church, to Jesus."

Her eyes grew round. "Will she have little baby Jesuses?"

Giles blew out a breath. He needed to get these girls to church more often.

Sister Bernadette, the older nun they had met last week, hailed him. "Monsieur Travert!"

"Sister Bernadette. Good day to you."

"And to you. How do you do, children? Rosalie, is it? And, let me think, Isabel. Oh dear, I've forgotten the little fellow's name."

"He's Felix," Isabel told her.

Sister Bernadette bestowed smiles on all of them, and then got down to business. "Monsieur Travert, let me introduce you to Harriet. She just loves children."

Giles drew a deep breath. Maybe this would be the woman he took home with him.

Harriet was a very thin woman, skinny, actually. Her face was long and sallow, her hair pulled from her face into a tight bun.

Giles reminded himself that this undernourished woman had been on land only a few weeks after having spent two months crossing the ocean in a ship no more than seventy feet long. He remembered how trying the passage from France was. Everyone was sick half the time and no one looked his or her best at the end of it.

"Harriet, this is Monsieur Travert, Rosalie, who is eight, Isabel, who is six, and Felix, who is three."

Harriet held herself stiffly but managed a curtsy. "Pleased to meet you," she said. But clearly she wasn't. Her hands were tightly clasped in front of her and her spine was stiff. She could not have been less at ease. Giles felt rather sorry for her.

"Louisiana is quite different from France, mademoiselle. Do you find it pleases you? The warm ocean, the sand . . ."

Clearly it did not please her, and neither did they. She not only did not look at the children, she did not look Giles in the eye either.

"It is very hot," she said, her mouth in a grim line.

She was frightened, he understood. Poor girl. It was a momentous thing to be taken from a sheltered life, transported across an entire ocean, and dropped into a foreign environment. He wondered if she had yet seen an alligator. That might be one challenge too many.

"It is hot, yes, but you'll appreciate this climate in the winter time. It doesn't snow here."

Harriet kept her gaze over his shoulder and had nothing to say about snow.

"Would you like to walk down to the water with us?" he asked.

"What a lovely idea," Sister Bernadette pealed.

Giles held out his arm for Harriet and after a moment's hesitation in which the poor girl looked at his elbow as if it might be infused with poison, she placed her hand on his forearm.

Rosalie dutifully arranged her brother and sister along the string and followed behind them.

"It is a long hard journey, sailing across the ocean. Do you find yourself well?"

"I am well."

"And you were raised in the convent?"

"No."

Plainly she was unwilling to talk about herself. Perhaps she would like to know about him and the children. "The children and I have four pigs, a dozen chickens, two dogs, and a friendly raccoon who often stops by to steal from the pigs. Do you have any experience with animals, mademoiselle?"

"They are God's creatures." Her mouth seemed to have only two expressions: either tightly closed or very tightly closed.

"I see."

At the shore where the settlers' boats were pulled up onto the sand, the children eased around him to stand at the water's edge. They were on a finger shaped barrier island between the mainland and the Gulf. Facing the sound, the water was calm and rather a dull greenish gray at the moment. Still, it was a peaceful scene with the lush growth of the mainland across the bay.

Giles raised his arm to point. "Over that way, a little east -- you see the mouth to one of the lazy little bayous so common around here. My wife and I built a homestead up that bayou." He smiled, remembering. "She was a great one for fishing off the bank of the river. Said it gave her an excuse to be lazy of an afternoon."

The woman beside him gave a curt nod of her head. As far as he could tell, she had yet to look directly at the children. He was contemplating asking her if she liked children at all -- perhaps she put them in the same category as dogs and pigs. But at that moment, Felix managed to fall into the water.

Rosalie shrieked, Isabel laughed, and Felix splashed with enthusiasm. With a grin, Giles reached a long arm down and hauled his son out of the shallow water.

"Look, Papa. Felix broke the string between him and Isabel."

"It'll be all right, *ma petite*. Don't fret." He stood Felix on his feet and wiped the hair out of his face. "What a mess you are, young man."

Felix grinned at him. Giles put his hand on his boy's head and turned to see Harriet scowling. At least now she acknowledged one of the children existed.

She backed up two steps so as not to be dampened by Felix's dripping form.

She wouldn't do, that's all. She really wouldn't.

"You are not fond of children, are you, mademoiselle?"

She drew a deep breath. "Of course I am."

And that was a lie. Sobered, Giles escorted her back to Sister Bernadette. If the good sister thought Harriet was the best a man with three children could do, he might as well go home.

He took the children back to the shoreline where he'd left his dugout. The younger nun was there waving off a couple heading into the sound.

"Ah, monsieur," Sister Joelle said. "We have a happy announcement. Sophie has just wed Monsieur Wasserman."

"I wish them well. Wasserman is a good man."

"Oh!" The nun whooped and covered her mouth. "Oh, you little dear." She knelt down to Felix and put her hands on his wet shoulders. "Did you fall in the water?"

Felix grinned at her. "I jumped."

She laughed. "And was it fun?"

"He is very naughty, Sister," Rosalie said.

Her eyes glinted with merriment when she looked at Rosalie. "Not so very naughty, though. I think he can be forgiven, don't you?"

8

Her head tilted, Isabel considered the nun's wimple. "Is that hat on your head very hot?"

"It is very hot. I would like to do like your brother and jump in the water."

Giles had a quick vision of the sister splashing about in her black robe and white wimple. He wondered if, under the wimple, she had red hair to go with those freckles. Well, he was in a sad way if he was thinking about a nun's hair.

"Time we headed home," he said, and hauled Felix up under his arm like a sack of wheat.

"Monsieur Travert?"

She was shy, this young woman. "Yes, sister?"

She gestured back toward the grounds where the prospective brides were. "If you would care to come again on Wednesday, we have a picnic planned for the settlers and the girls to get acquainted."

"Wednesday." It wasn't as if he had an appointment he had to keep with the pigs on Wednesday. He nodded. "Thank you. We'll be here."

# Chapter Two

*A Picnic, with Ants*
*First Wednesday*

Sister Joelle woke the women at daybreak for morning prayers and ignored the groans and complaints. "Father Xavier is already in the chapel. Get up, lazy heads."

A couple of the girls needed a nudge to wake up. Joelle didn't mind. Even after all these weeks together, on board ship and now here in Louisiana, Joelle still delighted in listening to the girls chatter to each other about, well anything. In the convent, idle talk was sinful, so any conversation centered around practicalities like getting supper on the table.

These girls talked about dogs and cats they'd had before they were orphaned, about strawberry tarts their mothers had made. They even told jokes to make each other laugh! What fun they had together, all day long. Sometimes, they included Joelle in their groups, and she drank in every word. No one here sat in a window watching the world go by. Everyone here *lived*.

A few of the girls shared Joelle's enthusiasm for this new life. Seraphina burst into song at odd moments, and Miranda whistled in the mornings as she got her shoes and stockings on. Of course, some of them wanted only to go home -- like Sarah. It was an ordinary morning, girls getting their hair put up, their shoes buttoned, and Sarah screamed. Loudly. Sarah didn't like spiders.

"It's only a little spider," Seraphina said.

"It's huge," Sarah wailed. "Didn't you see it?"

Joelle rushed to intervene before this escalated into yet another fuss about if it mattered whether a spider was big or not so big. Scared was scared, Joelle figured, so she took Sarah aside and soothed her as best she could.

Some of the girls hated the insects that insisted on sharing their cots and snuggling into their clothes. Some hated the heat.

Some feared the strangeness of this place, the odd plants and the relentless sun, the sudden torrential rains.

They would get used to being here, Joelle was sure. They would learn something new every day. Only yesterday, they had learned that rubbing their skin with mint leaves would discourage the mosquitos. Of course, the girls had immediately stripped all the mint plants on the island.

When everyone was ready, they filed out of the barracks together. That was the one stipulation Colonel Blaise insisted on. No young women wandering around the fort unaccompanied. In fact, he said, he strongly preferred that they remain in the larger group at all times. "These soldiers are a long way from home," he added, as if that were explanation enough.

Joelle, of course, had not been around men, not young men. They fascinated her though she was careful not to let her gaze linger on them. They spit on the ground whenever they wanted to, and they thought nothing of taking off their shirts to go swimming in the bay. They were so free, and big, and different.

Crossing the distance from the barracks to the chapel, Joelle breathed in the morning. The air smelled of earth and salt and pine. Spreading oaks made pools of shade, and the blue sea stretched out into the Gulf. Trees and water they had at home, of course, but the light was different here. The reds of flowers were redder, the greens of the trees were greener. Even the sky seemed filled with color.

The fort itself was modest, vertical logs fencing in the barracks, and outside the palisade were the chapel, a general store and an infirmary.

The women marched behind Sister Bernadette to the chapel, Joelle bringing up the rear. With muted grumbling, the wives-to-be took their places on the benches and prepared to listen as Father Xavier murmured his way through the devotionals.

Joelle closed her eyes and felt God's presence surround her. Breathing deeply, she gave herself over to the mass, finding comfort in the incomprehensible Latin of Father Xavier's droning voice.

When she opened her eyes she saw Nicole's head dip and then jerk up again. She wasn't the only girl nodding off this morning. If they were lucky, Sister Bernadette wouldn't see them.

Once mass was over, Joelle waited for the girls to file past, her mind wandering to the little Travert boy who'd jumped into the water. How adorable he was, his hair dripping, his face alight with mischief. His father seemed like a good man even if he did threaten to feed his children to the alligators. She grinned at the notion.

"Sister Joelle!"

Father Xavier's angry tone told her he had already spoken to her and she hadn't heeded him.

He eyed her shrewdly. "Day dreaming again, Sister Joelle?"

"Oh. I'm so sorry, Father."

"Wax dripped onto the altar cloth. See to it, please."

"Yes, Father."

Half an hour later when Joelle joined the others at breakfast, she saw Seraphina flirting with one of the soldiers. Again. That was a word she had not heard before, flirting, but Sister Bernadette had explained it meant a woman making a man forget himself so that he thought only of her bodily charms and not her character. A sure path to perdition, she'd added.

Seraphina was pretty, but no prettier than several of the other girls. She had curly brown hair and brown eyes and a woman's figure. What set her apart, Joelle supposed, was the way she smiled at a man like he was made of sunshine.

The young soldier was all smiles himself, his bright eyes keen with interest, and Seraphina was pretending to be modest while she sent out beckoning looks from under her lashes. Even Joelle could see this was flirting. With a sigh, she interrupted their tête-à-tête.

The soldier flushed bright red under his tan and hustled away.

"We were only talking, Sister," Seraphina complained. "I don't know what you and Sister Bernadette have against talking to a man. Men are God's creatures, too, you know."

Joelle nearly laughed. What an excuse for indecorous behavior. There was no point in scolding Seraphina. She would only pout and then promise to do better, which Joelle suspected put her soul in danger since she meant to do no such thing. Better not to tempt her to make a false promise.

Joelle sat down to her own bowl of corn meal mush and listened to the talk going on around her. Some of these girls had become devoted friends in the months of their journey. Joelle was happy for them though a little lonely. But that was nonsense. Of course she would not have a friendship like Cecile and Nicole's. Her path to become a bride of Christ was altogether different.

She was working her way toward her vows, after all, and her final vows were the dream of her life. She would belong to her order for as long as she drew breath. She would never be alone, never wonder who she was meant to be or what she was meant to do. She would be a professed nun and she would do all the things nuns did.

Her eyes strayed to Seraphina down the length of the table. How did it make her feel, when a man forgot all about manners and propriety when she smiled at him? Maybe she simply felt *more*. More alive? More important?

Joelle stirred the unappetizing mush in her bowl. Whatever benefit Seraphina derived from flirting, she realized, she was not likely to ever feel it herself. Joelle brought herself up short. That had been self-pitying and quite sinfully envious. Joelle sighed. She would have to confess it to Father Xavier.

But that would wait until later. Ah! That Seraphina! She'd folded under the top inch of her bodice to expose just that much more of her bosom, but Sister Bernadette was barreling down on her. That bared skin would soon be covered.

And poor Harriet. It wasn't that she was physically unappealing -- well, perhaps a little -- but she was so sour.

Joelle swallowed the last of the mush and made her way between the plank tables to sit beside Seraphina.

"Do you think human skin is disgraceful, Sister?" Seraphina demanded. "This is the skin God gave me and I don't know why I should be ashamed of it."

Joelle held her hand up, a quirk in her smile. "You won't get me between you and Sister Bernadette." She leaned in and spoke softly. "How would you like to do a good deed? A sort of penance for all the times you upset Sister Bernadette?"

Seraphina narrowed her eyes. "What sort of penance?"

Joelle nodded toward Harriet sitting down the row. "She doesn't know how to make herself pretty like you do."

"As far as I can tell, she doesn't want to be pretty."

Joelle thought about that. "I don't know about these things, Seraphina, but I wish you would help her."

With a slanted look, Seraphina smiled at her. "You think God would forgive me my sins if do?"

"It could only help."

With a put-upon sigh, Seraphina hauled herself up and sauntered over to Harriet.

Joelle didn't have time to see how Seraphina went about coaxing Harriet. It was time for the Wednesday picnic, and she had a thousand things to do, starting with supervising the soldiers as they set up long narrow planks on sawhorses to spread the food on. The women were contributing dried apples, corn fritters, and dried peas ground into flour and mixed with oil and garlic. Colonel Blaise told them to expect dried venison, stewed squirrel, even baked possum from the men.

By midday, prospective grooms began to arrive. Joelle kept her eyes open for the three children she'd met on Sunday, the adorable little one named Felix, the two sisters Rosalie and Isabel. There would be other children coming today, too. Joelle had been thinking about this since Sunday and had decided that it would be a Godly act if she kept the children while their fathers looked for new mothers.

She wouldn't ask Sister Bernadette, she decided. She would just do it.

"But why aren't there any kittens, Colonel?"

It was Seraphina, again, this time with the formidable Colonel Blaise. She was looking up at him with her head tilted and her eyes wide. The Colonel stood with his arms crossed and a glint of amusement in his eye.

"The pumas eat the cats, mademoiselle. And if the pumas don't get them, the gators will."

"Seraphina," Joelle called. "Will you help me, please?"

The flirt batted her lashes at the colonel and sauntered over to Joelle.

"Hold this end of the cloth, please."

"You asked me to come over here just to hold one end of a cloth?"

Seraphina had her there. It did not take two people to lay a cloth over a narrow table.

"You don't want me to have any fun at all, do you?"

"The colonel is not looking for a wife, Seraphina. Anyway, he's too old for you."

Seraphina eyed the man across the grounds and smiled. "I don't think so, Sister. Besides, he's delicious, don't you think?"

"Delicious?"

Seraphina's gaze didn't leave the long-legged figure of the fort's commander.

"Delicious, you mean like food?"

"Like cream for the cat."

Where on earth did she get such ideas living in a respectable orphanage run by nuns?

Nearby, one of the girls stood alone under a pine tree. Joelle squinted. Who was that? Good heavens, it was Harriet. Seraphina had done something miraculous with Harriet's hair. Ruthlessly contained in a tight bun until now, her hair floated in a soft cloud around her face.

Joelle strode toward her, smiling, expecting perhaps a shy smile from Harriet herself now that she was feeling pretty and feminine. Well, no. Seraphina's efforts had not changed Harriet's nature. How was she to find a husband when she scowled so?

Joelle would have to help. "Monsieur Ouellette?" she called. Another widower with a child, he seemed a nice man, he and the boy neatly dressed with their hair combed and tied. "Have you talked to Harriett yet, monsieur? Come, and I will introduce you."

Monsieur Ouellette followed her dutifully, the boy in tow. He bowed to Harriett and asked her how she did.

"Well enough." Why couldn't the girl smile? Every other woman from the *New Hope* smiled when a man addressed her.

"This is my boy Daniel."

Harriett's gaze darted to the boy and then slid off.

Monsieur Ouellette nodded to the Bible in her hands. "You are a pious woman, I see."

"I am a Godly woman, sir. You no doubt are Catholic?"

The man seemed taken aback at the question. "I am Catholic, of course. Are you not, mademoiselle?"

"I am a follower of John Calvin, Monsieur Ouellette."

He glanced at Joelle, confused. "Did you not come from the convent? Or the convent's orphanage?"

"No, I did not. My uncle, the magistrate, gave me a choice. Convert to Catholicism or board the *New Hope* for Louisiana."

"I see."

"I will not become a Catholic."

"No, I don't imagine you will."

Oh my, Joelle thought. She had not realized Harriett would refuse to convert when she married. But how many Protestant Huguenots would she find in a French colony?

Monsieur Ouellette met his son's gaze for a moment, and then he looked at Joelle. The unspoken message was clear: he had no interest in Harriet.

He bowed to Harriet and nodded to Joelle. "I wish you both a good day." He strode away more quickly than was quite polite, Joelle thought.

She looked around, wondering how she could be most useful, when she saw the three children that belonged to Monsieur Travert had arrived, and their father as well, of course.

She marched across the grounds. "Bonjour!" she called and raised her hand.

Isabel, Monsieur Travert's middle child, ran to her and hugged her around the waist. Her little brother Felix followed his sister and grabbed on to her, too.

A surge of feeling flushed through Joelle. She had not been hugged since she herself was a child, and oh how wonderful it felt. Laughing, Joelle squeezed Isabel and Felix before letting them go.

"Good morning, Sister," Monsieur Travert said. "You've made quite an impression on my two imps."

Joelle beamed at him, and at his oldest daughter. "Good morning, Rosalie."

Solemn-faced, Rosalie dipped a curtsy. "Good morning, Madame Jesus."

Monsieur Travert tried not to smile. "There has been some confusion at my house, Sister, about what it means to be a nun."

Rosalie's brow creased. "You are not married to Jesus?"

"I will be, in a way. Maybe next year."

"You may call her Sister Joelle, Rosalie," Monsieur Travert said.

Rosalie sighed. "Good morning, Sister Joelle."

"Do you like picnics?"

"Yes."

Isabel had a less restrained answer. "I love picnics! Papa brought fried squirrel and pecans and mayhaws." She pulled back the cloth on a little basket to show her. "See how pretty they are?"

Joelle agreed the mayhaws were red as red can be. "Monsieur Travert, I will be pleased to entertain the children while you enjoy the company." She hoped she didn't sound too eager. When she was a child, Sister Bernadette had snapped her hands with a switch for wheedling, and she had never forgotten it.

Monsieur Travert raised a brow in silent consultation with his offspring.

"Yes!" from Isabel. "Yes!" from Felix. "All right," from Rosalie.

Monsieur Travert's eyes were alight when he looked at her. "I believe you have an enthusiastic group of picnickers here, Sister. Thank you. I will be just over there, Rosalie," he said, nodding toward the women and men gathered around the plank table.

As their father ambled off to be sociable, all three little Travert faces turned to her expectantly. "Well. Let's get you some dinner."

Joelle helped each of them to a napkin of food from the long table where the dinner was laid out, then noticed Monsieur Ouellette with his son Daniel at the other end of the table. She invited Daniel to join them and led the four children to the shade under a trio of pine trees.

Joelle had envisioned a sedate luncheon with her charges. They would sit quietly, talk quietly, and eat their dinners. Felix, however, could not sit quietly. He would eat a few bites, hop off to explore the other side of the pine trees, come back, eat a little, and wander off again, but he never went far. Isabel ate, but somehow managed to chatter the entire time.

Did Sister know that mockingbird eggs were blue with brown speckles? That the birds with the skinny, curved beaks were called ibis? And did she know that bears ate fish and mice, not little girls, that's what Papa says.

Daniel tossed the leg bone of a squirrel on his napkin. "Actually, a bear would eat a little girl if she was handy and it was hungry."

Isabel got very still and very quiet. Her lip trembled.

Rosalie sighed. "Now you've done it."

"What?" Daniel said. "It's the truth."

Tears began to trail over Isabel's cheek, her little face crumpled, and she let out a loud wail.

Oh no. Joelle had never dealt with a crying child in her life. She stared for a moment, bewildered and a little frightened.

"You should probably hold her in your lap," Rosalie said.

"Of course." Joelle gathered Isabel up and held her close, her hand stroking her little back. What a delightful feeling, to have a child lean against her, needing her, even if she were crying noisily.

"I'm sure Daniel is mistaken, Isabel. Bears don't even like little girls. I don't imagine they like little boys either." She gave Daniel a meaningful look. "Isn't that right, Daniel?"

His face betrayed his disgust, but he made an effort to soothe over the upset he'd caused.

"They'd rather have berries," he conceded. "Or honey." He turned to Rosalie to share the next interesting fact. "They even eat bees."

"They eat bees?"

He nodded, just as solemn as Rosalie. "They do."

Joelle wiped Isabel's cheek with her fingers. "See? You don't have to worry about bears."

"Papa promised her he would never let a bear eat her, not even a little bit of her," Rosalie said.

Joelle swallowed a laugh. "I'm sure he --" A shriek tore through the air, stopping her heart, shredding every nerve.

In an instant, she realized Felix was not with them. She made a frantic dash to find him on the other side of the biggest pine.

He still shrieked, his face red, his hands flailing at dozens of ants on his legs and arms.

Joelle grabbed him up, ran for the water, and plowed in. Surprised at being plunged in, Felix hushed as Joelle washed off every ant with trembling hands.

"What fine mess have you gotten yourself into this time?" Monsieur Travert stood on the sandy shore with his hands on his hips.

"Oh, Monsieur Travert, I'm so sorry. I didn't --"

He held up his hand. "Every child I ever knew got into the ants at least once, Sister. The trick," he said, addressing his son, "is to do it only once. You think once will be enough, Felix?"

The child was still snuffling up his tears. "Yes, Papa."

Monsieur Travert leaned over and lifted Felix out of the water and set him on his feet. "Sister?" He held his hand out to help her.

Her sodden habit was heavy, but she could not accept his hand. She looked down to lift her skirts so as to step onto the low bank when she realized the wet cloth clung to her body, outlining her breasts.

She flushed in furious embarrassment. Monsieur Travert didn't seem to notice, but he was a man, and Sister Bernadette said men --

"Here we go," he said, gripping her elbow and hauling her up.

Joelle couldn't meet his eyes. She flapped at her wet skirts and tried to compose herself. She had never been touched by a man before, and she'd certainly never displayed any part of her body as it was now displayed.

If Sister Bernadette saw her like this, well, Joelle could only imagine how furious she would be.

The other children came up to stand around the tableaux of a half-drowned sister and a child with red whelps all over his legs and arms.

"That's going to itch, but you're not to scratch, Felix," Rosalie said.

If only she had some of her special salve to put on his bites, but Joelle had not had time yet to look for the herbs she knew would relieve itching. This was all her fault and she had nothing to soothe the stinging.

Daniel looked him over. "If those were fire ants, that many bites, he'll probably throw up."

"I am not going to throw up!"

Monsieur Travert straightened Felix's clothes and pushed the hair off his face. "All right, now?"

"He's all wet," Rosalie said.

"He'll dry soon enough. Thank the sister for giving you a picnic, all of you."

Four young voices uttered their thanks. "And I thank you, too, Sister Joelle. I've been talking to your Miss Emmeline and she wants to meet the children."

She was ready to look him in the face now and he seemed very pleased. Maybe Emmeline would become his wife, and she'd be mother to his children.

"That's nice." She probably should say something more, but she could think of nothing else to say. Isabel had sat in *her* lap. Felix had clung to *her* in the water when she washed away the ants. But it would be Emmeline who tucked them into bed at night, who fed them their breakfast, who became their mother.

Joelle clasped her hands together. She must stop comparing herself to these women. Everything was as it should be. Emmeline was meant to become a wife and mother. Joelle was meant to become a holy sister, just as she had always wanted.

"Come along," Monsieur Travert said, and strolled off with his brood.

"Well, Daniel," she said.

"Fire ants are very painful."

"With a name like that, I should imagine they are."

"Do you want me to show you their nest?"

"The ants' nest?" What strange things boys found interesting. "Very well. But be careful. I don't want you getting bitten too."

"I'm ten years old," Daniel said, not quite able to keep the indignation out of his voice.

Children were so much more complicated than Joelle had realized in spite of all those hours she had spent watching them on Rue des Boulangers.

# Chapter Three

*The First Brides*
*Second Sunday*

It did Marie Claude good to be here at the fort, among people. She could push aside her grief, at least for a little while, and concentrate on her friends. Even her healing ribs seemed less sore with so much going on around her.

Agnes nudged her. "Here comes that young nun. What do you bet she has red hair to go with those freckles?"

"Waste of a lot of good freckles if she doesn't."

What would Marie Claude do without Agnes? In those dark days after her husband had beaten her so badly that she'd lost the baby she carried, Agnes and Catherine had nursed her battered body and nurtured her broken spirit. These few weeks later, Marie Claude could now walk and talk and at least seem normal. A heart bereft of hope and love didn't show, after all.

"Bonjour," the young sister called to them. She seemed harried, trying to keep an eye on all the girls newly arrived at the fort.

"Bonjour, sister. You expect to marry off some more girls today?" Agnes said.

"That is our hope, Madame Villiers. You were both on the last voyage? And you each married a settler?"

Catherine strolled up and joined them, a big smile on her face. "We all did, Sister."

"It's all very exciting, isn't it?" Sister Joelle said. "Choosing a partner, starting a new life in a new world."

Catherine laughed. "I don't know if I felt excited at the time. Scared to death, more like it."

And yet, Marie Claude mused, she had come through it all right, Catherine had. And Agnes too. Both married to good men, both in love.

Marie Claude let the conversation go on without her, her mind on fate, chance, luck.

"But it's like Sister Bernadette says, isn't it?" The young sister's face was open and trusting. She had no idea how hard life could be. "People grow to love each other even if they don't know each other very well at first."

Well, Marie Claude thought to herself, she wished these new brides better luck in their husbands than she'd had. She squeezed her eyes shut against the image that flashed in her mind. Her husband's hands around her neck, her desperate scramble for the knife. Fear, pain, blood. So much blood.

Marie Claude blinked away the horror. Her brute of a husband was dead now. She was free of him forever. Why waste another thought on him?

And why feel sorry for herself? She was not alone in the world. She had Agnes and Catherine. And she had Thomas. He leaned against a tree twenty yards away, close enough to keep an eye on her but not so close that he hovered. He stood alone, as always. His black skin marked him as a man enslaved, which meant that other men, white men, didn't even see him. But Marie Claude saw him. She knew where he was, always, even when he was out of her sight.

"Ah," Catherine said. "Here comes Bridget."

"She's big as a house already," Agnes said. "That baby won't keep much longer."

Bridget approached them with a big smile pasted on her face, about as false a smile as Marie Claude had ever seen. Must mean she wanted something.

"Ladies, such a pleasure to see you."

"Hello, Bridget," Catherine said. Did Bridget notice the lack of warmth in that greeting?

"Your baby is due pretty soon, looks like," Marie Claude said. Bridget delivered that brittle smile again. If Marie Claude had to guess, she would say that was fear in her eyes. Well, Bridget had insulted everyone she knew at one time or another. She might very well fear she'd have not a single friend to help her when it was time.

"I'll just sit with the others and see what's going on in your little *école*, shall I?" Bridget lumbered over and managed to lower herself to the ground. Not a single woman turned a friendly face her way. Marie Claude felt a twinge of pity, but it didn't last.

"Everyone's here," Catherine said. "Sister, we're about to begin our Sunday *école*."

"You have a school here?"

"A sort of school," Catherine said. "Paris, as you can imagine, did not require us to know how to cook possum or make flour from cattails."

"Will you tell all the new women that they are welcome to join us?" Agnes said. "The more they know and the sooner they know it, the easier life will be."

"How very kind you are. Harriet," she called as some of the newcomers passed by. "And Miranda. Jocelyn."

The three young women dutifully walked over, but Marie Claude saw the pinched look on their faces.

"These women came over a few months ago," Sister Joelle explained, "and they teach each other the skills they've learned to cope with life here in Louisiana."

"You're welcome to join us. We get together on Sunday afternoons while our husbands meet for their own pursuits," Catherine said, waving a hand toward the area where fencing and wrestling and other manly entertainments were going on.

Marie Claude noticed the one with a cloud of dark hair had a mean look in her eye. The other two made their faces blank, a little bit more mannerly but still not friendly.

"Today," Catherine, ever gracious, said, "Rachel is going to show us how to smoke the chiggers out of moss before we try to sleep on a moss mattress. They say if a chigger bites you, you will itch for the rest of your life. It may be true. My bites have been itching for weeks."

The one with all the hair narrowed her eyes at Catherine. "They say the last voyage brought women from the streets and prisons of Paris."

Marie Claude stifled a laugh. It was just too funny that this plain woman without fortune or family -- or else why would she be here -- scorned Catherine, whose grandfather was a count in King Louis' court.

Agnes, her face expressionless, said, "Yes. Most of us came from the Salpêtrière."

The sour one tossed a meaningful look at Sister Joelle, turned on her heel and left them, the other two women following with their noses in the air.

"I guess they're more intent on getting themselves a husband right now," Catherine said.

"I'm sorry." Sister's face turned bright red under all the freckles.

Marie Claude shrugged. "They may change their minds when they find they don't know how to make candles or brooms or hats or how to preserve meat or -- " She shrugged again.

"If they do, they'll be welcome later on," Catherine said.

~~~

Sister Joelle felt shamed by her charges' ingratitude. These women offered to share their hard-won knowledge of living in the wilderness, and Harriet, Miranda, and Jocelyn scorned them for their pasts. Sister Bernadette would say they were not behaving as good Christian girls should, and Sister Joelle would have to agree.

She did wonder, however, why women who seemed so nice had been in the Salpêtrière, the most notorious prison in Paris. What was even more curious was that Agnes and Catherine both spoke with educated accents while the other women all spoke the language of the streets, or so Joelle thought. She shook her head. She knew so little of life outside the convent and out of sight of Rue des Boulangers. She would have to make her judgments on present behavior. That was what Jesus would want her to do. And she judged Agnes, Catherine, and Marie Claude were very good women.

With a sidelong glance, Joelle measured her height against Marie Claude's. She was the biggest woman Joelle had ever seen, but she was gentle and kind. Agnes was a tiny woman with bright brown eyes. And Catherine, with her blonde hair and gliding stride, had the bearing of an important person, like Mother Superior herself.

An imposing man strode toward them, purpose in every step. He included all of them in one sweeping bow although it seemed to Joelle he hadn't actually seen her. Men often didn't see nuns, she had discovered.

"Bonjour, mesdames." *And Sister Joelle,* she added silently. He focused on Marie Claude. "I believe I address Madame Joubert? I am Michel Moncrief. Madame Joubert, perhaps you would walk with me?"

Marie Claude turned her attention from a bird soaring overhead and stared at Monsieur Moncrief as if he'd spoken in tongues.

A line appeared between her brows. "Walk with you?"

Catherine nudged her. "Go on."

Marie Claude stared at Catherine then as if she too spoke an incomprehensible language.

Catherine tilted her head toward the gentleman and softly repeated, "Go on."

Monsieur Moncrief held out his arm for her, but Marie Claude ignored it and strode off with him a step behind her until he caught up.

Catherine smiled after her friend. "Marie Claude is not accustomed to courtship."

"So she is unmarried? A woman alone, here?"

"She was widowed a few weeks ago. I don't think she wants another husband after the one she endured."

"But she must marry."

Catherine shrugged. "She knows what she is doing on a farm, and she has men to help her work it."

Joelle waved at a fly. They seemed most attracted to her when she was damp with sweat, like now. She wiped her upper lip and wondered whether Father Xavier knew Marie Claude lived alone, with men? Joelle watched the two as they crossed the grounds in conversation. The man was as tall as Marie Claude and nice looking. Joelle couldn't see any fault in him, on short acquaintance, except for his lamentable manners toward a holy sister. Marie Claude walked with her hands behind her back as Monsieur Moncrief made elegant gestures with his.

"But surely -- surely she needs a husband."

"I don't think she does, Sister. But perhaps she would like one anyway. We'll see. Would you like to see how Rachel smokes her moss?"

Joelle did. She stood to the side with Catherine while a dark-haired woman built a light-weight rack to spread the moss on. Using dry tinder, she built a small fire underneath the rack, and once she had a decent blaze burning, she added wood she'd been soaking in a bucket.

Joelle had never built a fire. In the convent, lay sisters kept all the fireplaces going in the wintertime, laundered the sisters' linens, cooked and cleaned. When she thought about it, Joelle had learned to do very few things. She could mend and sew and knit. She could plant a garden, and she was quite good at drying herbs and using them to make healing infusions. That skill she could be proud of, but she reminded herself quickly not to indulge in vanity. What else? She could recite long passages of the catechism, and she had the capacity to kneel in prayer for an hour or more.

All Joelle had ever wanted was to be like Sister Bernadette and Mother Superior. Now she wanted to know how to build a fire, to make a mattress, to cook a rabbit.

"So many new things to learn here," she'd said to Sister Bernadette.

"New?"

"Oh, like how to turn meat into jerky or weave a basket."

"What nonsense," Sister Bernadette had insisted. "Your job is to see to Father Xavier and to worship God alongside him. Such a willful girl you are, Sister Joelle. Learn how to make jerky indeed."

So many things to know and she was not to know any of them. Joelle had sighed and resigned herself once again to Sister Bernadette's strictures.

Marie Claude came striding back, her face thunderously angry.

"No?" Catherine said.

"That man wants my slaves -- my friends -- because they know how to make indigo dye. I told him smelling those fumes makes people sick, that Pierre died from it just a few weeks ago. You know what he said?"

Catherine put her hand on Marie Claude's arm. "What did he say?"

"Before they get too sick, they can teach other slaves what they know about making dye."

So that black man who followed Marie Claude around was her slave? Though she hadn't given it any thought, Joelle knew there were slaves in the colony. There was even a little slave market at the other end of the island though Joelle had not been down there herself. Sister Bernadette had forbidden it because the slaves were all heathens and some of them were only half dressed.

It seemed harsh, slavery did, but she didn't think the Church forbade it. She would ask Father Xavier what to think about it.

Catherine squeezed Marie Claude's arm. "Of course you said no."

Marie Claude's face was still red and her eyes blazed. "As if I would sell Thomas or Remy or Simon to anyone, much less someone who meant to use them up until they died."

"I thought all the colonists were planting indigo," Joelle said.

Marie Claude glowered at her. Oh, she'd said something wrong?

"Many will plant indigo," Catherine said kindly. "And some of them will become very rich. But not everyone will because Marie Claude learned that the process destroys a man's lungs. So some of us will never plant indigo."

When Marie Claude pressed a hand over her eyes, Catherine caught the tall black man's eye and he came quickly.

"I don't like to see you upset like this," Catherine said. "You don't have all your strength back yet."

The black man gently touched Marie Claude's elbow. "Let's go home."

When he had led Marie Claude away, Joelle turned to Catherine. "She's been ill?"

Catherine, who had seemed so friendly and open, suddenly seemed remote. "More of an injury than an illness."

Joelle could see she should not ask any more. "Well, I am remiss in my duties. Thank you for including us in your school."

Catherine's face softened. "Any time. Everyone is welcome."

Joelle was meant to be minding her young women as they strolled the grounds, meeting and talking to potential husbands. They mostly chaperoned each other, but Joelle and Sister Bernadette both kept a watchful eye out. One never knew, for instance, whether Seraphina might wander off with a soldier and perhaps come back with swollen lips.

How different people were, Joelle thought. She could imagine Seraphina with swollen lips, and a big grin. Whereas when a man presumed to take Imogene's hand, she had blanched, jerked her hand back, and ran to stand next to Sister Bernadette where she would feel safe.

And how would Joelle feel if a man took her hand? Her face would certainly flush hot, but she blushed easily anyway. Would she mind very much to find her hand held by a man? His hand would be rough from hard work, and perhaps quite warm, like

Monsieur Travert's hand when he helped her out of the water. If she hadn't been ashamed to be seen in a clinging wet habit, she would not have objected to that moment's contact with a man.

Even her own thoughts brought the heat to Joelle's face, but then she was very hot anyway. Sweat trickled down her back under the dark habit. Sweat beaded on her forehead around the edge of her wimple. Dear Lord, she prayed, help me through this day. The heat was suffocating and it was only mid-day. By the afternoon . . .

*Ah non.* There was Seraphina, flirting again. With a sigh, Joelle headed toward her and the gentleman to make sure Seraphina remained in plain sight. The man was quite handsome with a long thin face, an elegant black moustache, curling black hair, and a lanky grace about him. He stood smiling down at Seraphina, his arms crossed and one leg cocked at the knee. And of course Seraphina was smiling at him. She tilted her head and said something Joelle could not hear. The man threw back his head and laughed.

Sister Bernadette had warned Seraphina, all the girls really, that no man would wed a girl who flirted like a wanton woman. Oh! And she had tugged her bodice down again. Joelle could shake her.

Before Joelle reached the two of them, that tiny little woman, Agnes Villiers, marched up and took the man's arm, quite firmly. The fire in her eye could have burned a tree to ashes.

"Bonjour," Joelle called. She was just in time to keep Seraphina from being immolated by Agnes Villiers' fury.

"Good day, Sister," the gentleman said. Joelle noticed he had placed his hand over his wife's where it rested on his arm.

"This is Monsieur Valery Villiers, Sister." Seraphina made a vague gesture at Madame Villiers. "And . . ."

"My wife," Monsieur Villiers said with a twinkle in his eye, apparently amused by Seraphina's rudeness.

"We are acquainted, aren't we, Sister? But you have not met my husband," Agnes said with subtle emphasis on the last word.

"I am Sister Joelle, Monsieur. How do you do?"

"My wife and I, we are very well." Joelle saw Monsieur Villiers' eyes linger on his wife's rounded abdomen. Then it was as she had thought when she first met Agnes. They were to have a baby. How wonderful.

Agnes gave a brisk tug on her husband's arm. "You will excuse us, Sister. We have business to attend to."

The man seemed happy to accompany his wife elsewhere, but he bestowed a smile on Seraphina before he turned away -- and winked at Joelle! He winked at her! She could only shake her head, but she had to deal with Seraphina before she could contemplate what kind of man would wink at a sister. When his wife was pregnant!

"Seraphina." Joelle used her firmest voice.

"Yes, Sister?" Seraphina's innocent look could not fool a three year old.

"Do you intend to marry one of these men or not?"

"Of course."

"You have already made your choice?"

"I suppose."

"Why are you not with him then?"

"Well, he isn't here yet, is he?"

"Seraphina."

"Hm?" She seemed more interested in the lock of hair she curled around her finger than she was in talking to Joelle.

"You cannot flirt with married men. And when you are married, you can't flirt with unmarried ones either."

Seraphina blew out a breath. "It's only flirting, Sister."

Joelle studied the girl, genuinely curious. "Seraphina, how did you learn to flirt living in an orphanage with only nuns and other girls in the whole compound?"

"Well, I wasn't born in the orphanage, was I?"

"So you flirted before you were orphaned?"

"I might have learned a little more afterward, too. Someone had to deal with the butcher's boy and the brewer and the stable lads."

Joelle just looked at her. She had no experience whatsoever with butchers' boys or stable lads.

Seraphina pursed her lips. "You make it sound like it's sinful. But it isn't. I'm as pure as the rest of these girls, you know. I just like men, that's all. And they like me."

"Sister! Sister!" Monsieur Travert's little girl, disentangled from the string attaching her to her brother and sister, dashed across the grounds with a big smile on her face. "Sister," she said once more as she plowed into Joelle so hard Joelle had to take a step back to stay upright.

"We came to see you!" Isabel told her.

While Seraphina slipped away, Joelle knelt and hugged the child, her heart as full as it had been ever in her life. What joy, to receive such a welcome. What pleasure to feel the warmth in a child's touch.

As Monsieur Travert neared, looking very rustic in his straw hat, Felix ran ahead to grab her, too. Rosalie, of course, approached with more dignity, but she too was smiling.

"Bonjour, Sister Joelle." Monsieur Travert said, and then he frowned. "Did they hurt you, Sister?" He leaned forward to disengage the children from wrapping themselves around her.

Joelle swiped at her cheeks, embarrassed at the tears that spilled from her eyes. "No, no, not at all, monsieur. I was merely surprised."

He studied her a moment, and then nodded.

"You want to see my ant bites?" Felix asked. He held out his arm still marred by red welts.

"Do they itch?"

"Yes, but Rosalie fusses at me if I scratch them. So I wait till she's not looking."

"A strategist, that's my boy," Monsieur Travert said.

"It's a hot day, isn't it?" Joelle said, just to have something to say. Her underclothing was clammy under her habit, but at least she had quit sweating. She resisted running her finger underneath her collar. Sister Bernadette would be disgraced to see such behavior. "I hope this is as hot as it gets."

He blew out a breath. "Pretty much. We'd all feel better if we walked into the shade, Sister." He motioned with his hand for her to accompany them into the tall pines.

Isabel swung Joelle's arm like a great pendulum as they walked while Rosalie quietly took Joelle's other hand. Joelle couldn't stop smiling. This is how it must feel to dance. How she had wanted to join the people on Rue des Boulangers when they danced around the May Pole on the little green square. Light and joy-filled, Joelle laughed out loud and the little girls laughed with her.

Joelle quickly put a damper on her high feelings. She could hear Sister Bernadette's scold in her head, see her scowl. *A nun is meant to be serene, contemplative, calm. At all times.* She sobered just remembering the many lectures on proper comportment, but didn't let go of Rosalie and Isabel's hands.

"Your life will be very quiet once all these young women have become wives and gone to their homes. Will that suit you?"

Joelle did not in fact look forward to moving out of the barracks assigned to the women. Never before in her life had Joelle enjoyed so many people, new faces, new sights, new everything. And never before had she known she could talk to men just like they were, well, anyone else.

Once the brides had gone away with their husbands, she and Sister Bernadette would move into the second of Father Xavier's two small rooms behind the chapel. What would she do all day? It was not the first moment Joelle had wondered about what life would be like here. She supposed she could start a garden. She would have her devotionals to perform with Sister Bernadette and Father Xavier. She worried, however, that she would spend much of her time standing on the shore, looking across the sound to the mainland where the wives and husbands were building their lives together.

"I might be of use in the infirmary," she said. "If Father Xavier allows it." After a moment she added, "And of course I will continue preparations to take my vows."

"Oh, yes. You're still a novice."

Joelle pressed her hand to her forehead as if that would ease the pounding in her head. "Yes. But perhaps by Christmas . . ."

"Ah, I see Mademoiselle Emmeline. Will you excuse us, Sister Joelle? Come girls, Felix."

Joelle watched the family walk away from her without a backward look. Emmeline smiled as they came to her, and Isabel ran to her just as she had run to Joelle. A little bit of shriveling seemed to be going on in Joelle's chest. Well, that was foolish. Monsieur Travert needed a wife and mother. Why should he waste time talking to her?

Across the yard, Sister Bernadette was beckoning to her with discreet waves. Joelle crossed the open grounds again, the sun beating down on her head like hammers. Dark spots appeared in her vision. She only vaguely registered it when her knees hit the ground.

# Chapter Four

*Heatstroke*
*Second Sunday Continued*

"Papa!" Rosalie cried. "Look!"

Giles tore his gaze from Emmeline's dark eyes to see Sister Joelle collapsed on the ground twenty yards away.

He dashed for her, calling out, "Water, someone!"

He scooped her up in his arms and headed for the nearest shade. There he knelt to lay her down and searched for the fastenings to the wimple behind her neck. Quickly he unwound the heavy linen until he could remove the whole thing, neck and head piece. Under that was another linen cap tied under her chin. No wonder the woman had fainted. He tossed the cap aside revealing tight, wet, copper curls pressed closed to her head.

"Sister," he said quietly. He took her jaw and turned her face to him. "Sister Joelle."

Her eyes didn't want to open, it seemed. They fluttered and then closed again.

"Joelle," he said again.

Laurent Laroux knelt next to him. "Fleur has a flagon of water."

Giles glanced over his shoulder at the young Biloxi woman. She handed him the flagon and he gently poured water over Joelle's hair. Her eyes popped open. Her hand flew to her naked head and her overheated cheeks flushed even redder.

"You should not have -- "

"Shh," he said. "Drink this." He held the flagon for her and helped her drink. "You just fainted from the heat, that's all. No wonder, trussed up in all this linen."

Sister Joelle put her hands to her bare head again and then reached for the wimple. "Please."

Sister Bernadette bustled up and immediately shooed everyone away. "This is ungodly, this is, uncovering a sister's hair. Go, go."

"Sister, do not put that contraption back on her head," Giles said. "She has heat stroke."

"But she is uncovered, monsieur!"

"Here." Giles plopped his own straw hat over the curls on Sister Joelle's head. "Now she's covered. Let's get her inside and give her some more water."

Giles picked her up again and strode toward the barracks.

"I can walk, monsieur. Put me down. Please."

"Hush now. Heat stroke is no small thing." She needed to be stripped and cooled, but Sister Bernadette would certainly not let him tend to her. He turned to the Biloxi woman. "You'll come, Fleur?"

Inside the shadowy barracks, the air was still and hot. "Open those windows," Giles said.

Sister Bernadette flapped her hands. "But the mosquitoes, monsieur, we cannot abide the mosquitoes in here."

"Air is more important at the moment. We need the breeze."

He lay Sister Joelle on a cot next to a window and looked for the buttons on her back. "Monsieur! You forget yourself," Sister Bernadette said.

Yes, he had, for a moment. "I'll leave you with Fleur. Listen to her, please, Sister Bernadette. She has experience with this heat."

"Thank you, monsieur," Sister Joelle said.

He touched her cheek. "Stay out of the sun for the next few days. Drink plenty of water."

And then he remembered he'd left his children with Emmeline. Lord knows what they'd got up to. He hoped he wouldn't find they'd tied Emmeline to a tree.

As he strode across the grounds, his mind drifted from Emmeline and the children. Joelle's fair skin was not meant for this climate. She didn't have anyone looking out for her, either. She needed --

"Papa," Isabell cried and ran for him. "Mademoiselle knows how to make string ladders. Come and see."

~~~

Fleur had been inside a French house before, when she went with her brother Mato into the general store. Straight up walls, a wooden floor, and glass windows. She had put her hand on the glass expecting her fingers might go right through as if it were clear water. It had been solid, and yet she could see the people outside, the sky, the earth, as if there were nothing there. She had touched it again, marveling.

There were four windows in this house where Laroux's friend Giles had brought the sister. Light came in from all around, and the beds were raised on wooden legs up off the floor. French people did not like to sit on the earth, she had noticed this.

"We will take the sister's dress off," she told the older woman. When the sister gaped at her, Fleur smiled. "I learned to speak French when I was a child, Sister. And I am a very good nurse."

"But . . ." The sister did not seem to know what to say next, so Fleur went about unbuttoning and untying the young sister's clothing.

"I can do that," the young one said.

"I will do it for you. Lie still."

This young one was different from any French person Fleur had yet seen. Her hair was the color of autumn leaves, and it was short as a baby's, and curled in tight ringlets. Her face was speckled with brown dots, and the skin of her body was white as the clouds. Blue veins even showed through the skin at her wrists.

"You are very kind to help me," the young one said.

"I am happy to help you. Your friend Giles is a friend of Laroux's."

The other sister hovered, indignation thrumming through her. "That man saw your hair, Sister Joelle."

The young woman's skin flushed red from her chest right up to her hairline. Even if she had never seen such a bright blush, Fleur recognized the color of shame.

"Giles has seen a woman's hair before," Fleur said.

"He has not seen the hair of a holy sister before."

"Sister Bernadette," the young woman said, "please. He did not show my hair on purpose, and you too must be careful not to get too hot."

"I heard Giles call you Joelle. It is a pretty name. Joelle," Fleur said again, feeling the syllables in her mouth.

"She is *Sister* Joelle," Sister Bernadette said.

"What is your name?" Joelle asked.

"When I am with French people, I am Fleur," she said as she bathed Joelle's face and chest with a damp cloth.

"I feel much better," Joelle said, trying to sit up. "Thank you, Fleur."

"Good. Then you can get dressed again immediately," Sister Bernadette said.

"Her dress is too hot," Fleur said evenly. "And the hat you wear is too hot. She must lie in bed the rest of the day. With the windows open."

"As Sister Joelle said, thank you, Fleur. I will take care of her now. You may go."

The young sister's light brown eyes apologized to Fleur, but she did not contradict the older woman. Fleur left the house, hoping Sister Bernadette did not make Joelle put the terrible hat back on.

Outside, Laroux waited for her, as she knew he would, so that he could walk her back to her people's blankets under the trees where they traded skins and baskets to the white men. Laroux seemed to think Fleur could not walk from here to there without getting lost, but she did not complain. Sometimes when he walked beside her, Laroux would touch her elbow or even the small of her back.

Only a few weeks ago, Fleur had thought she would be the one to close Laroux's eyes after he'd taken his last breath. His friends had brought him to her with a terrible wound in his shoulder. She had done what she could to keep the wound clean and to keep his fever from devouring him, but there were days she believed he would not wake to another morning.

Perhaps she loved him because, in his illness, he had been like her child. He'd been weak from loss of blood and helpless in his fever, and she took care of him until he was strong enough to leave the village and go to his own home. She worried about him there. He lived all alone, and he did not eat enough.

At her father's blanket, Fleur found her boy waking from his nap. Mahkee had no father, not since the days of the yellow fever, but he had his uncle and his grandfather. He would grow to be a man who could hunt and give counsel as well as any other man. She scooped him into her arms and tickled his tummy to make him laugh.

"Will you walk with me to my canoe?" Laroux asked.

Fleur glanced at her father who chose to look at a squirrel chasing around a tree.

She walked beside Laroux, quietly, as Biloxi women did with their men. Was Laroux her man? Perhaps he was. Or perhaps he could be. But not today.

At water's edge, Laroux said, "Will you come to my cabin? Just to see it?" His eyes were hungry on Mahkee as they were on her sometimes.

Her Laroux was a lonely man. It pulled at her, the need she saw in him. It made her want to take him in her arms. But when he had lain in her cabin, deeply asleep in his weakness, she had wanted to touch him then, too, when he was not at all lonely.

His eyes drifted back to Mahkee. "I will have a puppy in a few days. The mama dog at Griffin's is ready to let it go." He gave Mahkee his finger and smiled when Mahkee tried to put it in his mouth.

"We will come soon. To see this puppy."

Laroux did not smile at her as he had at Mahkee. He only said, "Good," and then got in his canoe and paddled away.

# Chapter Five

*Courtship*
*Second Wednesday*

Mademoiselle Emmeline had invited Giles to the next Wednesday picnic, and he would very much like to see her again. The children seemed to like her, and he liked her, too. But if he left his little farm again today, he was afraid he'd be inviting the encroaching forest to march right back into the land he'd cleared.

Since Bella died, it was hard to keep the farm up. Aside from missing her, there were the children to see to while he tried to clear more land, tend the crops, keep everyone clean and fed and safe. If he didn't have Rosalie to keep an eye on Felix, he didn't know how he'd manage.

Should he go all the way back to the fort to court Emmeline again today? He needed a wife, but he really needed to be in the field and to get some meat into the house. Food first, he decided. Then on Sunday he'd court Emmeline again.

"Rosalie," he said, gently nudging her shoulder. "Wake up, *ma petite.*"

She woke with a little jerk, instantly alert. Surely that was not a good thing, that his girl should be so tense even in her sleep. He put too much responsibility on her, he knew he did. But what else could he do, except get her a mother so that she could be a child again.

"I'm up, Papa."

"I'm going to work. Can you manage breakfast?"

"I can do it."

Giles collected his hoe and his picking basket and headed to the garden. The deer jerky he'd dried earlier in the summer was nearly gone. Well, he'd find time to fish, and he could try his hand at trapping again. Dupre had shown him how to make a noose trap, but so far all Giles's efforts had yielded were empty nooses.

A yell and a scream from the cabin had him running right through his bean plants. He burst through the door to see Felix on the floor, crying and rubbing his head, and Rosalie standing on a chair, both hands covering her face, sobbing piteously.

With one arm, Giles grabbed up Felix and then pulled Rosalie in to his chest and sat on the bed with both of them held close.

"What happened?" He directed his question at Isabel who was the only one who seemed coherent.

She let out a huge sigh. "Felix lost his balance on the bed post and hit his head when he fell."

"Why was Rosalie on the chair then?"

"That is a good question, Papa. She doesn't seem right in the head, does she?"

Felix's cries were becoming just a little bit forced, like he was not quite ready to give up the pleasures of his suffering. Rosalie, however, was sobbing into his neck.

Giles patted her back until her crying diminished to harsh breathing.

"Rosalie, sweetheart, what is it?" Felix had fallen off chairs and table tops and beds and tree stumps every other day since he could walk and climb. It couldn't be a bump on the noggin that had her so upset.

"I ruined breakfast," she managed to tell him between hiccups and sniffles.

"You ruined breakfast?" That's all?

"Felix was balancing on the bed post and I yelled at him to get down and then the porridge boiled over and I ran back to the pot and then I knocked it off the hook and it all spilled into the fire and now we don't have any breakfast and there isn't any more corn meal to make more porridge and everybody will be hungry and I can't feed us any porridge -- " Her voice had risen into a fine wail and then the tears came again.

"Hush, baby. It's all right."

This would not do. He was expecting too much of his girl. She shouldn't have the responsibility of feeding a family and looking after a three year old.

"Here's what we'll do." He set Felix on his feet but kept a hand on his shoulder. They didn't need any more climbing boys falling off some perch this morning. He took Rosalie by the chin and made her look at him.

"We'll eat some nuts and some mayhaws. We'll go to the fort and buy corn meal. And we'll visit the pretty ladies again. How's that?"

Instantly excited, Felix actually bounced. "Madame Jesus! I'll show her the lump on my head, Papa."

"Call her Sister Joelle, Felix, remember?"

"Will you tell her I ruined breakfast?"

"Of course not, darling. Although I may tell her about all the times you put steaming bowls of perfectly cooked porridge on the table. She would be mightily impressed."

With a shuddering sigh, Rosalie climbed off his lap. "I'll get the hammer to crack the nuts."

Now he had his children calmed down, Giles felt like weeping himself. How they missed Bella, all of them. They needed her, and not just to fix their breakfast. *I'm trying, Bella. I'm trying.*

Well, there was work to do. He got busy seeing everyone was fed, their faces and hands washed. Once that was accomplished, Giles herded his children into the dugout and pushed off into the river. The sun was high and hot when they arrived, and the picnic was well underway.

Giles wondered if Sister Joelle was sensibly staying out of the sun. What an amazing head of copper curls the girl had. Pity it was hidden under her wimple. Such a medieval contraption, those wimples, and in this heat.

"There she is!" Isabel hollered. She leapt out of the dugout before Giles had finished pulling it onto the beach and dashed toward Sister Joelle. Felix ran after her, and Rosalie followed.

She wore that awful habit, of course, but at least she was in the shade, standing with Dupre's wife Catherine and Madame Joubert.

The sister held her arms open as his children ran for her and laughed as all three of them grabbed her. Giles caught up to them as Sister Joelle bent to look at Felix's latest lump.

"My goodness, it's as big as a goose egg. Do you think there's a baby goose in there?"

As Felix giggled, Joelle put a hand on Rosalie's shoulder to show she knew she was there, that she was important, and at the same time smiled and nodded at Isabel's chatter.

"No, Isabel, I never have seen a baby bird peck its way out of its shell. Did you see it, too, Rosalie?"

Rosalie nodded. "It was a mockingbird baby."

"We know it was a mockingbird," Isabel explained, "because the egg was bluish with brown blotches. Isn't that right, Rosalie?"

Joelle turned to his eldest, who was not inclined to vie for attention when her sister was excited. "You've learned the color of birds' eggs?" the sister said. "What a wonderful thing to know."

She'd make a good mother, this young woman. Except, of course, she would never be a mother. A quick image of her extraordinary hair flickered across his mind again. Nor would she ever be a wife, he reminded himself.

Giles nodded to the dugout moving into the sound carrying Yves Aubel and a woman. "You've had another wedding today, have you?"

"We have," she said with a big smile. "Genevieve and her Monsieur Aubel."

"You are well? You're staying out of the sun?"

"Me?"

She looked surprised he would ask after her.

"Yes, you. You will have to watch the sun now you've succumbed to it once. It can happen again if you're not careful."

She seemed so very uncomfortable. Not used to being noticed, he would guess.

"Shall I take the children again while you visit with . . . with Emmeline?"

"Yes!" Isabel said.

"You're sure?" he asked Sister Joelle.

Her freckled face beamed at him. "I'm sure. And I promise not to let Felix get into the ants."

Giles laughed. "And you three," he said to his own, "you're to see Sister Joelle stays out of the sun."

He left his treasures with Sister Joelle and went looking for Emmeline. He'd thought of her often since last Sunday, and not just as a mother for his children. She had lovely wavy brown hair, and a sweet way about her. Her bosom was high and her waist small. Of course, the girl's figure was not -- well, of course it was. It was *of interest*, to put it in polite terms. It had been over a year since Bella died. He didn't think he would ever stop grieving for her, but he could learn to care for someone else, and he didn't hide from his need for a woman in his bed. Emmeline was desirable.

Very. And she had smiled at the children. She had even smiled at him.

Yes, he decided. Yes, he would be happy to take Emmeline home with him. Now he had only to help her make up her mind about him. About all four of them.

There were more men here today than there had been last week. And fewer women. They were spread out among the shade trees, some of them shy and maybe a little fearful. These were the ones who kept together as the men approached them. But not the flirtatious one he had noticed before. She was looking up at a stern-faced man, a little pout on her face. The man who took her on would need a strong constitution to keep that one in line.

He scanned the pretty faces looking for Emmeline and finally saw her leaning against a tree, a man in a velvet coat standing at ease before her, his weight on one fine, polished boot, the other boot placed just so to present an elegant picture. That velvet coat might be very fine, but it must be hot as blazes.

Should he approach? It would be rude, but he did have something of a prior claim with Emmeline. Or anyway, a prior acquaintance. He needed to cut out the competition, that's what he needed to do.

"Mademoiselle." He lifted his straw hat and was keenly aware of how rustic he looked next to this gentleman. "Monsieur."

"Monsieur Travert." Emmeline blushed. She glanced at the other man and then back to him.

"I am Pierre DuPont," the man said and offered his hand.

"Giles Travert."

"I hope you will congratulate us," he said. "Mademoiselle Emmeline has just agreed to become my wife."

Oh, hell. He'd waited too long. He forced a smile. "I do wish you well, and you, too, Emmeline. I hope you have a happy union for many long years to come."

"Thank you, Monsieur Travert."

He touched his hat to take his leave when Emmeline put her hand on his sleeve.

"Monsieur. I know you need a mother for your children." Emmeline nodded toward the woman Giles had met the first Sunday. "I could introduce you to Harriet. She hasn't yet chosen anyone."

Harriet again. He should feel some compassion for her, and he did. She was unappealing and cold and likely to be left here when all the other women had taken husbands. But Oh good Lord, he could not take her home for his children, nor for himself either.

"Thank you, Emmeline. Harriet and I have met." He nodded to the gentleman, smiled at Emmeline, and went off to nurse his pride.

He supposed he should try someone else. On a sigh, he looked around the grounds.

At the moment the women all seemed to be entertaining one or two gentlemen. All except Madame Joubert. She was talking with Catherine Dupre and Villiers's wife Agnes.

Giles considered her. She was a widow. Maybe she would take on a widower with three children. She wouldn't get many offers, poor woman, big and homely as she was. Emmeline was certainly prettier and more desirable, but he couldn't have Emmeline, could he?

This morning had been wrenching, seeing Rosalie weighed down with too much responsibility. At this point, he would be glad of someone who didn't mind hard work and would be good to his children.

Well, he could say hello, see how it went.

As he approached the three women, he felt uncomfortably self-conscious, each of them looking at him as if wondering what he could possibly want. He lifted his hat. "Madame Dupre, Madame Villiers, Madame Joubert."

"Good day, Monsieur Travert," Catherine and Agnes said. Madame Joubert scowled and said, "I don't go by Joubert. I'm Marie Claude. That's all."

Giles nodded. So she wasn't grieving over her lost husband anyway. He eyed her big, rough hands and the strong arms and shoulders. Clearly, she was a capable woman.

Should he mention the heat? Or the clouds to the west likely bringing a rain storm later? He'd bore even himself.

"I heard you speak about indigo a few weeks ago," he said.

"And what did you do about it?" Marie Claude said. A blunt woman. But he'd been impressed by her courage that day. The indigo broker, of course, had not wanted her to tell the colonists how poisonous the fumes were when the indigo was processed into blue dye. The man had tried to push her from the platform until she grabbed his fist and forced him to his knees.

"I will not plant indigo, Madame . . . Marie Claude. I've no desire to see a man sicken and die so I can prosper."

Marie Claude gave him a long, considering look. "Then you are a good man."

She was a plain woman until you took the time to notice her hair and her beautiful skin. He had yet to see her smile, but most any woman looked lovely when she smiled.

Giles glanced at the black man leaning against a tree perhaps thirty feet away. He'd heard she had slaves, and this one seemed to always be nearby. He recognized him from market days when he sold metal goods he'd forged. Nails, mostly, but the man took commissions for more complicated work, too. A valuable man, he seemed devoted to his mistress.

"For now, I'm intent on growing food, enough for the family of course, but enough to sell, too." He looked at Marie Claude. "I have three children, you see."

"Where are they?"

"They're with Sister Joelle over there under the pines. Would you like to meet them?"

"Yes, I would."

Agnes Villiers raised her eyebrows and glanced at Catherine. They had expected her to say no?

The two of them walked across the grounds, three feet of space between them. The sun fierce in the sky overhead, Giles asked, "Do you find the heat difficult?"

"Sometimes."

She wore no hat and her honey-blonde hair shone in the sunlight. She was only a little taller than he, not enough to matter really. And from what he could tell under her loose dress, her shape was quite nice.

Sister Joelle had managed to tame his three imps. Felix was asleep in her lap and Rosalie and Isabel listened intently as the sister told them a story. A Bible story, he heard as he got closer. One couldn't expect stories of knights and dragons from a sister, after all.

Marie Claude surprised him by immediately sitting on the ground next to Sister Joelle and nodding to her as if she wanted to hear the rest of the story. Sister Joelle smiled and carried on telling about all the animals, lions and rabbits and crickets, every sort of creature filing into Noah's Ark.

Giles settled himself on the ground as well and Isabel climbed into his lap.

Sister Joelle was a wonderful story teller. She made sweeping gestures with her arms to indicate the torrents of rain, and then the torturous waves rocking the ark back and forth and up and down. With great animation, she told of lightning and thunder and fearsome winds.

When the rain stopped and the sun shone down on the ark, Isabel let out a sigh of relief, and Marie Claude smiled and clapped her hands. She did have a lovely smile.

Once the water had drained away and the animals emerged from the ark, Rosalie said, "Another one, please, Sister."

Sister Joelle looked at him. "I think your father needs your company now. How do you do, Marie Claude?"

"Hello, Sister."

"Do you know Monsieur Travert's children? This little one is Felix, and these are Rosalie and Isabel."

Marie Claude looked at each child, eye to eye. To Rosalie, she said, "I bet you take good care of your baby brother."

"I do, but he is not a baby anymore."

Marie Claude smiled and looked at Isabel. "Do you like stories?"

"Maman used to tell us a story every night. Do you tell stories?"

Now there was a smile, even sweeter than the last one. The woman liked children, and stories.

"I do. But I'm not as exciting as Sister Joelle."

"That's all right. Any story is a good story," Isabel said.

She was a moral woman, warning everyone what indigo could do to a man's lungs. She liked children. And her smile was something to see. A heart could find warmth in that smile.

He looked over at the blacksmith slave waiting for Marie Claude. Giles didn't hold with slavery. That would be something they would have to work out.

But he was getting ahead of himself.

Sister Joelle kissed the top of Felix's head. "I should see where I am needed." She handed his boy to Marie Claude without waking him, and then she did a curious thing. She looked full on at Giles, her pretty brown eyes clear and -- unreadable.

What had she meant by a look like that? If she were not a novice, he would think -- he shook his head. Nonsense. It had been merely a glance before she went on her way.

Marie Claude cradled Felix, one of his little hands in hers. She gazed down on him as if he were a wondrous creature, and Giles supposed he was.

"You have sweet children, Monsieur Travert."

"I'm Giles. And you know what they say about sleeping children," he said with a nod to his drowsy son.

"Nothing sweeter than. That's what my father always said. Easy to love a sleeping child."

"Are you used to children who run and yell and spill things and fuss at bedtime?"

"I have little brothers and sisters at home. I know all about the excuses they get up to at bedtime. My littlest sister, Evangeline, used to tell me she couldn't go to sleep until the moon did, but I told her the moon was just waiting for her to go to sleep so he could go to bed."

"Did it work?"

Marie Claude grinned at him. "Not once."

He rather liked this plain woman. And she liked his children.

Yes, he decided.

"Marie Claude, my children need a mother. I need a wife."

The smile on her face faded away.

"Giles, I will not marry again."

Every woman he had ever known, excepting Sister Joelle, of course, wanted a husband. Life was hard enough without a woman trying to make a go of it on her own.

"I don't need a husband. I can work my farm myself, and I have three good men to help me."

"Slaves, you mean."

"The law says they are slaves. But on my farm, they are not slaves."

"You don't want . . . a man in your life?"

Marie Claude's big hand gently smoothed the hair from Felix's forehead. She shook her head. "I don't want a husband ever again."

So marriage to Monsieur Joubert had not been good.

"I'm not a bully, Marie Claude," he said softly. "I would never hurt you."

She looked at him then, really looked. For a moment, he thought she might say yes. And then her gaze moved to the black man leaning against a pine tree, watching them. His face gave nothing away.

She shook her head. "I don't want a husband."

She reached her big hand to touch his knee. "But Giles, if you ever need help with the children, if you get sick, or . . . if you send for me, I will come."

He took her work-hardened hand in his own. "I'm sorry you don't want a husband, Marie Claude. I truly am."

She smiled, gave his hand a squeeze, and let go.

After a companionable silence, Marie Claude had a sudden thought. "Have you met Harriet yet?"

~~~

Once Marie Claude said goodbye to the man and his children, Thomas fell into step with her on the way to the dugout.

Thomas had watched the sparkle in Marie Claude's eyes dim these last weeks. Losing her baby from that evil man's beating had taken all the joy out of her. But just now, with the little boy asleep in her arms, she had glowed -- the way she had the first time he saw her.

The master had brought home this young woman whom he had met and married that same day. She'd stepped out of the dugout and the sun caught her hair and lit it in gold and bronze. She had smiled as she looked around the place, pleased to be alive, it seemed.

Marie Claude and her new husband were strangers that day, but Thomas knew Monsieur Joubert very well. He was not a good man, and so Thomas worried about the girl. Marie Claude was no weak thing like so many white women, though. She was big as a man, and she knew how to work. Most of all, she was a woman with heart.

That time Marie Claude had shown Joubert a tiny perfect frog in the palm of her hand -- Thomas had been nearby. He saw her face when Joubert knocked the frog from her hand and then ground it under his heel. She turned white as bone, her gray eyes filled up with tears, and in that moment, Thomas's heart opened to her.

He'd wanted to hold her and soothe her, but he was a slave. All he could do was bury the frog with tender hands, to show her that he cared.

Thomas had been a slave all his life, but that didn't make it right inside himself. Joubert had bought him and the other three because they knew how to make indigo. They'd cost him plenty, skilled as they were. Thomas was even more skilled than Joubert knew. He was a blacksmith, but he didn't reveal that to his new master. Only once the man was dead did he set up a forge and begin to earn some money for the place. For Marie Claude.

She'd been going through the days like she was half-asleep, until today when she held the little boy in her lap. Marie Claude was a woman meant to be a mother. And now she had no husband. But anyone would want to marry her, as strong and as good as she was. Maybe that Monsieur Travert. If Marie Claude married him, she'd have three children to mother and love, and later on, she'd have her own babies, too. He'd like to see that, Thomas thought, Marie Claude happy, the gladness back inside her.

"That man wants to marry you?" Thomas said.

Marie Claude let out a sigh and nodded.

"He has good children," he added.

"They are good children. I liked them, all of them."

"He seemed a good man."

"I think he is."

"Marie Claude, you should marry this man."

She kept her gaze straight ahead.

"You want children, Marie Claude. He has three. He could give you three more, or six or eight."

"If I had a husband, Thomas, everything would be his. My farm. My self." She looked at him from the side of her eye. "And you."

They did not speak again until they were in the dugout and half way across the sound.

"You should marry this man," Thomas said again.

# Chapter Six

*A Miracle*
*Third Sunday*

Joelle sat on her bed while Sister Bernadette finished dressing. In the past, Joelle had always used the moments before mass to compose herself, opening her mind to God so as to give herself over to His presence. This Sunday, she was having trouble concentrating.

She had felt not quite herself for some time, she realized. Her mind was too busy; too many new things in her life, that's all it was. Monsieur Travert's children, they were with her constantly. Their little faces had been alight as --

"You're daydreaming again," Sister Bernadette scolded. "What is it this time?"

Joelle tried to smile. "I was just thinking about the Travert children, Sister, that's all."

"You have spent far too much time with those children. Your job is to see that these girls behave themselves until they are married. Not to frivol away your time playing and telling stories."

Sister Bernadette attached the rosary to her belt, but that didn't distract her from berating Joelle. "You are to set an example to the young women by being attentive to Father Xavier. Is he not our priest, our father here on earth? For shame, Sister, forgetting your duties."

"Yes, Sister." What else could she say? The life of a nun was one of obedience, after all. To God, of course, but to her order, to her superiors.

"Come along," Sister Bernadette commanded and led the way into the chapel to the first row of benches.

Joelle eyed the rough bench, no more than a split log on legs, hoping not to catch her skirt on a splinter again. Mending was not her favorite chore.

She sat down gingerly and folded her hands in her lap. As Father Xavier began the prayers, Joelle closed her eyes, shutting out the distractions of fidgeting people, the smells of heated bodies pressed together, the sweltering heat.

Father Xavier's voice droned on, and Joelle's mind wandered to the memory of Felix asleep in her lap, how she'd felt with his sweet, hot body nestled against her. And how thrilling it was to see the children's and even Marie Claude's face light up as she told her story.

A hard pinch to her arm shocked Joelle back to the present. "Pay attention!" Sister Bernadette hissed. "Remember what I told you."

Joelle swallowed a sigh.

Even when she'd stared out the window at the life below the convent, wishing she could talk to the people on Rue des Boulangers, she had been happy. Now she had all the company, all the conversation she could want, and yet here she was, in chapel, and she couldn't concentrate. Was it because Sister Bernadette was right about her extravagant hair, that it signified a sinful nature?

But how could it be sinful to think about children? Getting dressed, cleaning the chapel, urging the sleepyheads to get up in the morning -- she found her mind on Felix's sweet face, on Rosalie in her solemn need, or Isabel in her exuberance. And they seemed to care for her, too. How could she resist such a pull?

But she must. She was not what the children needed, not her.

Joelle wiped the sweat from beneath her eyes, breathed deeply, and renewed her attempt to connect to Father Xavier's voice, to enter into the channel he opened to God's loving mercy.

Moments later, pulling at the sweat-drenched linen tied around her neck, she thought of those moments when she'd had heat stroke and been allowed to lie in her underdress in front of an open window -- she longed to lie like that again, a breeze wafting over her bare skin.

Nausea rose in her throat and she feared she would faint.

She got to her feet and pushed past Sister Bernadette, ignoring her astonished protests, and hurried out of the airless chapel. Stumbling her way into the shade, she leaned against a tree and gulped in air.

"Sister?" Seraphina took her elbow. "I saw you leave. Are you all right?"

Joelle's head pounded and bile rose in her throat. "I'm fine."

Seraphina peered into her face. "I don't think so." She took Joelle's arm and hustled her toward the little cove behind the barracks. This is where the women washed their clothes, and where they bathed after dark when no one could see them in their shifts.

At the water's edge, Seraphina insisted she sit in the shade. She took Joelle's shoes and stockings off, wet one of the stockings and wiped Joelle's face with it.

Joelle shoved Seraphina away, leant over and vomited into the sand.

"That's it. I'm taking this off." Seraphina batted Joelle's hands away and unfastened the linen neckerchief, unwound it, and pulled the entire headdress off Joelle's head. "The cap, too," Seraphina said.

Joelle felt blessed relief, the breeze cooling her sweat-soaked hair and her bare feet.

"You sit right here. Nobody can see you. You just wait and I'll go get some water."

With Seraphina gone, weariness and shame took hold of her and she leaned her head into her hands, remembering Monsieur Travert had seen her with her hair uncovered. No man had ever seen her hair before, not since she was a child, and it was such awful hair. Not only was it practically orange, it curled itself into tight ringlets. It humiliated her every time Sister Bernadette cut it, the red ringlets shining bright on the floor.

Joelle huffed a breath, and then another. God, she reminded herself, had given her this hair. She was foolish to act as if it were the mark of Cain. It was merely hair, and she kept it decently covered. She mustn't let Sister Bernadette's worst notions fill her head.

By the time Seraphina returned, Joelle had composed herself. She drank from the flagon of water and dug her toes into the cool damp sand.

"Thank you, Seraphina."

"It was nothing. Just think how much credit I'm accumulating for the next time I err."

Joelle smiled at her. "You plan to err again, do you?"

"It is inevitable."

They sat in companionable silence for a while.

50

"I don't think God wants you to wear a wimple in this heat."

Joelle looked at her, shocked. How could she say such a thing?

"I mean it. That headdress is meant for people living where it's hot only a few days a year, and never as hot as this. Why would God want you to suffer heat stroke?"

Joelle rested with her eyes closed. It was too hot to argue.

After a few quiet moments, Seraphina said, "Can I ask you something?"

"Why wouldn't you?"

"Because it is not done, this kind of question."

Joelle opened her eyes enough to glance at Seraphina and smiled. "Go ahead."

"It's just that I don't understand. Why do you want to be a nun? You have to give up so much. A husband. Children. Seems like you give up *life*. I don't see how that helps God any."

Joelle had been shocked at the idea of not wearing the wimple. She was horrified at this. Surely it was blasphemy to suggest the life of a nun did not serve God.

"I don't mean any disrespect, Sister Joelle. You'll be a good nun, you *are* a good nun even now. But don't you yearn for a man in your life? Don't you want to be touched? Isn't what happens between men and women one of the great mysteries of life? One that God approves of?"

"But I . . . "

"Don't be angry. I wonder, that's all. How you could give up so much?"

"I just . . . " Joelle couldn't think how to explain. "I want to be a nun. I want to love God."

"I love God," Seraphina said. Whatever she saw in Joelle's face caused Seraphina to grab her hand. "I'm sorry. I really am. I didn't mean to upset you."

"I don't know how to tell you." She shook her head, struggling to explain. "It's all I've ever wanted, to be a nun."

"All right. I shouldn't have asked. It is not my place. Here, I'm going to wet your cap before I put it back on you, both your stockings, too. That'll keep you cooler."

Joelle and Seraphina rejoined the men and women on the grounds. "You won't mention this to Sister Bernadette, will you?" Joelle asked.

"If you'll stay in the shade and drink plenty of water, she won't ever know."

Joelle touched Seraphina's arm. "Thank you."

Seraphina grasped Joelle's hand.

Such an odd sensation, Joelle thought, to have her hand in someone else's. It was . . . nice.

"You are most welcome, Sister."

A large man was striding toward them. Tall, muscled, no fat on him. No one here carried any fat, except for Sister Bernadette, and she was noticeably slimmer than she was when they left France. "Is that the man you've chosen?" Joelle said, nodding toward him.

Seraphina drew in a long slow breath. "That's him. Excuse me, Sister."

Joelle watched her go to the man she meant to marry. The man did not smile when she stopped a few inches in front of him. As Joelle walked toward the shade trees, she could see that Seraphina wasn't smiling either. Instead they were simply looking at each other. Well, what did Joelle know of men and women?

She scanned the grounds, seeing who was alone and in need of help finding a suitor to talk to. Harriet, yes. Ariadne was alone, but there was a young man walking toward her with a bunch of wild flowers in his hand. So, Harriet then.

How kind Seraphina had been to help her cool off, Joelle thought as she crossed the ground toward Harriet. But those questions. Why did she want to be a nun? She'd never thought to be anything else. Of course she wanted to be a nun.

But what if after all she were like Seraphina, or Miranda? What if she were meant to marry a man and be a mother to his children? What if that's what God intended for her and she simply didn't know it? Joelle stopped mid-step. How does one know what God intends?

Eyes closed, Joelle searched for God, for a connection, right now. Surely he had already chosen the life of a nun for her. Why else was she here, wearing this habit, preparing to take her vows? *Show me, God. Please show me.*

She heard nothing, felt nothing. Maybe instead of showing her the way, God was watching to see what she would do.

She would do what she was supposed to do, of course. At this moment, she was supposed to help Harriet find a husband.

Harriet's hair hung down her back again, loosely tied with a piece of twine. She did have remarkable hair. Dark, but so curly and full it was as if she wore a dark cloud around her head. Gorgeous hair, really.

"Hello, Harriet."

"Sister Joelle. How do you do?"

"I am well. Is there someone I could introduce you to?"

Harriet looked at her with a squint. "You know all these men?"

"I know many of them. The ones I don't know I can still introduce you to. I don't have to be shy with gentlemen like you do. I'm a nun."

"Well, you're a novice."

Joelle refrained from grinding her teeth. What good would it do to be annoyed with Harriet?

"Yes. I'm a novice. I see two gentlemen over there. Would you like to meet them?"

"It is not lady-like to put myself in front of gentlemen. If they wish an introduction, they may approach me."

"Very well." Joelle marched off across the grounds, remembering too late she was to avoid the sunlight. Her cap and stockings were still wet, however, and she would cross quickly.

"Gentlemen," she began, smiling at them. One of them was Monsieur Laroux, the one who was friends with the Indian girl Fleur.

"Good day, Sister. Are you keeping out of the sun?"

"Mostly, I am, sir." She looked at the other man. "I am Sister Joelle."

"Aubrey Baer, sister."

"Are you looking for a wife, Monsieur Baer?"

"I've not made up my mind to it. Perhaps."

"Would you let me introduce you to some of the girls? Harriet is available at the moment."

Monsieur Baer narrowed his eyes and gazed across the grounds at Harriet. "This is the woman who carries her Bible with her everywhere? A Huguenot?"

*But doesn't she have lovely hair?* Joelle wanted to say. Instead, she said, "Harriet is strong in her faith, yes, but -- "

"I don't think we would suit, Sister."

"I see. Perhaps you will see someone else who interests you." She left the two men, annoyed with Monsieur Baer on Harriet's behalf. Then again, perhaps she should be annoyed with Harriet for being so obstinate. And unpleasant about it as well. What would they do with Harriet if she found no one to marry? Perhaps she could work at the fort, take in laundry or mending.

She remembered she must drink and walked over to the water table where a young soldier handed her a ladle. She sipped it slowly and then asked for another. Her gaze wandered over all the people spread out on the grounds, and then she realized what she was looking for. Whom she was waiting for. Monsieur Travert, with his children. It was well past mid-day. Weren't they coming?

"Sister Joelle." The petite woman, Agnes Villiers, came to her. "We are about to begin our little *école*. Would you like to come?"

"Oh, yes, I would."

Joelle fell into step with Agnes. "What are you teaching today?"

"Selina is going to show us how to make a kind of flour out of cattails, the tall rushes growing on the edges of ponds and lakes."

So Joelle settled down to learn how to make flour out of rushes. Maybe someday she would gather herbs and teach the women what she knew about making healing teas and salves. Sister Marguerite used to swear by the tonic Joelle gave her.

A dugout pulled into the landing carrying, not the Traverts, but a woman and three slaves. One of them helped her step ashore and Joelle could see it was Bridget, hugely pregnant now. Why had she made the trip from her homestead when she looked ready to drop that baby at any moment?

Bridget walked with one hand pressed into her lower back, her gait clumsy and slow. She paused once, her body shuddered, and Joelle wondered if she were already having pains. She looked around. Who here knew how to help her if she began her labor?

The poor woman's velvet gown must have been hotter than Joelle's own habit. Sweat trickled down Bridget's cheeks and her face was very red.

Selina halted her presentation and stared. The other wives turned to look at her. No one spoke or moved for a long moment. Why did no one rush to help her sit in the shade?

Joelle must welcome her then, but Marie Claude rose and stepped around her friends to come to Bridget's side. The poor woman leaned all her weight into Marie Claude and groaned. "It's time," she panted.

Marie Claude looked over her shoulder. "Catherine."

Catherine called to Joelle. "Sister, we can use the infirmary?"

"I'll go ahead and see there's a bed ready."

In only a few moments, Marie Claude and Catherine half carried Bridget into the infirmary and laid her on a cot where she immediately arched her back and groaned.

"You are midwives?" Joelle asked.

Catherine shook her head. "We attended a friend's birth on the passage over. That's all."

"There must be someone among the Biloxi who delivers babies," Marie Claude said.

"You're right. I'll go ask," Catherine said.

"Let's get this hot dress off her." Marie Claude held her up while Joelle unfastened the buttons up her back.

"What are you doing here, Bridget?" Marie Claude asked. "You might have had to deliver your baby in a dugout canoe."

Bridget only groaned. "It hurts."

"I'll make you a cloth rope out of something in a minute and you can bite on it if you need to."

Catherine came in with a Biloxi woman of middle years who quietly assumed control. She called for warm water and cloths, for clean moss and a fire to cleanse her blade.

The afternoon wore on, Bridget suffering, either panting or wailing. Joelle's nerves were ragged with Bridget's cries, with waiting, with heat, but she continued praying the rosary, praying that it would soon be over.

The Biloxi woman's patience was deep as the ocean. Even the most piercing scream didn't seem to ruffle her. Joelle added such poise to her list of qualities to aspire to.

In the next half hour, Bridget's contractions came one after another, her lungs grasping at air as she panted.

The Biloxi woman pantomimed for Bridget to push down with her belly muscles, push, push again.

Joelle had never seen a naked body before, certainly never seen a female's lower parts, but she could not look away. Slowly the baby's head emerged, and then the whole little body slipped out of its mother.

Joelle recoiled. "What's that?" she whispered.

"That's the cord," Marie Claude said. "It's just as it should be. We'll cut it off and he'll have a fine belly button."

It took a moment for Joelle to understand. A belly button. She'd had no idea. She had never even wondered what the nub was in the middle of her belly.

The Indian woman held the child up, but he remained still and silent. Gently she massaged the baby's back, and then the child gasped and let out a cry. Joelle pressed her fingers to her mouth, and her eyes filled with tears. She had never been so overwhelmed as she was at this moment. Surely this was one of God's miracles, and she had seen it!

She knelt and prayed for God to bless this child and its mother, to see them to health and a life lived in Jesus' name.

She heard Catherine say, "It's a boy, Bridget."

Joelle heard the trickle of water as Catherine bathed the child, and then Joelle rose to see Bridget hold her arms out, eager to have him in her arms. When she put the babe to her breast, Joelle looked away.

These other women, they thought nothing of seeing Bridget's naked body. Of seeing . . . that . . . down there where the baby came from. Joelle felt suddenly deprived. Why didn't she know what other women knew? She had not been at all sure how the baby was to get out of its mother, but she knew now.

The sun coming through the window indicated late afternoon. She was exhausted. She herself of course had not felt the pangs of labor, but she had listened to Bridget's suffering, she had sweltered through the hours with her, and she was light-headed again. She needed to get some air.

"I will come back in an hour to sit with her," she told Marie Claude. She stepped outdoors and squinted at the bright light.

"There you are," Sister Bernadette said.

"Oh, Sister. A baby was just born!"

"There was a birth? Why did I know nothing about a birth? Not one of our girls, surely?"

Joelle tilted her head to look at Sister Bernadette. Even she knew babies took most of a year to grow inside a woman. How could one of their girls have a baby?

"No," Sister Bernadette answered her own question. "Of course not. I have been an attentive guardian. Yes I have."

Joelle could see the next thought cross her face.

56

"But what were you doing in there? You should not have been in there. You should know nothing about babies being born! I don't know what Father Xavier will think."

Hot and tired and unnerved by the afternoon's event, Joelle wanted to tell the sister she did not care what Father Xavier would think, but she held her tongue.

As she walked through the shady pines, she thought about what Sister Bernadette said. That she should know nothing about how babies were born. But it had been glorious, that moment when the baby took in a gasping breath and let out a loud lusty cry. At that moment, another being came into life. How could it be wrong to have seen this miracle?

The thought that Sister Bernadette could be wrong about something would not have occurred to Joelle a few weeks ago. She was astounded at herself. She doubted Sister Bernadette's warnings that her hair marked her as likely to sin, and she knew in her bones it was not wrong for a nun to know about birthing babies.

Joelle pondered her own boldness. Who was she to decide an older, wiser nun could be wrong? But Sister Bernadette was wrong. And believing that, Joelle decided, did not amount to a transgression that must be confessed to Father Xavier. She could think her own thoughts and still be a good nun.

# Chapter Seven

*A Baptism*
*Third Sunday Continued*

Marie Claude ached to hold the baby in Bridget's arms. He was so beautiful, his delicate skin smoother than silk, each tiny finger perfect. Yearning carved a hollow in her chest where all the tears and lost hope collected. She would never have a child now, never be a mother.

If she didn't get hold of herself, she was going to have to leave, and she didn't want to do that. She was feeling sorry for herself, that's all, and she wouldn't do it anymore.

Catherine wiped the sweat from Bridget's face. "When you don't come home this evening, your husband will be worried."

"Is it so far?" Sister Joelle asked. "We can send word, and maybe he can be here by mid-morning tomorrow to collect you and the baby." She looked puzzled. "He didn't realize it was time for the baby, I suppose."

The young nun, Catherine too, was so innocent, but Marie Claude knew there was no way the man hadn't known the baby was due, not with how huge Bridget's belly had been, with how she could barely waddle across the grounds. He wouldn't be coming for them.

Bridget smoothed the black hair across her baby's forehead, unwilling to look at any of them.

"So you came here for help, and he won't have you back," Marie Claude concluded.

Bridget shook her head.

"But he has to. He married you. Didn't he?" Sister Joelle said.

Marie Claude blew out a long breath. "The baby is not his, Sister."

When Sister Joelle frowned, Marie Claude wondered if she understood how babies came to be. Did she even know a father didn't have to be a husband?

Marie Claude tapped Sister Joelle's chin. "You're gaping, Sister. This is not the first child conceived in sin. It's no fault of his."

Sister Joelle blushed. "Of course it isn't."

Marie Claude took the baby from Bridget and handed him to Joelle. "Come on," she said as she and Catherine took Bridget's arms to help her out of the bed. "We'll get you to the privy and then you can sleep a while before the baby wakes."

Joelle was left alone with a tiny baby in her arms. She swallowed, a little frightened, but more, she was awed. What a wondrous thing, this brand new person in her arms. His eyelids were graced with dark lashes, his cheeks were smooth as cream. His lips pursed and worked even in his sleep. She took his hand in hers and marveled at the perfect little fingernails.

Never in her life had she thought she might hold a baby. Her breath shuddered and she feared she was about to be overcome, and that would not do. Sister Bernadette had warned her time and again not to let emotions discompose her. Was not tranquility the mark of God's favor?

But how could she not tremble in the face of such a miracle? The baby's fingers curled around her own and she hoped he never let go.

Sister Bernadette bustled in with Father Xavier in tow. "Here she is," Sister Bernadette said, her tone brisk and censorious. "I had to tell Father Xavier, Sister Joelle, that you had deliberately participated in the actual birthing of this child." She turned to the priest. "I told her it was shameful to be here with such nakedness, but she never listens to me. And now she has stepped past her duties again."

"I was here," she said, her gaze still on the baby in her arms. He slept so peacefully, with perfect trust he would be taken care of. And he would be.

Father Xavier stepped around Sister Bernadette. His sharp cheekbones and sunken eyes seemed less severe in this light. He looked on the child for a moment, and then he placed his bony hand on its forehead and closed his eyes.

"Here, Father." Sister Bernadette interrupted his silent prayer to hand him a vial.

"You are going to baptize him now? Should we not wait a moment for his mother to be here?" Joelle dared to say.

"Yes. We will wait," Father Xavier said, his hand caressing the baby's head before he stepped back.

No one spoke. Father Xavier and Sister Bernadette stood perfectly still as if waiting involved a state of suspension. Joelle gently rocked side to side, all her attention on the beauty of the child in her arms.

Bridget returned, leaning on Marie Claude's arm. Seeing the priest, she flushed a deep red, but she raised her chin and took her baby from Joelle.

"The child must have a name for baptism," Father Xavier said.

Bridget hesitated.

"What was your father's name?" Marie Claude asked.

When Bridget scowled and shook her head, Marie Claude suggested, "You could name him after the king."

"Or one of the saints," Joelle added.

Bridget thought a moment. "Matthew, then."

"And your husband is Andrew Guerin? So, Matthew Guerin."

Bridget's jaw hardened and her lips thinned as she threw a defiant look at Father Xavier. "My child's name is Matthew Moreau."

"Matthew Moreau Guerin, then."

"No. Matthew Moreau."

Father Xavier's thin brows rose. He looked at Sister Bernadette, who seemed confused.

Father Xavier's penetrating gaze settled on Bridget. "What will your husband say when he hears what you have named his son?"

Bitterness in her laugh, Bridget said, "He will be pleased his name is not attached to this child."

"Matthew Moreau is a fine name," Marie Claude said.

Joelle echoed her softly. "Matthew Moreau."

Father Xavier's whole body radiated disapproval. "This cannot be. The child must have his father's name."

Marie Claude glanced at Bridget. "Father, you remember Bridget and me, lots of us, were whores before we came here. She doesn't know the father's name."

With sudden understanding, Father Xavier's body jerked back as if he had never been in the presence of sin before. He cast a glance at Bridget that, had he the power, would have sent her straight to hell.

Joelle stared at the priest. Had he not often been in the presence of sinners in the confessional, only a screen between him and the sinner? Would he have been one of the people in the Bible who would have cast stones at a sinful woman? But he was a priest. Joelle's stomach knotted as she realized she was again questioning her elders, her very guides to virtuous conduct.

"Very well." Father Xavier opened the first bottle and sprinkled holy water on the baby's head. "I baptize you, Matthew Moreau, in the name of the Father, and of the Son, and of the Holy Spirit."

From the second vial, he poured three drops of sacred oil onto the babe's head and gently rubbed it over his scalp. "May the Holy Spirit dwell within the heart of this new Christian child."

The baptisms Joelle had attended had been solemn, lengthy affairs with singing and prayers. The priest had worn splendid vestments, the baby had been dressed in lace and linen, and the joyful parents and grandparents and godparents had crowded round to watch the baby accept the holy water on its head, or else scream lustily in protest. Either way, everyone smiled.

Still, Bridget's baby was baptized now. That's what mattered most, that he be readied to enter heaven if some illness overtook him. She had had nightmares as a child when she first heard what befell babies who died before being baptized.

As Bridget kissed Matthew's forehead, Sister Bernadette tugged at Joelle's sleeve. "Come away, now."

Outside, Father Xavier strode away from them, his black robe swirling around his legs.

Joelle looked at Sister Bernadette's pinched face. "You are displeased with me, Sister."

"I don't know what you were thinking involving yourself like this. First you remain during the baring of a woman's body. Then you remain when you know what kind of woman she is. If you are to be a nun, Sister Joelle, you must keep better company. I warn you, if I must I shall insist Father Xavier take steps to discipline you."

This was new, to threaten rather than to simply scold. But Joelle was not a child. She was not frightened at the prospect.

Instead, she simply kept step with Sister Bernadette as they joined the women at supper. She didn't argue, and she did not try to excuse herself either, nor express contrition. Perhaps she would, later. But at the moment, she needed to think. A holy sister should not mix with sinners? Did not holy sisters commit sins as well? And there was Father Xavier judging Bridget when only God was to judge. And here she was, questioning and doubting. And was that not a sin?

After supper, Joelle walked down to the water to catch a cooling breeze. To be by herself for a while, and to think, but she did not have the landing to herself.

"Monsieur Travert," Joelle called. He and the children were heading toward the dugouts, Felix asleep on his shoulder. "You're leaving?"

"Time I got these children home." He waited for her to catch up to them.

"Did you meet someone you like today?" She shouldn't ask. That was too personal.

Monsieur Travert's sad smile seemed touched with a little resignation, a little humor, a little regret. "No one pining to be Madame Travert. All we saw were very nice young women hoping for a less demanding life than taking on the four of us."

"We're very discouraged," Rosalie said.

Isabel took Joelle's hand and looked at her father. "We haven't asked Sister Jesus," she said.

Joelle felt the heat rise in her face, but Monsieur Travert only bit his lip to keep from smiling.

"Sister Joelle, Isabel. And she won't marry anyone, remember?"

"Except Jesus."

"That's right." He grinned at Joelle. "We didn't see you this afternoon. You did well to keep out of the sun."

"Oh, Monsieur Travert. The most wonderful thing. I was at the birth of a baby."

He gave her a big happy smile. He understood what she was feeling.

"That is a momentous thing, is it not?" He glanced at his three. "There is nothing like it, when a little one comes into the world."

"I've never felt such -- I've never felt such . . . " She didn't know what she wanted to say.

"Such joy."

"Yes. As if my heart was too big for my chest. As if I could sing."

He was smiling at her, and looking at her with an odd expression. She flushed again. She was being exuberant. Sister Bernadette wouldn't like it.

Isabel swung their hands. "You could come home with us. I'd tell you a story and you could tell us a story."

Oh! Joelle had a sudden picture of herself in a cabin with Monsieur Travert, Rosalie, Isabel, and Felix, all of them gathered in front of a cozy fire. Sister Bernadette would delay her taking vows for another year if she knew she had even thought of it.

Monsieur Travert touched her arm. "Don't fret, Sister. Isabel doesn't realize, that's all."

"Oh, I'm not fretful, Monsieur Travert." She did not want him to know how unsettled she was, at the thought of being part of this family, at being touched.

"No, of course not." He looked to his children. "Well. One more Wednesday and one more Sunday. We'll try again, shall we?"

"Yes, do, Monsieur Travert. There are still women who have not committed themselves to anyone."

"Maybe you can point them out to us next time." They were at the landing now. "Good night, Sister."

Joelle watched Monsieur Travert settle the children in the dugout and push off into the sound.

Rosalie and Isabel waved to her and she raised her hand good-bye.

How extraordinary. He had touched her, just there where she could still feel the press of his finger. Not a necessary, practical touch like helping her from the water. Joelle pressed a hand to her heart. He had touched her just because he wanted to touch her.

# Chapter Eight

*A Baby and a Puppy*
*Third Sunday Continued*

Fleur sat in the dugout with Mahkee in her lap as Laroux paddled them across the sound toward his homestead. She watched him, this slender French man whom she had nursed back to health.

Fleur's husband's body had been large, his arms, chest and shoulders shaped by the bulk of muscle. Her beloved's skin had been the color of walnuts, and as smooth as her own.

This man's open shirt revealed a tanned triangle of skin at his throat, but Fleur had seen him in his nakedness, and touched him too, when she'd cooled Laroux's feverish body with damp cloths.

The skin under Laroux's clothing was as pale as the inside of an oyster shell. The muscles of his arms were slender, but defined. His abdomen was lean and hard, each muscle distinct from the others. And he had hair on his chest. As he lay unconscious in his fever, she had been tempted to trail her fingertips along that dark trail down his belly, but she had not.

The sun would set in a few hours. Perhaps, after she had seen his home, instead of paddling the bayou in the dark and then stumbling along the path to the village, perhaps she would spend the night with Laroux in his cabin.

Laroux hauled the dugout ashore at his farmstead, then reached for Mahkee, who went to him eagerly. With Mahkee in one arm, the French man held his other hand out to help her from the dugout. Fleur noticed again how the French seemed to think women were delicate, like flowers, or small children, guiding them across open ground as if they could not see with their own eyes, helping them over fallen logs as if they could not lift their own feet. Fleur had found it comical at first, but she had come to like the little touches that came with such assistance.

Laroux led them up a short trail into open ground where his cabin stood. "This is it," he said, looking at her.

It seemed a nice cabin, built on log posts in case the bayou should flood. She knew that it would, the next time a storm came. So Laroux thought of the future.

He opened the plank door and motioned her in ahead of him. As soon as she stepped in, the puppy began whining and begging to be let out of his box. She knelt and picked him up, letting him lick her chin. "Look, Mahkee."

Mahkee reached for the puppy, laughing as it licked him in the face. He rolled on his back, giggling, and the dog pounced on him, his tail wagging madly.

Fleur looked at her Frenchman watch her child play with the puppy, his eyes and his mouth smiling. She had not seen this smile before, unguarded and completely happy.

This man was not like the men of her tribe. He did not seem like the men of his either. He was pretty, like a woman. His lashes were long and thick and his eyes big and deep. His mouth was wide, his lips soft and slightly pink. Pretty, like a woman. But she did not forget how his naked body had stirred her.

He saw she looked at him, and he took her hand in his. "Welcome to my home."

She looked around the room, seeing how a French man lived in a log house. A wooden floor that would stay dry when it rained. Windows that let in light and air. A table. Two stumps for stools.

A rabbit hung from the rafters. Fleur wondered if the mice climbed down the rope in the night to nibble at Laroux's supper.

A clay fireplace covered with soot showed where he did his cooking. She bent to look inside at the tunnel going up. "This is a chimney?"

"Yes. It funnels the smoke through the roof to the outside."

"What happens when it rains?"

He laughed. "If it rains hard enough, it puts my fire out. I haven't figured out yet how to make a chimney cap that will let the smoke through and keep the rain out. At least, not one that won't catch fire or melt in the rain."

Fleur knew how to fire clay so it would not melt. She could show him how, if she lived here.

On the other wall was his bed, a platform raised from the floor in the French way. The French did not like the floor. It was only for feet, she supposed, and children and puppies.

Laroux knelt to Mahkee, grabbed him and the puppy up. "Let's take this fellow outside to do his business."

Mahkee wrapped an arm around Laroux's neck. Her little one liked this man.

While they were outside, Fleur fingered the book propped atop the mantle. She had seen a book once before, at the fort. This book was not filled with the same marks. Laroux drew pictures instead.

She set the book on the table and pored over the first drawing. It was of a heron, its long legs bent in its stalky walk. The bird's eye seemed to look right at her. She turned the page. Three turtles sunned themselves on a log at the edge of the bayou. Carefully she turned the pages, admiring the gator, the ibis, a spreading tree, a single flower.

The next page stopped her breath. It was a picture of a woman. It was a picture of her. Fleur touched a fingertip to her own mouth rendered in paper and ink.

The next page was a sketch for a dugout seen from the side and above. The next was another picture of her, laughing.

And the next, Fleur feeding Mahkee at her breast.

What did it mean, that Laroux drew her picture again and again? Did it give him some kind of power over her? She didn't feel as if he had power over her. She could leave at this very moment, if she chose. He would not stop her. He could not stop her, if she made up her mind to go.

It meant he was a lonely man. It meant that he thought of her.

She returned the book to the mantle so that she would be sitting at the table when Laroux returned with her boy and the puppy.

She was not good at simply sitting. She would fix their supper. She cut the rabbit down, took it outside, and cleaned it. If she were here tomorrow, perhaps she would tan this skin.

Laroux had taken Mahkee and the pup down to the bayou so they could splash. Such happy sounds, when a child laughed, when a small dog yipped. She was glad if they made Laroux happy, too.

He came back to the cabin as she was spitting the rabbit. "I'll build a fire. We can cook out here."

When they had the rabbit over the flames, they sat together on either side of the fire, the puppy asleep in Laroux's lap. Mahkee fussed and pulled at her tunic, so she took it off and gave him her breast.

She knew Laroux watched her as his fingers stroked the puppy's fur and caressed its soft ears. She felt as if his fingers stroked her skin and caressed the swell of her breast.

The fireflies came out as dusk crept in. The forest around them sparkled with tiny flitting lights and Fleur thought of the old stories of magic and mystery.

"Do you have such lights in your country?"

"We do, though not so many as here. They are company on quiet nights."

"Yes. They are."

She put Mahkee to sleep on a nest of blankets from Laroux's bed. They ate their supper as the stars came out.

"Too dark a night to return to the village now," she said.

"Yes."

He extinguished the fire and held his hand out to her. She took it and walked with him into the dark cabin. He helped her take off her clothing, then took off his own. They lay together on his narrow bed, touching, exploring.

His body was not her husband's body. His touch was not her husband's touch. Yet when Laroux kissed her, his touch and his kiss were all she needed and all she wanted.

~~~

Laroux woke when Fleur brought Mahkee to lie between them. She gave the babe her breast and Laroux reached a finger out to touch the baby's cheek. He had never seen a more beautiful sight, Fleur and her child at the breast.

Laroux had loved her twice last night. She had wanted him, too. Maybe now his obsession with her would ease. He had never known a woman like her with no artifice, no attempts to manipulate. It's true he did not always know what she was thinking, but he knew she was honest and straightforward.

He had wanted her long before he'd been taken to her hut with his wound. He'd seen her at the Sunday markets, laying out her blanket and the baskets she made. Her hair was marvelously black and straight and thick. Her cheeks were high and curved sweetly down to a strong jaw. He'd bought a basket just so he could come close, and she'd looked at him with her calm dark eyes. He'd had to swallow before he could speak to her.

At first he told himself he had been too long without a woman, that's all. And that was true. But he had never had to gulp down his attraction to a woman before he could speak to her.

But she had a child, and therefore a man of her own. He walked away after exchanging a few words, only enough to complete the transaction.

He had no room for a woman in his life, he had reminded himself that day. He would be going back to France in a few years, as soon as he made enough profit here to start him on his way to buying back his family estate. Father had not been himself the last months of his life and had wagered the entire property on a game of chance, and lost. If his sisters had not already been married, they would have been like him, not only homeless but penniless. Regaining the home that had been in his family for four generations was what kept Laroux going in this lonely place.

That and hopes of marrying one of the daughters on the neighboring estate. Monsieur Foucault had a houseful of girls, all of them pretty and blue-eyed. The two youngest would be of age when he returned. He would marry one of them, and they would make a home on the estate. They'd raise their children. They'd be a family.

And then had come the skirmish with the renegade Indians who had kidnapped one of Fleur's cousins. In the rescue, Laroux had taken a knife to the shoulder, and his friends took him to Fleur and her healing hands.

Once the fever had passed, it had been an agony to be so close to her and not touch her. She thought nothing of pulling off her tunic to nurse her child in front of him. Thought nothing of sleeping next to him, her bare skin aglow in the firelight.

Fleur had protested when he made ready to go home. "You are too weak. You must wait."

But he could not bear it, day after day, wanting her and not having her. He had gone home, but not seeing her had been worse than being within arm's reach of her.

And now she lay in his bed. He played with her long braid, tickling her with the end as she fed her little one. She giggled, a sound he had not heard from her before. She turned and switched

Mahkee to the other side, leaving Laroux free to trace the lush curve of her breast. He touched the bluish drop of milk on her nipple and put it in his mouth. Sweet. He hadn't known that.

He glanced up and found Fleur's eyes intent on his hand as he fondled her. He lapped the tender skin under her breast. Fleur's breathing deepened, and thus encouraged, he laved her skin, loving her with his mouth.

Sated, baby Mahkee slept. Laroux took him from Fleur's arms and laid him on the blankets, then turned to look at this woman quietly watching him. A beam of morning sun lit her golden brown skin and flashed dark lights in her hair. Long, strong legs, lush hips, a narrow waist and soft belly, and breasts proud and firm. She opened her arms to him and he settled himself between her legs. As she raised her hips to him, he eased his body into hers. He felt wholly enveloped, inside her body, inside the circle of her arms and the clasp of her thighs.

In the night, the first time and the second, they had nearly fallen off the bed in their eagerness, had nearly set the bed ablaze. This time, he moved in her slowly, tenderly. Instead of her fingers digging into his back, her touches were gentle. Yet as softly as they began, her scent, her smooth skin, her small sighs and then her moans overwhelmed him. Looking into her black eyes, their bodies thrusting and taking one another, he abandoned control, soared and burned and fell into this woman, into Fleur.

This loving, though still intense and consuming, this time there was a sweetness between them. A sense of knowing and being known.

Laroux pulled her to him and held her close as they both drifted back into sleep.

♪

# Chapter Nine

*No More Daisies*
*Third Wednesday and Fourth Sunday*

The day for the mid-week picnic at the fort, Giles decided again to stay home and work. He had few hopes now that he would find a wife and mother among those women from the *New Hope* who were still unattached. Perhaps the next time a ship delivered women from France.

Some men he knew had taken Indian women to wife. He did not fault them for it. But he wanted his children to be French, to be able to return to their homeland someday if that's what they wanted. They would need to know French ways, and that meant they needed a French mother.

He took Felix to the field with him so that Rosalie could cook breakfast in peace. "See here, the shape of this leaf, rounded on top and pointed at the bottom? That's a bean plant. You don't want to pull those up. Now this," he said, gesturing to a weed, "has lots of little leaves, and it grows close to the ground. Those are the ones you pull up."

Felix, for all his rough and tumble ways, was a peaceful kind of boy. He worked steadily and quietly, a good companion out here in the field. Isabel, on the other hand, would already have told him every single thought that passed through her head. Not a restful companion, but entertaining just the same. A lot like her mother, in fact.

The grief welled up again, as it often did when he was thinking of other things. Chopping firewood, his mind might wander to the day when, just a boy, he'd watched the men chopping wood on his father's estate. And that thought led to remembrance of Bella riding by in her carriage just as he'd hefted an axe to give it a try himself. She'd thought he was one of the laborers, and still she had looked at him and smiled.

Felix would not remember his mother. Perhaps Isabel would have some few vague memories of her. Rosalie, however, would always miss her. He had only the one miniature of Bella to show the children, and when it was time, he would give their mother's likeness to Rosalie.

Giles and the children passed a peaceable, productive day. As he and Rosalie prepared supper, he decided he was glad he'd stayed home, but that meant he had only one more day, next Sunday, to find a wife among the women from the *New Hope*. He shook his head. If that meant only Harriet was left, he'd come home without a woman. There were worse things than loneliness.

"Papa, Papa!" Isabel thundered into the house with Felix right behind her. "The nice lady is here! Come see!"

Sister Joelle had come up the bayou? What would she be doing this far from the fort?

Wiping his hands, Giles walked down to the landing with buoyant steps, but he found it was Marie Claude and her slave who had come ashore.

Not Sister Joelle. Why had he thought she'd be up this way?

"Welcome!" he called. When he stood a few feet from Marie Claude, he hesitated. Should he take her hand? As if they were in Paris and she were a grand lady and he a courtier? Shake it like they were two men?

It hardly mattered because she was distracted by his noisy children. Isabel was talking at her, of course, and Felix had taken her hand. That she was happy to see them was in no doubt with her plain face alight with pleasure.

He might have had this woman to wife, he thought with some regret. Well, she would not have him, and that was that.

"We were on our way home from seeing to Bridget. You knew she had her baby?"

"I heard. So you've been tending to mother and child?"

Marie Claude's smile was shy and a little sad. "The baby needs a lot of attention."

As the father of three, Giles didn't remember the newborns needing attention as much as the mother did. The busy part came when the baby no longer stayed where you put him.

"You're in luck. We have three ducks for supper, more than we can eat. You and your man come on up to the house."

"Stay to supper?"

Isabel jumped and shouted "Stay stay stay."

Giles placed a calming hand on her shoulder. "We would enjoy your company."

Marie Claude glanced at her man still standing at the dugout. It seemed the man pretended he was invisible most of the time, but Giles could see he observed everything. There was the slightest nod of his head to indicate he was willing. Odd that, that Marie Claude consulted her slave.

Giles had no idea what to do with him. Should a slave be invited into the house? Or would he expect to eat on the step outside?

"We'd be pleased to stay for supper, then. I have a new bag of cornmeal with me."

"Nothing better than corn fritters," Giles said.

The big woman was good company even if she was from a different class than Giles. Not that he was an aristocrat, of course. His father had land and a manor, but no blue blood, and Giles himself was the fifth son of the house. He had to make his own way just as Marie Claude did. And here in the Louisiana wilds, he had learned that class had very little to do a man's, or a woman's, character.

There was not a quiet moment throughout dinner with the children chattering, Marie Claude answering them, and even, occasionally having a moment to talk to Giles himself. She had only been on the bayou half a year, but she knew a lot about how to live out here. Most interesting to Giles, however, was her delight in his children. She spoke to Rosalie as if she were a little adult, to Isabel as if she had faith the child would not float to the ceiling in her exuberance, and to Felix as if he were six instead of three. The children adored her.

When Felix finished his supper, he slid off the bench and joined the man Thomas on the stoop outside. Giles could see them in the shadows, sitting side by side, Felix expounding, Thomas answering quietly in his deep baritone.

Giles felt tension ease out of his shoulders, a tightness he was so accustomed to he no longer noticed it. It was good to have people on the place, good to have friends.

Fireflies were beginning to wink among the trees when Marie Claude said goodnight. "We don't live but a mile up the bayou, you want to come visit us. I'll fix supper next time." She stepped toward the dugout, and then turned back. "Bring your mending. I like to sew."

Giles and the children waved them up the bayou and then hurried back to the cabin to keep the mosquitos from eating them alive.

One by one, his darlings fell asleep, Isabel first, which seemed right since she spent inordinate amounts of energy in just being Isabel. Giles took his pipe outside to watch the stars. The mosquitoes didn't seem to like the smell of the blend of wild lettuce, mint, and grass he used instead of tobacco. He didn't much like the smell himself, but it was better than no smoking at all, and it did keep the bugs away.

A hazy ring circled the moon. There'd be rain before morning.

He rubbed the center of his chest where sometimes the loneliness lay like a lead weight.

Well, there was one last Sunday before the ladies from the *New Hope* were expected to make their choices. Giles thought he had probably already spoken to all of them, and had not found a kindred spirit. Was he lonely enough, did the children need a woman badly enough, that he should try to bring someone home even if he were not enthusiastic about her nor she about him?

Sunday morning he got everyone fed and dressed and into the dugout. They arrived at the fort in time for mass and took their places amidst the other colonists who'd come in from the river and the bayous.

Sister Joelle sat with Sister Bernadette on the front bench. Emmeline sat nearby with her new husband. He'd missed a good thing there with Emmeline, but he couldn't find any wounds in his heart. He hardly knew her, after all. He knew Sister Joelle better than he knew any of these unmarried women.

He had to stop thinking about Sister Joelle. He had so far managed not to remember her red hair more than once a day. Not to remember her face alight as she told the children about all the bunnies and puppies boarding Noah's ark. Not to imagine unwinding that ridiculous strip of linen from her neck and removing the wimple and the cap, then running his fingers through her curls. If he let himself . . . well, he wouldn't let himself. Eventually, maybe, he'd be able to look at her without seeing anything but nun.

After mass, Sister Joelle flitted from one picnic to another, no doubt trying to finalize these courtships and get the couples into the chapel to be married. She'd be too busy for him and the children today. Even from here he could tell her freckled face was flushed. He'd have to keep an eye on her, see that she didn't overheat again.

A newcomer strolled up from the landing. A rougher looking man Giles had never seen. He was dressed in worn buckskins and moccasins like the Indians wore. He was bareheaded, his greased hair held back in a long queue, his beard long and unkempt. When he passed close by, Giles could smell him. It wasn't that he smelled unwashed as much as he smelled of forest and animal and something essentially male. So they would all smell, he supposed, if they lived as this man apparently did.

Giles guessed the man was a *voyageur*, one of the French Canadians who traded furs all up and down the continent's big rivers. HIs canoe was probably full of furs he'd like to sell to the general store.

Giles didn't imagine he would find a friendly reception from any of the women of the fort, if he was interested in them, that is. He must be a man who preferred solitude anyway, living the life he did.

It would kill Giles to live that life, alone, no one to take care of, no one to love. Thank the Lord he had a family who needed him and loved him.

The voyageur seemed intent on eyeing every woman in sight. So he was interested. No telling how long since he'd seen one, living in the wilderness as he did. Giles remembered how he'd felt when he first saw the *New Hope* girls. Daisies, he'd thought, when he saw them.

The voyageur smiled and nodded at Harriet in a civilized, well-mannered greeting. She startled as if a bear had spoken to her.

The man halted his progress, said something else to her. Reassuring her he was human?

Harriet put a hand to her hair and focused her gaze on the ground.

Giles waited for her to freeze the man with her frosty glare. Instead, he heard the man chuckle, saw him put his fingers in that lush hair of hers. Now she would blast him.

No. Harriet, of all people, blushed.

Well, Giles thought. Maybe it was true, what people said. There was somebody for everyone.

74

# Chapter Ten

*A Precious Gift*
*Fourth Sunday Continued*

Bridget's baby Matthew was tuning up for a wail, poor little fellow. His tummy was empty and he didn't know what else to do but make a fuss about it. Marie Claude put her little finger in his mouth and let him suck on it. That would hold him for a while.

By the time Bridget bustled in, her son was tired of Marie Claude's finger and was proving how robust he was with loud, healthy cries.

"I'm coming, I'm coming," Bridget fussed as she opened her dress and held her arms out for him.

"You're going to have to feed him regular, Bridget. It's not good for him to have to holler so hard every time his tummy is empty."

"I know that," Bridget snapped.

They sat quietly for a time, Bridget staring out the window, Marie Claude watching Matthew nurse. He was a fine baby. In a year, he'd be walking, and not long after that he'd be running. If Bridget lived here at the fort, Marie Claude could see him every Sunday.

"Would you like to have a baby, Marie Claude?"

Bridget didn't know she'd lost a baby, didn't know how it grieved her still. And here was Bridget with a child. Did she even want him?

"Monsieur Prejean is going to New Orleans to open a dry goods store. I could go with him."

Marie Claude's pulse sped up. Did Bridget not want to take Matthew with her, was that what she was getting at?

"And if you went with this Monsieur Prejean?"

Bridget absently played with Matthew's foot. "He says New Orleans is going to be a city before long, not like this little backwater. I might start a business of my own."

"What kind of business?"

Bridget gave her a mocking smile. "What do you think? I don't know how to do but one thing. But I'm good at it."

"A brothel, you mean. You'd start a brothel." Marie Claude looked at Matthew, her throat gone dry. "A brothel is no place to raise a son."

"I happen to agree with you. I need to get my figure back. You know what nursing does to a woman's breasts. And I'll have to work hard at first to establish a place, bring in more girls. He'll be in the way."

That a precious child like this could be in the way. Marie Claude swallowed past the dryness in her throat. "Then you should leave him with me."

"That's what I think, too."

Marie Claude's heart thudded in her chest. "You'd never come back for him."

"No. Why would I?"

"Then I'll take him."

As easily as that. Marie Claude gripped her hands together. As easily as that, she had a baby. Matthew Moreau. Whatever his name, he would always know he was her son.

She took a deep shuddering breath. "I need to find a wet nurse."

"All right. Matthew and I will take a little nap together while you're gone. Don't take too long though. Monsieur Prejean wants to leave this afternoon."

"I won't take too long."

Marie Claude left the infirmary and looked for Thomas. He was squatting in the shade of the fort's palisade talking to somebody else's slave.

When he came to her, she said, "Thomas." She pressed her fingers to her mouth, unable to speak another word.

He led her to a private spot on the other side of the infirmary. "What's wrong?"

She laughed on a sob. "Nothing's wrong. Thomas, we have a baby."

He just stared at her with his deep brown eyes.

76

"Bridget is giving me her baby. Forever."

He still stared at her.

"Don't you see? We can take Matthew home with us. Today. And he'll be ours from now on."

She wanted to wrap her arms around him, she wanted to cry into his shoulder. Of course she couldn't do that. Not here where people would see.

He still hadn't said anything. She couldn't bear it if he didn't want a baby on their place. "Aren't you glad, Thomas?"

He looked her over like he sometimes did, at her face, at her hair, her ear, even at her neck. A slow smile built in his face until it lit his eyes.

"You'll be a mother."

She bit her lip to keep from crying. "I'll be his mother."

He grabbed her by her upper arms and she thought for a moment he would hug her to him. He squeezed her arms, patted them, and then let go.

"When we going to get this baby?"

"Today. Just as soon as I can find a wet nurse."

Thomas glanced at the slave he'd been talking to. "I got an idea about that."

"Who?"

"Henri was telling me, down at the slave market, they got a girl just had a baby that died. She's got a bad foot and won't ever be any good in the fields, so nobody will buy her. The broker might let her go cheap."

"Thomas, I don't have enough money to buy a slave."

Thomas grinned and rattled the coins in his pocket. "I got paid for those iron hooks I forged. And we got the money we saved up for a pig. You got it with you?"

She touched her pocket. "I have it."

"Then let's go buy us a wet nurse."

# Chapter Eleven

*A Red Ribbon*
*Fourth Sunday Continued*

Joelle heaved out a breath. She had all the weddings lined up, one after the other, to begin in about ten minutes. Finally, every woman who came aboard the *New Hope* would be married, except for Harriet.

Of course there was Monsieur Travert. He had not found a bride. Joelle didn't really want to see him and the children with Harriet though. She wouldn't make the Travert family happy.

"Sister Joelle." Seraphina hurried up. "I have something for you and I don't want to hear any protests."

"Why would I protest?"

"Because it is not a nun-ly gift, but you will take it just the same." Seraphina pulled a handful of ribbons from her pocket. "Monsieur Elliot has just given me all these ribbons." She held them out in both hands, a rainbow of satin glinting in the sunlight. "He brought them all the way from France hoping he would have a sweetheart to give them to someday. And that's me! Aren't they gorgeous?"

They were gorgeous. Joelle had never seen their like, ever. She touched a blue one with her forefinger, just to feel the light and the satiny texture.

"No, not blue for you. You will have a red one."

"Oh, goodness. I don't need a ribbon."

"You don't have to need one. You only have to want one. And you do."

"No, really I don't. Seraphina, nuns don't wear ribbons."

"You're not a nun. Not yet. And you don't have to wear it where it shows. It's enough for you to know that somewhere on your person is this little bit of gorgeous satin. Hold out your hand."

Joelle put her hands behind her back. "No, really. I can't."

Seraphina reached around her, grabbed a hand, and dragged it forward. "I will be hurt if you don't let me give you a ribbon. After all you have done for us, ever since we left France. You have to let me do this or you will commit a sin."

Joelle laughed. "What kind of sin?"

"I don't know, but it seems like most everything is a sin if you listen to Sister Bernadette. Now stand still."

Seraphina pushed Joelle's black sleeve up and tied the red satin around her wrist. Then she slid the sleeve back down. "See? No one will know but you."

"And God."

"Pff. God doesn't care if you wear a red ribbon."

"But -- "

"No buts. Come say hello to my husband-to-be. In about an hour, you can be the first to call me Madame Elliot."

The tall quiet man Joelle had seen Seraphina with before walked over at Seraphina's beckoning wave.

"Sister Joelle, this is Monsieur Elliot."

Joelle couldn't think what she was supposed to say. She couldn't think when she had ever been formally introduced to a man other than Father Xavier on the day of their arrival.

"How do you do, Sister?"

Yes, of course. That's what one said. "How do you do, Monsieur Elliot?"

Seraphina giggled. "She's fine, Monsieur Elliot. And he's fine, too, Sister." She cast a flirtatious look up at her husband-to-be, and he gave her an amused half-smile, a little gleam in his eye. Joelle was glad to see he was not a humorless man. He didn't seem someone Seraphina would be able to get around by flirting with him, either. That was probably a good thing.

Seraphina slipped her hand into his, right out in front of everyone. Joelle was embarrassed for her, but his big hand gripped hers and didn't let go. "We'll see you at the wedding?" Monsieur Elliot said.

"I'll be there. I only want to speak to Bridget first. I see she's left her bed, and Sister Bernadette says I am supposed to scold her if she does that."

Bridget was carrying her baby, Marie Claude walking beside her. They were deep in conversation when Joelle joined them.

"You might as well know," Bridget said. "Marie Claude is going to take my baby."

"Take your baby?"

"She's going to raise him."

Joelle felt her skull must be very thick. "Raise him? Where will you be?"

"I'm going to New Orleans."

"You're going to New Orleans?"

"Have you turned into a parrot, Sister Joelle?"

They were approaching the landing where the boats were all pulled ashore.

"How are you going to get to New Orleans?"

Bridget nodded toward a well-dressed man standing next to a proper boat with four men at the oars. It was laden with boxes and chests with only enough space for two people on the forward bench. "Monsieur Prejean has agreed to take me with him. He has business interests to pursue there, and I may do the same."

"But your husband?"

"That's finished." Bridget gave a quick kiss to her baby's forehead and handed him over to Marie Claude.

She turned to the man in the velvet coat, gave him a brilliant smile, and allowed him to help her into the boat. As they pushed off into the sound, Bridget waved and smiled.

And that was that. Bridget had just given her child away and left without a single tear.

"How could she do that?"

Marie Claude was tracing the baby's smooth cheek with her finger. "Some women don't want to be mothers. I'm just as glad Bridget is one of them."

"But what will she do in New Orleans? She can't marry this man. She's already married."

"Being married or not married won't matter with what Bridget wants to do."

"Not matter?" She couldn't seem to understand anything anyone said.

"Men don't ask whether a whore is married or not."

"Bridget wants to be a whore?" Joelle was not sure what a whore did, but she knew women were once stoned for it.

Marie Claude smiled at her. "You may be part parrot, after all. Yes, Bridget plans to be a whore again. Whether or not that's what she wants, that's what she sees as her best bet since her husband kicked her out."

"That was very wicked of him."

"Yes. But she didn't tell him she was pregnant when he married her. Enough sin to go around for everyone, I've always thought."

"Marie Claude," Joelle said, quietly. Perhaps she shouldn't ask, but she wanted to understand. "When you were a whore, was that what you wanted?"

Marie Claude snorted. "Sister, most women become whores because they'd rather whore than starve to death."

"Oh. I see."

They both gazed at the sleeping infant, Marie Claude with a smile on her face, Joelle with a sudden overpowering need, a yearning to cradle this baby close to her body, to touch, to cherish. She'd never felt such a bodily ache in all her life.

"Can I hold him?" she asked.

Marie Claude gently handed Matthew into her arms.

He hardly weighed anything at all. His tiny hand was open and relaxed on his chest and his rosebud mouth made little sucking motions. Joelle didn't want to breathe. She wanted only to watch him, to take his tiny hand in her own.

"Come along," Marie Claude said. "I want to register him in the chapel book. Then he'll be mine."

"But Father Xavier will be performing weddings all afternoon."

"Then I'll wait."

They passed through the dappled shade toward the chapel, ambling slowly, stopping to tell anyone interested that Marie Claude was now a mother. Joelle had hold of herself now, the foolish yearning tamped down to a very reasonable pleasure in having a baby in her arms. Even nuns could love a child. God was good to allow her this small pleasure.

~~~

Giles was stretched out under the pines digesting his dinner while his children played around him. Rosalie and Isabel had brought the ragdolls their mother had made for them and were having a special luncheon just for them. Felix lay beside him in the same posture, arms behind his head, legs crossed at the ankle.

After Felix had contemplated the treetops overhead and the blue sky and white clouds beyond, he said, "What are we looking for, Papa?"

"I once saw a dragon in the clouds. I'm waiting to see if he comes back."

Felix seemed content to help him keep watch, and Giles thought he might just doze off. Instead, a shriek from Isabel sent a jolt of alarm up his spine.

"Can I see? Let me see?"

Giles got to his feet to rein in his over-enthusiastic child. She was jumping up and down in front of Sister Joelle and Marie Claude, begging to see the babe in the sister's arms.

Rosalie was stretching up to see the child's face, just as interested as Isabel but more subdued about it. It occurred to Giles that with a sister as ebullient as Isabel, maybe Rosalie held herself back a little. Maybe she would be more spontaneous herself if she were not the eldest, if she had not embraced her role as the responsible sister. He should try spending more time with Rosalie alone, letting her be a child with no chores to look after, including her brother and sister. But when would he ever have the opportunity to do that?

Marie Claude sat down against a tree and patted her lap. "If you sit right here, I can help you hold him."

"Me first," Isabel said.

Yes, he needed to curb Isabel and see that Rosalie didn't lose all of her childhood to being the mature, responsible sibling. "Rosalie first, Isabel," he said, holding her back with a hand on her shoulder.

Rosalie was biting her lower lip but that didn't keep her from smiling. She settled on Marie Claude's legs and Sister Joelle bent and gently handed the baby down to Rosalie's arms, Marie Claude's hands steadying him.

As Sister Joelle straightened up, she pulled down her loose sleeve, but not before Giles saw a red ribbon tied round her wrist. Bright satiny red against her pale skin. Completely out of the blue, Giles felt a stab of lust so intense it stole his breath. Lust, for Sister Joelle. A young woman destined to be a nun. What was the matter with him?

He glanced at her and realized she had seen him see her ribbon. Her face was bright red, and he wondered if a sheltered young woman like Sister Joelle could have any idea what had gone through his mind in that moment.

He gave himself a mental shake and crossed his arms to watch his children coo at the baby. Even Felix peered at the little fellow.

"Whose child is it?" Giles asked, just to have something to say.

"Bridget's. Remember, he was born last Sunday?"

Good. She was also going to pretend that moment of lust had not happened. He nodded to indicate his mild curiosity was satisfied.

"She's given him to Marie Claude."

He tilted his head and raised a brow as if that could not be true.

Sister Joelle nodded. "Bridget has gone to New Orleans and doesn't plan to come back. She doesn't want a child." A line appeared between her eyes as she met his gaze. "I can't understand it. A gift from God like this, and she doesn't want him."

"Then the child is better off without her." Marie Claude would be a good mother, anyone could see that. And having her own child meant that she really would not need a husband, so he might as well put away the hope she might change her mind and marry him.

Thomas stood nearby, as always, this time with a young black woman whose thin dress strained across her breasts. A wet nurse? Giles could see even from here that something was wrong with the girl's foot. Good heavens, half of it was destroyed and raw. What a ghastly injury.

Beside him Sister Joelle sighed. "I should be at the chapel, helping with the weddings."

"It'll be quiet for you here, after all the women have gone to their new homes."

"Yes. It will. But Father Xavier will keep us busy."

She strode off, keeping to the shade, he was glad to see.

He stood there, feeling superfluous in this scene. But the children were enjoying themselves, and Marie Claude seemed happy to have them clustered around her and on her.

"Giles," Marie Claude said, "I have all afternoon here and I'm happy to have Rosalie and Isabel and Felix with me. You can go shoot or wrestle or something with the other men."

Giles had no desire to wrestle in this heat, but he would enjoy the company of other men, and he was interested in learning more about making a bow.

"I'll be back in an hour," he told his brood. "Mind your manners and mind Marie Claude."

They hardly seemed to notice he was leaving, so he left.

# Chapter Twelve

*The Letter*
*Fourth Sunday Continued*

Catherine Dupre leaned her head to better hear her friend Agnes whisper. "Marie Claude gets to keep Bridget's baby."

"You mean, keep it, forever?" She kept her voice low because one of the women was in front of the group explaining how much sunshine it took to cure strips of deer meat.

"Bridget's gone. For good, I think, so yes, forever."

Catherine drew in a deep breath. "Best thing that could happen to Marie Claude, and to the baby, too."

Agnes nodded. "I've been worried about her. She hasn't been herself for weeks."

"No, she hasn't. I had wondered, well, never mind." Catherine had wondered if Marie Claude would turn to her friend Thomas after her husband died. But that would be dangerous, even fatal, for Thomas, a black slave, to touch a white woman. But there was a closeness between the two of them.

"Where is Marie Claude?"

Agnes nodded toward the trees. "Over there, with Giles Travert's children."

At the edge of the pines, they paused and looked out over the open grounds. The fort was a busy place today, the last of the newcomers marrying at the chapel. Catherine looked for her husband Jean Paul on the other side of the grounds where the Biloxi had laid out their blankets to sell furs and corn and beans and leather. As a former musketeer, he was a keen swordsman and a crack shot, but he had left his days as a musketeer behind him. Now he wanted to learn to use a bow and arrow as his friend Mato did. She spotted him with a length of wood, measuring it against his height.

She and Jean Paul had been married since early February, but the love they'd found for each other was only a few weeks old. She felt warm and safe and cherished every time he looked at her.

There must be something physically magical about love, she thought, for at that moment he raised his head and looked right at her, as if there were an invisible connection between them. She raised her hand and he raised his.

"Newlyweds," Agnes said smiling.

Catherine nudged her with an elbow. "I've seen you and Valery mooning over each other as recently as . . . why, I believe it was about an hour ago."

Agnes sighed. "I can't help it. He is the dearest man."

Colonel Blaise, the fort's commander, approached them. "Good morning, Colonel."

"Madame Villiers, Madame Dupre. I have been looking for you, madame," he said to Catherine.

"Yes?"

"A packet ship arrived yesterday with a mail pouch from home. I have a letter addressed to Catherine de Villeroy." He pulled an envelope in heavy paper from his breast pocket. "It is meant for you, I believe."

Catherine's entire body went cold, and her lungs couldn't draw in enough air. She reached for Agnes's hand to hold her steady.

The colonel looked at her curiously. "That was your name, before your marriage, was it not? I looked through the chapel records to see if we had a Catherine de Villeroy. You are in the registry, married to Jean Paul Dupre."

"Yes. I'm Catherine de Villeroy. No. I *was* Catherine de Villeroy. I'm Catherine Dupre now."

He handed her the letter. "I wish you joyful news from your home, Madame Dupre."

The envelope seemed heavy, the fine paper smooth under her trembling fingers. Agnes wrapped an arm around her waist. "You need to sit down."

When she'd settled with her back against a tree, Catherine stared at the letter in her hands.

"I'm going to get Jean Paul," Agnes said.

How she had yearned for a letter from home the first weeks she had been in the colony. It would mean Grandfather had discovered Cousin Hugo's perfidy in kidnapping and stowing her aboard the *New Hope*. It would mean Grandfather had tracked her here to Fort Louis, and would tell her to come home, she would be safe, all would be well.

She could go home. She wouldn't have to wear the same dress every day, eat the same bland food, she wouldn't have to work until her blisters had blisters. She could resume her life as the daughter of le comte de Villeroy, a woman of wealth and glamor who bathed every day and drank chocolate from a fine china cup.

Jean Paul could put away his axe. He could become a gentleman. If farming was what he really wanted, he could have his own vineyard. How splendid he would look in silk stockings, embroidered waistcoat, and powdered wig.

She saw Agnes go to him. Jean Paul leaned over to hear her, and then he raised his head to look at Catherine. He stood very still, staring at her across the distance.

Her heart thudded. This letter -- Oh, what if it were not a summons home? What if Grandfather had died? What if Hugo had taken over all of the estates, all of the wealth and power? And all that stood between him and final possession was her, Catherine. Maybe the letter was merely to find her so that he could send someone to kill her. No. That was mere melodrama. Hugo knew where she was.

Jean Paul came to her across the sunlit ground, unhurried, deliberate, his eyes never leaving her.

~~~

Jean Paul could see from yards away how his beloved's face glowed. He covered the ground slowly, dreading to find the letter was from her grandfather, summoning her home.

It would make her happy, to go home. And why shouldn't it? Only a few months ago, she had dressed in silk and danced the night away at parties where the king himself made merry. And now her hands were rough, her complexion sun-darkened, and she toiled from morning to night.

If Catherine could go home again, she would step back into her old life, surrounded by noblemen who would flatter and court her. Jean Paul found it hard to get enough air into his lungs.

There would be no place for him in that life.

She wouldn't need him anymore if she went home.

He was going to lose her.

He forced himself to keep going until he reached her. He stopped, studying her teary eyes, her watery smile.

She held the unopened letter to her breast. "Jean Paul, it's from Grandfather."

He swallowed. How was he to make himself smile when what he wanted to do was howl. He couldn't do this here, not now. He needed time before he could put on the face she deserved to see. She needed to know he was glad for her to go home -- how could he make her believe that when his heart was thudding in his throat?

He held his hand out to help her up.

"Let's go home. We'll read it there, shall we?"

Catherine laughed and put her hand over her mouth, the letter still clutched to her chest. "I'm about to cry and make a fool of myself. Yes. Let's go home, Jean Paul."

# Chapter Thirteen

*Even Harriet*
*Fourth Sunday Continued*

Joelle remembered to stop long enough to take a long drink of water. She didn't have time today to be sun sick. Keeping to the lightly wooded areas either side of the sun-beaten open ground, Joelle searched for Seraphina and her Monsieur Elliot. They were next to be married and Father Xavier was in no mood to have his schedule disrupted.

Of all her charges, Harriet was the one Joelle worried about the most. She seemed determined to remain unmarried, and none of the men seemed inclined to argue with her about it. Ah, one more man had decided to attempt it. The voyageur she'd seen earlier, the wild-looking man, approached her slowly, as if she were a deer or a squirrel or a duck that would dash off at the first moment of alarm.

Joelle didn't intend to spy on them, but she couldn't help but see them as she scanned the area looking for brides and grooms. He had a charming smile, it seemed from where Joelle stood, but Harriet merely stared at him.

He talked to her a few minutes, Harriet's face blank. Then Harriet's head reared back as if she smelled something truly foul. The man laughed, took a step closer, and touched that magnificent black hair of Harriet's. And Harriet allowed it. Well, he'd gotten closer than any of the other men. But Harriet certainly wouldn't have a man who lived out of his canoe if she wouldn't have one of these men of property, however small their farmsteads were.

Enough scanning. Joelle would have to go looking for Seraphina. She passed close by the men in their self-imposed separation from the women. She'd never seen sword play before and was tempted to stop and watch, but there wasn't time. Among another group of men she saw Monsieur Travert and felt a rush of heat from her toes to the top of her head. He had seen the ribbon when her sleeve had pushed up handing the baby over. He had noticed it, too, not just glimpsed it. What must he think of her?

She was not meant to have such things. If Seraphina wouldn't take the ribbon back, she'd have to give it to one of the girls.

She seemed to spot everyone but Seraphina and Monsieur Elliot. Miranda had apparently decided on the suitor who wore the costly brown velvet coat. She'd have to get them to the chapel soon. Cecile and Monsieur Ouellette were strolling toward the chapel, so they were seen to. But where was Seraphina?

A swish of blue fabric behind a tall pine caught her attention. Joelle marched over there and caught Seraphina and Monsieur Elliot kissing! His arms were all the way around Seraphina's body and in front of her very eyes, Monsieur Elliot's hand drifted down and caressed Seraphina's bottom! And Seraphina didn't even try to stop him!

Her mouth dropped open. How could they? They weren't even married.

"Seraphina!"

Monsieur Elliot's head jerked back, startled, but Seraphina only grinned at her over her shoulder.

"Hello, Sister," he said. At least he looked shame-faced. Seraphina did not. "Don't worry, Sister Joelle. We're on our way to the chapel right now, aren't we, Leo?"

If Seraphina did not blush, Joelle felt a flush heating her own face. Again. This was a day for embarrassment and -- oh! Monsieur Travert had his eyes on her. Somehow her face felt even hotter. He had seen Seraphina and Monsieur Elliot, and he'd seen her watching them. She hadn't been watching, really, because it had only been a moment between the time she saw them and the time she spoke, but he'd seen her see them kissing.

He was getting to his feet. No. She could not talk to him now. She ducked her head and hurried back to the chapel where everything was as it should be, men and women marrying under Father Xavier's loving care. Yes. That's where she should be. Not talking to a man. No need to talk to a man at all.

It took a moment for Joelle's eyes to adjust to the dimness in the chapel, and then she saw Father Xavier was marrying Annamaria to a man clad in rough homespun.

She congratulated Annamaria as she passed down the aisle, a married woman now. Seraphina and her Monsieur Elliot took their places in front of Father Xavier.

In only a few minutes, he had performed the rites and pronounced Seraphina and Monsieur Elliott man and wife. Seraphina turned her face up and Monsieur Elliott gave her a kiss. This wasn't like the all-enveloping kiss Joelle had seen behind the tree, but the look on his face promised there would be other kisses.

Joelle felt her chest inexplicably tighten. She would be glad when this day was over. Then it would be just Father Xavier, Sister Bernadette, and, she supposed, Harriet. Thank goodness she wouldn't see any more kissing.

By the time the very last couple was married and Joelle stepped outside, the sun was throwing long shadows. People who hadn't already left would soon be packing up to go home. She walked down to the landing with Sister Bernadette to wave their friends off. It was pleasant on the shore where the water cooled the wind.

Sister Bernadette nudged her. "Would you look at that?"

Harriet walked right down to the shoreline with that voyageur. He carried her little chest under one arm and held the dugout steady while she climbed in.

Sister Bernadette frowned. "I didn't know Father Xavier married Harriet and this man."

Joelle bit her lip. "I don't think he did."

"Wait!" Sister Bernadette hurried over. "Harriet, what are you thinking? You can't go off with this man without marrying him."

Harriet merely settled her skirts around her and balanced her chest on her knees.

"Get out at once," Sister Bernadette insisted.

"Excuse me," the voyageur said. He gently moved Sister Bernadette aside and shoved the canoe into the water. Harriet's body swayed a little, adjusting to the canoe's motion.

"Harriet!"

Harriet gave a curt nod to Sister Bernadette, and then she turned her attention to the man carrying her away into the unknown. She fixed her eyes on him and seemed oblivious to everything and everyone else in the world.

Monsieur Travert came up beside her, Felix riding high on his shoulders.

"I can't believe it," Joelle said.

Monsieur Travert gazed at the canoe carrying Harriet away. "I am all amazement, myself. Was he a Huguenot, was that it?"

"I have no idea."

Isabel leaned into Joelle's skirts. "I'm tired."

"Are you, darling? Your papa is taking you home, now, I think."

Rosalie wrapped her arms around Joelle's waist and pressed her face into her apron. "We didn't get a new mama and now" -- her voice soared into a wail -- "now all the ladies are gone."

Monsieur Travert forced a smile and gathered Rosalie to him, Felix still balanced on his shoulders. "There will be other ladies, *ma petite*. Come, Isabel. Let's go home. Good night, sisters."

As Joelle watched the family move into the sound, Sister Bernadette rubbed her hands together in satisfaction. "Well. We've done it. Every single girl married. Or at least off our hands."

And there would be another ship in a few months bringing more young women to be married. Maybe one of them would marry Monsieur Travert and be a mother to his children. The thought should make her happy for the Traverts. But it did not.

# Chapter Fourteen

*News from Home*
*Fourth Sunday Continued*

The letter Colonel Blaise had given her sat in her lap all the way home from the fort. While Jean Paul paddled the canoe, Catherine noticed the clouds and wondered if it were going to rain later. She watched fish darting under the water as they entered the bayou, and spotted a wild orchid high in a tree.

And while she pretended the envelope was of no consequence, merely paper folded into this interesting shape, she felt a thrumming hope, a tremulous excitement.

She didn't really need to open the envelope. If the letter had found her, it had to mean Grandfather knew what Cousin Hugo did to her. It meant she could go home again.

Had Hugo confessed? She couldn't imagine he would ever admit to such treachery. He was too busy enjoying the wealth he'd stolen from her through betrayal and abduction. She could almost smell the sweet vitriol he'd drugged her with even now. Could still feel the nausea, confusion, and fear waking on a ship at sea, no idea where she was going.

Those first weeks, Catherine had burned with the need for vengeance. She would see Hugo stripped and dragged through the pig sty, she would see him caged with hungry rats, she would stake him in the forest for the wolves. Somehow, someday, she would make her way back to France and reclaim her rightful place.

And that someday had arrived. She and Jean Paul would take the next ship home to France. Grandfather would open his arms to her and she would be home. She and Jean Paul would sleep in her bed, the rose silk canopy arched over them, and wake to a fire already lit and hot coffee brought to them while they still lay abed.

Jean Paul pulled the dugout ashore and his hound bounded from the boat and raced up the path ahead. Débile liked to be the first one home, to sniff all around the cabin and reclaim his territory.

When Jean Paul helped her out of the dugout, she squeezed his hand and smiled at him. He'd be glad to go home. This was not the life he had expected to lead, either. He'd been a dashing musketeer, a man of urbanity and cachet. He belonged in Paris just as she did.

As soon as they got inside, she'd open the letter. They would read it together, and then they'd have a feast to celebrate. She'd use the last of the honey to make a mulberry sauce to spoon over the rabbit stew as Agnes had taught her to do. Instead of wine, they'd toast each other with spring water and be as gay as if champagne bubbles tickled their throats.

Jean Paul untied the leather door for her. "I'll check the traps, get a bucket of water from the spring."

Ever practical, her husband. She would wait then. When he came in, they would sit together and open the letter.

She sat on the side of the bed and fingered the heavy envelope, tracing the spiky handwriting in dark ink. It must have been written weeks ago, maybe months ago; the ink had developed a purple cast to it.

What was taking him so long? Catherine peeked out the doorway and didn't see her husband, so she returned to her seat on the bed, determined to be patient. Jean Paul had probably had a hard time getting the rabbit out of the noose. Sometimes the poor things panicked and got themselves entangled in the line and then suffered until Jean Paul put an end to them.

Catherine waited an eternity, listening for Jean Paul's footsteps. Where was he? She set her letter in the center of the rough table and went looking for him. He wasn't at the spring, she didn't see him at the usual traps, not in the garden. At the woodpile, she found he'd left a skinned rabbit and the bucket of fresh water.

She found him at the bayou, his arms crossed, staring at the moon rising over a darkening sky.

"Jean Paul?"

He half turned to look at her over his shoulder.

"You're not happy about the letter? You won't come in and read it with me?"

He dropped his arms and reached for her hand. "Of course. Forgive me."

"You mustn't worry, Jean Paul. It'll be good news, I'm sure of it."

He gave her a tight smile. "Then let's go in."

Inside, Catherine sat at the table and waited while Jean Paul lit two candles, an extravagance, but this was a special occasion. When he took the other stool, Catherine placed the envelope on the table between them and smoothed her fingers over the writing.

"This is Grandfather's hand, Jean Paul. Grandfather wrote this himself." Her hands trembled only slightly as she broke the wax seal and unfolded the heavy paper.

*My dearest, darling Catherine.* She needed a moment to clear her throat before she continued to read the letter to Jean Paul. *I have searched everywhere for you, my men covering all of Paris, then all of Île-de-France, and then all of France. I could find no trace of you, and my heart was shattered.*

*But I have discovered you at last if you are reading this letter. Because Hugo betrayed no sign of grief for his vanished cousin, and he had much to gain by your disappearance, I searched his apartments and found your sapphires hidden in the false bottom of a bureau. Hugo now resides in the basement of the old castle ruins.*

"He means a dungeon," Jean Paul said.

Catherine shivered. "I've seen that dungeon. Underground. No windows. No light."

"You're feeling sorry for your cousin?"

"I have wished for much worse to befall him, I admit. But the dungeon is a fearful place."

Jean Paul touched her hand. "Go on. Read the rest."

*"I have interviewed the captain of the* New Hope *and so know you arrived at Fort Louis on the Gulf coast. His cooperation in revealing your destination saved his life, for I have such a rage in my breast for what befell you that I would have ended his days with pleasure. Though I have not taken their lives, neither the captain nor Hugo will trouble anyone ever again.*

*Come home, Catherine. Come home, my beloved child.*

Catherine put her hands over her face and cried with deep gulping sobs. She had thought she would never see his loving face again. But she would, she and Jean Paul together.

Jean Paul came around the table to wrap his arms around her. "He loves you, your grandfather."

"Yes."

"And misses you."

"Yes."

When she recovered, Jean Paul's arms still encircling her, Catherine spread the remaining pages across the table. "Look."

The additional pages each bore the seal of the Bank of France. "Promissory notes. More than enough to pay our passage back across the ocean, to clothe ourselves, to hire a carriage to cross the country to Grandfather's estate."

Catherine twisted on her stool to hold Jean Paul around the waist, but she did not see a smile on his face. "Jean Paul?"

He pulled her into him before she could look more closely, before she could read his eyes.

~~~

Jean Paul held Catherine to him until he could master his face. His darling wanted to go home, needed to go home, and he didn't know if he could bear it. To lose her now, after all they had been through to find their love, it would break him.

She pressed her face into his body. "Just think, Jean Paul. Home. Paris."

"No more hard work for you, my darling," he said. "Pretty dresses, maids, chocolate. All the things you've missed." All the things she deserved.

"And a fine cocked hat for you. I want to see you in a black velvet cloak, lined with scarlet satin. The kind that swirls around your knees when you turn." She looked up at him. "You'll be the most handsome man in France."

Her smile dimmed. "What's wrong?"

He kissed her forehead and moved away to build the fire.

"Jean Paul?"

He couldn't tell her she would be going home alone. Not yet. "It's a shock. I had not expected this letter, had you?" he asked.

Her smile broke his heart.

"I suppose a little bitty corner of my heart hoped for one, but no, I did not expect it."

He wouldn't tell her tonight. Let them have one more night together, one more chance to love while she was filled with joy.

Tomorrow would be soon enough to disappoint her. She loved him, he knew that, and it would hurt her to leave him behind. But that is what she must do. He would insist on it.

"You get the rabbit in the pot? I'll bring in some more firewood."

"I'll cook you the best rabbit stew you ever had," she promised.

When they sat down to supper, Catherine raised her gourd of spring water and waited for Jean Paul to raise his.

"To France. To home," she said.

Jean Paul managed a smile as he touched his gourd to hers. "To France."

After supper, Jean Paul helped Catherine off with her new calico dress and hung it on a peg. Moonlight bathed her hair in silver and gave a pearly glow to her pale skin. He touched her cheek with just the tips of his fingers and gazed at this woman who held his heart.

"Come to bed." She climbed onto the narrow cot and held her arms out to welcome him. After all these weeks it still stunned him that she wanted him. The first weeks of their marriage, she had slept facing the log wall, as far from him as she could get. Thank God that time of frustration and heartache was over.

He lay down and drew her to him. Her body trembled and her hands were icy cold.

"Catherine?"

"Hold me."

He wrapped his body around her to hold her steady, to warm her. "Are you frightened, about going home?"

"I guess I am, a little."

"Hold on to me. I've got you."

When the trembling eased, he planted soft, slow kisses all along Catherine's neck, over her jaw, on her eyelids. She moved under him to take his mouth with her own, to drag her hands across his sides and down his back.

"Love me," she whispered.

"I do love you." He rolled her to her back and nestled himself between her thighs. In the ghostly moonlight, he pushed the hair from her forehead and looked into her eyes. "I'll always love you."

Sometimes when Jean Paul and Catherine made love, they were in too much of a hurry to savor or indulge in tender kisses.

Other nights, each kiss, each touch, was full of sweetness and exquisite care. And some nights they laughed and did silly things, like when he stuck his tongue in her ear and she shrieked, or when she'd dared him not to move while she tickled him with a mockingbird feather.

This night, *this* night, plundered the depths of his heart. Every touch was precious to him, every taste, every scent. This was not the last time he would love her . . . she would be here in this bed tomorrow and the next day . . . but it felt like the last time.

Slowly, he made love to her, holding still inside her while their bodies thrummed together in low, pulsing vibration. Gently he rocked into her, then again held himself still, letting the heat build, letting her feel what she meant to him.

He took her panting breath into his own mouth, tasted his Catherine, breathed in his beloved. His body throbbed with hers, and she moved beneath him, wanting more. He kissed her softly. "Easy. Easy."

He pressed in deeper, and held, pressed, and held, until Catherine arched her back and dug her fingers into his shoulders.

A moan erupted from deep within her chest, and it was time. Jean Paul pushed himself against her in a hard fast lunge, and again, and Catherine cried out, her body bowing him off the bed, releasing him to plunge into her in desperate thrusts until his own cry burst from his lungs.

As their hearts steadied, Catherine fell asleep in his arms, her boneless exhaustion enviable. Jean Paul could not let go of the ache that one small envelope had brought into their lives.

Sweat trickled down his neck, and tension hardened the muscles in his back. Late into the night, he gave up trying to sleep and eased out from under Catherine.

Down at the bayou he watched the water flow under the moonlight. Not a breath of wind stirred, but frogs called to each other, owls hooted, and the ever-present cicadas played their music.

Débile nosed his leg to let Jean Paul know he was right there with him. Before Catherine came into his life, Débile had been his only friend. Jean Paul had sometimes thought he would lose himself in the great loneliness of this forest, living here alone, not seeing another soul for weeks at a time. And then he had gone to Fort Louis in frantic need to bring home one of the brides brought over from France. He hadn't thought, he hadn't planned, he had simply rushed headlong down the bayou and across the sound to find someone, anyone, to come home with him.

The last woman unclaimed, Catherine had been as desperate as he. She'd chosen him, filthy as he was, had married him, and had come into this wilderness to live and work beside him.

What an ass he'd been the first weeks, convinced he had nothing to offer her, too broken to let another woman into his life after the only woman he'd ever loved had betrayed him. He'd wanted never to love again, had resisted his need for her and his attraction to her, yet Catherine had steadily pierced all his barriers until he could no more live without her than he could live without breathing.

But he had to let her go. Catherine was not born for this life. Ahead of her was only labor, risk, and a life of deprivation if she stayed with him. He could never buy her a silk dress or a painted fan, never take her to a ball at the king's palace. But if she went back, she could dance at Versailles again with royal dukes and princes.

That letter meant she could be restored to her grandfather and resume her rightful place among the nobility. She could avenge her abduction and put Cousin Hugo to whatever punishment she chose. She wouldn't have to grow old before her time in this sun, in these fields. She wouldn't have to eat possum and sweet potatoes ever again. Her hands would soften once more, and her sun-darkened complexion would return to the creamy paleness of an aristocratic woman.

Even if he were not a wanted man back home, there would be no place for him in a life like that. His people were common farmers, and though he had acquired a little polish as one of the king's musketeers, he would be an embarrassment to her. She would grow ashamed of him. No, his place was here. Hers was in Paris.

She would forget him once she was among her own people. Eventually, this time in the wilds of Louisiana would become like some dream she barely remembered. Her feelings for him would be replaced by the attentions of gentlemen in elegant garb and powdered wigs.

Jean Paul would do this last thing for her -- he would insist that she go home where she belonged.

# Chapter Fifteen

*A Little Beauty*
*July*

All the young women who had sailed across the Atlantic with Joelle and Sister Bernadette were gone, embarked on their new lives. Fort Louis was quiet. And dull.

Settlers still came on Sundays for mass, to shop, to trade, to socialize, but the rest of the week Joelle had little to do.

She busied herself keeping the chapel free of cobwebs and palmetto bugs. She did Father Xavier's and Sister Bernadette's laundry with her own. She attended to her devotionals and prayers. And she spent a lot of time at the shore staring at the lush green banks on the other side of the sound.

The Rue des Boulangers had been more stimulating. Beyond the green banks, however, Joelle actually knew people, in person, by name, and they knew her. Seraphina lived up the river with her Monsieur Elliot. Miranda and her new husband lived on the sound further west. And Monsieur Travert and the children lived up the bayou to the east.

Joelle looked for the Traverts every Sunday, but they had not been back to the fort, not even to attend mass. She wondered if Rosalie was still sad not to have a new maman. She imagined Isabel getting into all kinds of mischief. She had so much energy, she might climb on the roof to see the sights. Joelle laughed to herself. It was entirely possible, this notion of Isabel scaling walls.

An image of Felix drowsy on his father's shoulder pained her unexpectedly. It would feel wonderful to have a sleepy child in her arms. Not her own child, of course. She would feel blessed to hold Felix. Or Marie Claude's tiny son. Well, she needn't dwell on it.

Joelle edged a finger under the windings at her throat. After a week's wear, the linen was limp and smelled of sweat. She would take a minute to change into a fresh wimple before she fetched the water for Sister Bernadette's feet. In this heat, the older woman's ankles and feet had begun swelling, and it eased her for Joelle to bring her a basin of cool water to soak them in.

In the back room of the chapel, Joelle unwound the neck cloth and removed her wimple and cap. She ran her fingers through her short curls, enjoying the air on her neck, the relief from the hot linens. It was time for Sister Bernadette to cut her hair again. That would make her the tiniest bit cooler, she supposed. She dreaded it though because whenever Sister Bernadette had a handful of shorn red curls in her hand, she felt compelled once again to warn Joelle against her natural inclinations. It was well known that a woman with hair the color of the brightest of autumn leaves had a sensual nature, a rebellious nature, and Joelle must guard against these tendencies to sin in order to become a true holy sister.

Before this, Joelle had always felt chastened after such a lecture, but today, alone in the quiet room, it occurred to her: God gave her this hair.

She'd never heard a Bible story about women with red hair being wicked. Oh. Had Mary Magdalene had red hair? But she was a saint. At any rate, Joelle had never sinned, at least not in the ways Sister Bernadette said her hair predicted.

Joelle opened her small chest and dug deep under other clothes to get out a fresh wimple. Before she fully understood what she was seeing, she jerked her hand back as if she'd been bitten. There, nestled among the white linens, was Seraphina's red ribbon.

But she had given it to Cecile after her wedding. Then she remembered, she had seen Cecile and Seraphina talking before they went off to their new lives as married ladies. Cecile must have slipped back into the dormitory and hid this ribbon among Joelle's things.

Joelle sat back on her heels. She didn't know whether to be annoyed or amused. Some of both, she supposed. She ran the ribbon through her fingers, the feel of satin as smooth as, what? Marble? The statue of St. Anne back at the convent had been carved in marble, but marble was cold. Nothing this red and this soft could be cold. Smooth as a rose petal, then, though she had never seen a rose as deeply red as this ribbon.

She touched the satin to her lips and closed her eyes. Was it possible to feel a color, to smell a color? Her eyes flew open. This must be what Sister Bernadette meant about her sensual nature.

She hastily stuffed the ribbon under her linens and closed the chest.

With a basin of water, Joelle hastened to Sister Bernadette and found her under the spreading oak fanning herself with a palmetto.

"There you are. I thought you had forgotten me." Sister Bernadette had become querulous in the last weeks. Perhaps she didn't sleep well at night either.

"Let me help you with your shoes and stockings, Sister. You'll feel better in no time."

Such relief it would be if the two of them could take off their wimples in the hottest part of the day. They could stay under the concealing limbs of the old oak and no one would see them. Or they could sit at the water's edge with their bare feet in the cool sand as she had done when Seraphina helped her recover from the heat.

Of course they would do no such thing. And here she'd had yet another thought that would scandalize Sister Bernadette. Joelle pondered whether these thoughts were weighty enough to mention in her confessions with Father Xavier.

Swallowing a smile, Joelle considered her small transgressions might be the most exciting sins Father Xavier had ever heard from a sister.

He would certainly be dismayed that she had a red ribbon in her chest.

A scrap of red ribbon.

A small bit of beauty.

Hidden.

What harm did it do to have such a thing? *God doesn't care if you have a red ribbon,* Seraphina had said.

"Now is as good a time as any for you to recite the catechism to me, Sister Joelle. Chapter Three, if you please."

Joelle closed her eyes. She had recited the first chapters of the catechism to Sister Bernadette dozens of times. Scores of times.

"Very well. *Christian, recognize your dignity, and now that you share in God's own nature, do not return to your former base condition by sinning.*"

Had Sister Bernadette chosen chapter three just to dig at Joelle's own sinful nature? A sinful nature proven by the color of the hair God gave her?

*Never forget that you have been rescued from the power of darkness . . ."*

Was not everyone, not just redheads, born a sinner? That's why Father Xavier baptized Bridget's baby as quickly as possible.

All her years in the convent, Joelle had found comfort in the routine and sameness of life. She had thought it a harmless diversion to watch the people living in the lane below the convent, but now she began to wonder if it was an indication of a weakness in herself, for she could not shake this malaise, this vague discontent. She did not understand why these rebellious thoughts contradicting Sister Bernadette came into her mind.

She would pray harder, study harder, and she would regain her peace of mind. She focused on the rote words . . . *Sin creates a proclivity to sin resulting in perverse inclinations which cloud conscience and corrupt the judgment of good and evil.*

Ah. The meaning was clear. She must burn her red ribbon.

# Chapter Sixteen

*Temptation*
*A Thursday*

Giles stilled his hoe and listened. Rosalie was fussing at Isabel again. His too-old-for-her-age child was fractious these last weeks. Ever since they came home from the fort with no hope of a new maman.

He stared at the tree line edging his cleared land. To tell the truth, he had himself been a bit blue. He had let himself imagine having a friend, a partner, a lover, a wife, which made him all the lonelier.

He stomped the dirt off his boots and stepped in to chaos. Isabel had cornmeal in her hair. Felix was naked. Rosalie was red-faced. All three of his children were crying.

Without a word, Giles scooped up his children and sat with them on the bed. Felix plastered himself to his chest and Rosalie and Isabel each claimed a knee and leaned into him.

He wrapped his arms around all three of them and rocked a little back and forth while they cried it out.

Sometimes, all you could do was laugh at misery. He kissed each little face and wiped away tears, and smiled at each of them to show them all would be well.

"Isabel, can you pour some water into the basin? Felix, my son, can you put your clothes back on?"

Sniffling, his two youngest set to work. When Rosalie meant to slide off his knee, Giles held her back.

"Just a moment, *ma petite*. Let me keep you a little longer." She snuggled into him and he held her close. "I don't have a chance to just hold my big girl anymore."

Isabel did a good job using the gourd to ladle water from the bucket into the basin. "See? I didn't spill a drop."

"Good girl. After you wash your face, you can help Felix get his socks on."

"I don't need help getting my socks on, Papa."

"He's putting them on wrong side out," Rosalie said.

He tightened his arm around her. "Everything doesn't have to be just right, my darling. If you chase after perfect, you'll be disappointed every time. Look there, Felix's shoe went over that inside-out sock just fine."

Isabel stood before him shiny faced, waiting for whatever came next. Felix got to his feet, fully clothed.

"Here's what we're going to do. Number one, Isabel will go outside and shake the cornmeal out of her hair, and Felix, you'll help her comb out the tangles. Number two, Rosalie and I will fix an early lunch. Number three, we will get ourselves into the dugout and go to the fort."

Isabel threw her arms in the air. "Hooray! Come on, Felix."

If there were a park nearby, or a bakery, or even a shady road to take a walk on, that's where he'd take the children to get their minds off their woes. There were none of those things, however, so the fort it would be. He too could do with a break in the unending toil with the forest hemming him in on three sides.

Giles put a finger under Rosalie's chin to see if he'd earned a smile. He had not. "You don't want to go to the fort? Sister Joelle will be there."

"I want to go."

"You don't look happy about it."

She leaned into his chest again. "Sister Joelle doesn't want to be our mother. And Marie Claude doesn't want to be our mother. Nobody wants to be our mother." And with that, the tears spilled over again.

Giles thought he might cry himself. Instead he let out a sigh. There had been other bad days since Bella died. They had survived them. They would get through this one too.

"You remember how special your maman was?"

Rosalie nodded.

"And Maman wouldn't want just anyone to take her place. She wants you to have another special maman. We just haven't found her yet."

"Will we find her?"

Lord, he hoped so. "We'll keep trying."

They were getting a late start, but if they didn't make it back before dark, there would be a full moon tonight. Giles made sure hands and faces were cleaned, gathered up the two piglets he meant to sell, and got everyone situated in the dugout. The piglets were excited to be on the bayou, and Giles hoped their busyness wouldn't tip them all into the water.

The sun beat down on their heads, but there was a breeze coming up the bayou to keep them comfortable. No doubt Rosalie, the fairest of them all, would have a sunburn. Why could he never remember to make them wear their hats?

By the time they'd entered the sound, Felix and Isabel each had a sleepy piglet in their laps, Rosalie seemed calm and happy to be on the water, and Giles found his own spirits lifted. He shouldn't have kept them all home the last few Sundays. People needed people, and that included children. Today was a Thursday and there would be few settlers at the fort, but the man who kept the pigs was a friendly sort.

The children would be glad to see Sister Joelle, as would he, but Giles needed to squelch his attraction to her. He had liked her very well, and then he'd seen that red ribbon peeping out from her black sleeve. His feelings about a young nun and that red ribbon did him no credit.

What on earth was a sister doing with a red ribbon on her wrist? It was meant to be hidden, he was sure, and when she realized he'd seen it, she'd turned scarlet. It didn't take much to make her blush though. That fair freckled skin, typical of red hair, seemed to go with blushes.

Which thought led him to remember the short copper curls he'd revealed when he took her wimple off.

Maybe he should have taken the children to visit Marie Claude instead.

Once he'd pulled the dugout ashore and helped his brood disembark, he guided them toward the pig sties set up at the far end of the island. Monsieur Porcher kept three pens of pigs for sale, piglets, sows, and one mean looking boar.

Monsieur Porcher lounged in the shade, apparently indifferent to the heavy odor hovering like haze in the air. Giles wished for a breeze to at least move the stink along.

"Bonjour, monsieur. What you got for me?"

"Felicité is a gilt and François is a barrow," Isabel explained.

"Excellent, my friends. No one seems to want old Gascon there. He's too old and too mean, but a nice little barrow, somebody will buy him this very Sunday, you wait and see."

"Felicité wants to go with François, Monsieur Porcher," Rosalie said.

Porcher's eyes gleamed with amusement. "She does, does she? Well, maybe that is what will happen. They'll go to the same nice family."

Isabel clapped her hands once and gave a little hop. "They can still play together then."

Thank heavens the man didn't mention Felicité's possible future on a roasting spit.

Rosalie was on her knees saying goodbye to Felicité and François. They put their snouts right in her face, and she kissed them back. No tears, however, Giles was relieved to see.

Giles pocketed his profit and nodded good day to Porcher. The man might look like a swineherd and smell like a swineherd, but he was one of the few people in the colony who dealt in silver instead of in trade goods.

"Now what, Papa?"

"Now we go to the general store." They needed candles and thread and soap. Bella had used to make soap from bear grease and lye, but Giles didn't have the time or the inclination to figure out how she'd done it.

Felix and Isabel took off running, their arms spread out like they were about to fly off into the sky. Rosalie took his hand. "They're very silly children, aren't they, Papa?"

"Silly is fun, sweetheart. I wonder. Do you think you could catch them if you ran very very fast?"

She turned her face up to him and he was happy to see a gleam in her eye. She took off running after her brother and sister just as if she were not a child who had to watch her siblings, help cook breakfast, help wash the laundry, help and help and help. He thought for the fortieth time, it was too much for a child, but he didn't know how he could manage without her.

Coming in from bright sunlight, Giles had to wait a moment for his eyes to adjust to the interior of the store. When he could see clearly, he found his children eyeing the jar of boiled sweets on the counter.

"This candy came all the way from France, imagine that," the storekeeper said.

Rosalie sighed. "They're very beautiful."

And they were. A beam of sunlight came through the window and illuminated the jar so that the red and green and yellow candies seemed to glow.

"We'll take three pieces," Giles said. He had a pocket full of silver from selling the piglets, and dear as candy from France was, his children had few treats in their lives.

Isabel grabbed him around the legs and squeezed. "You are the best Papa in the whole world."

Giles laughed and felt a surge of happiness. He didn't blame them when they all chose red. They were as beautiful as rubies and judging by the face Felix made when he tasted his first candy, incredibly sweet and delicious.

"One for you, monsieur?" the storekeeper asked.

He shook his head. He'd never had a sweet tooth, but Bella, she could have eaten a whole jar of sweets all by herself.

Giles picked up the candles, thread, and soap, and carried them out in the last basket Bella had made. A bit lopsided, but a treasure just the same.

"There's Sister Joelle!" Isabel took off running, Felix and Rosalie after her.

Sister Joelle walked with the older nun leaning on her, her free hand carrying an empty basin. When the children ran to her, she gently freed herself from Sister Bernadette so that she could open both arms to them.

When Giles caught up, Felix was showing her the candy he'd taken from his mouth and deposited on his palm. Isabel simply opened her mouth to show the red jewel on her tongue.

Sister Joelle laughed and caught Giles's eye. She blushed, poor girl. Did she realize how often she blushed, or how the blush made her eyes brighten? Of course she didn't. She would have no idea of being pretty, or desirable.

Felix held his hand out. "You can have a taste."

"Oh, what a kind boy you are, Felix. But do you know, it would make me happy to see you enjoying it all by yourself."

Judging by Felix's grin as he popped the candy back in his mouth, that was exactly the right answer.

Giles noticed a rivulet of sweat traveling down the side of Sister Joelle's face to disappear into her neck windings. He wished he'd bought a bright bit of joy for Sister Joelle, too. The look on her face when she first tasted all that sweetness, it would be a sight to see.

Of course, Sister Bernadette should have one, too.

Would it be improper to buy sweets for nuns, or almost-nuns? Not if they came from the children, surely.

Giles bent to whisper in Rosalie's ear. She turned her face up to him and nodded yes with a big smile on her face. He handed her a coin and sent her off.

Isabel took Sister Joelle's hand and pulled at it. "Will you tell us another story? Please?"

Sister Joelle's big smile told Giles she was about to say yes when Sister Bernadette interrupted. "Sister Joelle has duties to attend to, children. Come, Sister."

The young sister's face fell and a flash of guilt crossed her face. Giles clamped his jaw. The other sister and Father Xavier seemed to keep her on a short tether if she couldn't even sit with the children.

And then he reminded himself it was not his business to approve or disapprove. Giles was sorry for it, but that was the life she'd chosen, to be bound by the strictures of being a nun.

Rosalie came bounding back, a big grin on her face. Shyly, she opened her hand to show two jewel-toned candies on her palm, one red and one green. "The red one is for you, Sister Joelle."

Sister Joelle clasped her hands to her bosom and beamed. And then, her eyes teared up, and Giles's heart felt a little squeeze. He very much wanted her to put that piece of candy in her mouth and feel the explosion of flavor on her tongue. She had probably never experienced such a taste in her life.

She glanced at Sister Bernadette, whose eyes were focused on the candies in Rosalie's hand.

"The green one is for you, Sister Bernadette," Rosalie said.

"How very unnecessary," Sister Bernadette said. "Such invitation to frivolity." She tore her gaze from the candy and frowned at Giles.

Giles was not interested in Sister Bernadette's frowns. He turned to Sister Joelle and met her gaze.

"It's only candy, Sister," he murmured.

~~~

Joelle had never seen anything like this candy, glowing red in the sunlight. She reached for it -- and felt Sister Bernadette's nails bite into her arm.

Joelle could see from the hard glint in her eyes that there would be no kindness in the words to come. "Such worldly temptations are not for us, Sister."

Rosalie turned to her father. "Did I do something wrong, Papa?"

"No, darling. The mistake was mine. Say good day, children."

Joelle felt her throat close. Monsieur Travert was offended. Rosalie was hurt.

Sister Bernadette had already turned away to stride toward the chapel. Joelle watched her for a moment, then she turned back to the Travert family. Isabel and Felix looked at her like she was the thing they wanted most in the world and they were not to have it. Rosalie had her father's hand, her head bowed. Joelle couldn't bear it.

"Monsieur Travert, if you have the time, I would like to tell the children a story."

Monsieur Travert smiled at her. "We'll make the time." He tipped his head toward the trees where pine needles carpeted the sand. "Let's go sit in the shade."

Joelle settled on the ground and Felix promptly climbed into her lap as if that were his rightful place. How very glad she was to have his small body in her arms. She wondered if Sister Bernadette had ever known such a pleasure.

Monsieur Travert leaned against a tree, his legs stretched out in front of him, crossed at the ankles. Isabel laid her head on his thigh and Rosalie sat with her elbows on her bent knees.

"Do you know the story of the Creation?" Joelle asked them.

Rosalie shook her head for all of them.

"Well, it took God a whole week to create all of this." She swept her arm to include the earth and the sky, the gulls overhead, the trees around them, and the ants in their ant hill a few yards away.

"My favorite is the story of the third day. Do you know, in the beginning there was nothing growing in the whole world? Not a blade of grass or a single wildflower. No pine trees, no sweet potatoes, no corn."

"Then what did people eat?" Isabel asked.

"God hadn't made people yet. Imagine that."

Joelle told the story the way she'd always wanted to hear it, with details, embellishments, even humor. Her audience attended every word, and when she made Rosalie smile, she found a happiness new to her. To be noticed, to be listened to -- what heady gratification this was.

"But why did God make weeds?" Felix asked.

Monsieur Travert had seemed half asleep propped up against the tree, but he caught her eye and smiled, sharing his amusement. And Joelle could not look away. She felt suspended in that moment, captured by the warmth in this man's eyes. He stared into her own, the smile fading.

"Papa, maybe God doesn't want us to pull up his weeds."

His gaze shifted to his son, and Joelle's lungs took in a rush of air. What had just happened to her? She felt light-headed and her heart thumped hard in her chest.

"What a philosopher you are, son. I believe the answer is that when God made men, He gave them permission to manage all the animals and all the plants. Is that right, Sister?"

"Yes. That's right." She helped Felix climb out of her lap and shook her skirts as she stood up.

Monsieur Travert got to his feet and nudged Isabel. "What do you say?"

"Thank you, Sister Joelle. Will you tell us another story next time we come?"

She dared to look at Monsieur Travert. His face was mild and pleasant, as always, but now she knew there was more underneath. Something deep and . . . she didn't know. Something . . . feverish?

No, she was imagining it. He simply looked like a loving father, that's all. Then was that something feverish inside her instead? That something that Sister Bernadette warned her against?

"You're a gifted story-teller, Sister Joelle."

She ducked her head in a sort of nod. "Thank you. I . . . I have to go."

Rosalie and Isabel each hugged her around the waist. "Good bye, Sister Joelle."

Monsieur Travert took a step toward her. "I wish you'd take your candy, Sister. It's only a mouthful of sweetness." He dug in his pocket and held out his hand, the bit of temptation nestled in his palm.

She couldn't think. Her throat felt thick and tight. She plucked the candy from his hand and thrust it into her pocket. She had to get away, to think about what had just happened between her and this man. As she strode away from them toward the chapel, she finally raised her face to look where she was going. Sister Bernadette and Father Xavier watched her, their arms crossed over their chests.

Shame rose up in Joelle's breast as she saw the scowls on their faces. She had just experienced something extraordinary. When Monsieur Travert had looked into her eyes, she had suddenly become aware of her whole body. Her breasts had felt heavy and her belly . . . she had no words for such feelings. She had not even realized those parts of her body had feelings.

Did it show on her face, that she had felt something forbidden?

Was this what Seraphina felt when she flirted with men? Is this why women welcomed the touch of a husband?

But Joelle had not been touched in that way. Nor had she touched Giles Travert. Nor any man.

"Sister Joelle." Father Xavier's scowl had something of disapproval in it, but also something of disappointment. She gripped her hands together at her waist.

"Sister Bernadette says Monsieur Travert tempted you with a piece of candy."

"Tempted, Father?" Tempted, as in tempted to sin? By a piece of candy?

"She was about to accept it when I intervened," Sister Bernadette accused. "No doubt she put it in her mouth as soon as I left."

"I did not, Sister Bernadette." She had hardly realized she'd taken the candy from Monsieur Travert's hand, and now it felt like a burning ember in her pocket.

"But you wanted to."

When Joelle released her hands, they trembled. That was foolishness. She wiped them on her skirts and drew a deep breath. Once, when Joelle was quite small, she had cut up a stocking because scissors were still new to her and it was so very satisfying to slice the blades through a piece of fabric. She had, too late, realized it would anger Sister Bernadette and hid under the stairs for hours until an older child found her and dragged her out for her punishment. She was no longer a child.

"Yes. I did."

"She spends time with Monsieur Travert every time he comes to the fort, Father."

"Is this true, Sister Joelle?"

"With him and his three children, yes, Father."

"The children are with you always?"

"Yes, Father. Of course. I tell them stories."

His eyes narrowed. "What kind of stories?"

"The first time I told them about Noah and the ark. Today I told them about God's creations on the Third Day."

"Ah." The crease between his eyes eased. "Bible stories."

"Yes, Father."

Sister Bernadette turned so her shoulder was to Joelle and whispered loudly. "Father, Monsieur Travert saw Sister Joelle without her wimple."

The priest's eyebrows rose into pointed arches. "Indeed? But surely that was when Sister Joelle was taken ill."

"Yes. It was," Joelle said. She had succeeded so far in keeping the tremble out of her voice, but her insides were clenched tight.

Had what happened between her and Giles Travert a few minutes ago shown her any hint he remembered seeing her hair? The moment of searing awareness had not been planned. It had taken him by surprise as much as it had her. And immediately afterward, he had acted with great propriety. She looked her priest in the eye. "Monsieur Travert is entirely respectful, Father."

Sister Bernadette's chin jutted stubbornly. "Sister Joelle is not fully protected by her final vows, Father. It is not proper, a novice spending time with a man."

Father Xavier tilted his head and looked at Joelle, studying her. "You have delayed her vows, have you not, Sister Bernadette?"

"I have. You see why, Father. She strays now and then." Sister Bernadette raised her hand. "Not that she has committed sinful acts. I am ever vigilant, as you know. But she shows a lack of judgment, Father. You can see that."

"Hm."

Joelle's hands, again clasped tightly together, grew slippery with sweat. The linen around her neck was too snug. Sweat dripped across her scalp and she yearned to wrench the wimple off. But she must stand still. She must never feel impatient. She must never feel . . . anything. But she did. She did feel.

"Telling Bible stories to children is entirely appropriate, Sister Bernadette. I believe Sister Joelle has not erred in this matter." Father Xavier looked Joelle in the face. "But I agree with the good Sister. Accepting candy, that would be inappropriate. Remember your place, Sister Joelle."

With that, Father Xavier left them, his mind apparently already occupied with other matters.

Joelle quietly let out the breath she'd been holding. "I'm sorry I gave you cause to worry, Sister Bernadette."

"It is not I to whom you should apologize. God too has been offended by your willfulness." With a dramatic turn on her heel, Sister Bernadette marched off.

Joelle drew a deep breath and wandered down to the shore to calm herself. She was sorry to have displeased Sister Bernadette, and the sister was right. For that little while, she had forgotten that she was not like other women. She was to be a nun, and the feelings women allowed themselves were not for her.

She saw the Travert family in their dugout half way across the sound. She raised her hand in goodbye, but they didn't see her.

Joelle's fingers found the candy in her pocket. She took it out and looked at it, so pretty and bright in the sunlight. Only a mouthful of sweetness, Monsieur Travert said.

She raised the candy to her lips and gave it a tentative lick. She licked it again. Not just sweetness, but flavor. Cinnamon? Or was it anise?

Joelle placed the whole thing on her tongue and closed her mouth. Sweetness seemed to fill her entire being, seemed to rise into her head and down into her body. With eyes closed, she allowed the sensations to flood her senses.

She opened her eyes, the candy slowly dissolving in her mouth. The sky was still blue. The water still calm. If she were so very wicked, wouldn't she know His displeasure?

Joelle licked her fingers and smiled up toward Heaven. God still loved her. She could feel it.

# Chapter Seventeen

*No Selling, No Trading*

Edda, baby Matthew's wet nurse, brought him to Marie Claude.

"He needs to burp, madame."

Marie Claude set aside the basket she was weaving and held her arms up for her son. "Here, big fellow. Come to Maman."

She laid him against her shoulder and gently patted his back. When Matthew delivered an impressive burp, Marie Claude grinned at Edda. "He's a good eater, my boy."

Edda's intense gaze on Matthew reminded Marie Claude that Edda needed this baby as much as she did. Her own infant had died only two days before Thomas and Marie Claude took her from the market. Her breasts had been full and aching, and she gladly put Matthew to nurse.

Who the father of Edda's child was Marie Claude did not know. Had she cared for him? Or had she borne the child of a man who had used her? Either way, she could see Edda's need to love this baby. Whenever he nursed, she held him tenderly and gently smoothed the light hair as his eyes closed in the bliss of a full tummy.

"You can be happy here?" Marie Claude asked the girl.

"You are a kind mistress, madame," Edda said in the lilting speech of the Caribbean. "I am grateful to be here."

"I won't expect you to work in the fields, Edda. Not with your bad foot."

Edda took in a shuddering breath. "I will do whatever you ask, madame."

"Then first thing, you call me Marie Claude. I don't like madame or any of that. Just Marie Claude."

The new slave girl stared at her. Poor girl. She'd been with them for weeks now and she was still scared. She didn't need to be.

"Sit down, Edda. I need to explain how things go here."

Edda sat on the far end of the stoop and clasped her hands tightly. "I do something wrong, madame?"

"You do everything just fine, Edda. But I want you to stop calling me madame. I don't like it. Just call me Marie Claude, that's all. Like Thomas and the others do."

"Yes, ma'am."

"No. Just Marie Claude."

She stroked Matthew's back, feeling his little body slacken as he succumbed to sleep, and looked at Edda's foot, healed enough to be open to the air with just a layer of unguent on it.

"Your foot hurting you bad?" Marie Claude said.

The girl would never walk well again. The toes and the instep of her right foot had been crushed, the bones half-healed but misaligned. The toes were still raw and misshapen. Heaven knows the pain she had endured these last four weeks. Four weeks ago -- that's when she had tried to run away with her infant and that's when the slave trader had taught her a lesson.

Marie Claude didn't know how Edda's baby died. She was afraid to ask her. What if it had been because of something the trader had done? Marie Claude didn't think she could bear knowing that.

Someday, she would ask.

Edda didn't even look at her foot. "I got it to live with, that's all." She picked up the basket and started shelling peas.

"The other thing you got to understand about this place -- it's *our* place, not just mine. The law calls it mine, but Remy, Simon, and Thomas work just as hard as I do. It's *our* place. It's *our* home. And now it's yours, too. You belong to us, and we belong to you."

Edda's hands stilled over the basket of beans. "You bought me, madame. I know I'm a slave."

"Marie Claude, I told you." Why did people have so much trouble with a simple name? "You're not a slave as long as you're on this property. When you go off it, you'll be safer you act like you're a slave cause that's what people expect, but I don't hold with owning another body. You're free, far as I'm concerned."

Edda wouldn't look at her. Marie Claude thought that clamped jaw showed a stubborn nature. Well, none of them was perfect. They'd get along well enough.

"What about when the baby weans? You sell me off then?"

Marie Claude breathed a heavy sigh. "No. That's what I'm telling you. No selling. No trading. You can leave or stay -- that's what free means, but --"

"But I got nowhere to go."

"You don't have to go nowhere. You got a home here, and we got a baby who needs you."

At the edge of the clearing, Remy was felling a tree. In the garden, Thomas tied up the climbing bean plants. Simon was probably at the Biloxi village seeing that woman he was sweet on.

"You going to let one of them men make me his woman?"

"Nobody is going to make you be anybody's woman." She caught Edda's eyes on Remy as he wielded the axe. "But if you and one of the men decide you want to be together, he can build you a place for the two of you. We got lots more land than what's cleared."

And then there would be more babies born. Marie Claude rubbed her cheek across Mathew's soft hair. A fine thing, to have more babies in the family.

Marie Claude cuddled her sleeping babe. God was good. She had Thomas. She had Simon and Remy and now Edda. And she had her own son.

Smiling, she raised her face to the sun and closed her eyes. This was happiness.

# Chapter Eighteen

*Fever*
*August*

Laurent Laroux paddled his dugout into Marie Claude's landing and sauntered up the path. He raised a hand when he saw her sitting on the stoop with her baby on her shoulder.

"Good morning to you," she said.

"I hear you have a baby boy." She let him take her baby into his arms. "What do you call him?"

"Matthew."

Laroux held Matthew's head in one hand, his little body along his forearm, his other hand on the baby's belly, and looked into Matthew's sleepy gray eyes. How could you not smile with a perfect little person in your hands?

"I've come on business," he said, returning the baby to her.

Marie Claude gave him a shrewd look. He held his hand up. "Nothing to do with indigo, I promise." He knew as well as anyone how she felt about poisoning people to make blue dye for spoiled rich people.

They walked to the ruined cypress vats across the yard. Dupre had told him Marie Claude chopped into them to make them useless for processing dye, but he hadn't seen the damage before now. It had taken uncommon strength to splinter and split good cypress.

Laroux nodded toward the vats. "Dupre told me you had some good wood in those vats, and that your men were fine carpenters." He ran a hand over the smoothed cypress. "You think one of your men could cut this smallest vat down and make a bed out of it? A toddler bed, not for a baby like Matthew."

Laroux was pretty sure Fleur thought he only wanted to bed her. Maybe the men in her tribe, well, maybe they took the women for granted. None of them had lived alone in the woods for months on end, had no reason to have ever known what it meant to be lonely. Perhaps they did not need their women as he needed Fleur.

When Fleur saw the bed for Mahkee, she would understand what he wanted: to make a home for her and the baby, to have them live with him. To be a family together. And when it was time for him to return to France, Fleur would have the crib to take with her back to the village. He wouldn't have to worry about her. She would be taken care of among her people.

And he didn't want her to think he simply needed a woman. He didn't want just any woman. He wanted Fleur.

He had tried to tell her. He couldn't tell if Fleur didn't believe that he loved or didn't understand. Even speaking the same language, at least in its rudiments, their cultures were as different as French and Chinese would be.

They could get past that. He'd show her they could.

"Remy," Marie Claude called. She turned back to Laroux. "He's the best woodworker. We'll ask him."

Remy set down his axe and joined them. "Tell him what you want," Marie Claude said.

Laroux described what he had in mind, using his hands to sweep across the cypress, shaping a bed using the existing bottom of the vat and keeping a few inches of lip to keep Mahkee from rolling out.

"I don't intend a trade, Marie Claude. I have coins to pay for it."

She nodded at Remy. "They'll be Remy's coins then. He's the one who'll do the work. Remy?"

"Yes. I can do this for you, monsieur."

"Good." Then Fleur would see: Laroux would take care of her and her baby.

~~~

When Laroux entered the village, he felt like he was coming home. Those days he'd lain in Fleur's hut recovering from his wound, he had been welcomed and cared for, not only by his dark-eyed angel, but by her brother and his cousins. They had stopped by in the afternoons and talked like old friends.

Three little boys ran to him chattering, two of them with runny noses. That Laroux did not understand them and that they didn't understand him either seemed not to matter, and they happily ran off to other pursuits.

Children played, women visited while they worked together, and the men who were not hunting smoked or tanned hides. No idle hands here. In fact, the village was quite noisy with grinding stones whooshing across corn kernels, people talking, laughing, coughing and sneezing.

He stopped to talk to his friend Mato for a few minutes, said a few words to other men he had come to know, and made his way to Fleur's hut. The two young women who sat with her went away, tittering and looking at him over their shoulders. Girls were the same everywhere, it seemed. He smiled at them and turned his attention to Fleur.

Today she wore her hair loosely draped over her shoulders. He wanted to scoop her up and take her inside the hut, to make love to her until he had spent all his strength, and that would take hours. But he was in her home, not his, and he would be a gentleman even in a village of thatched huts.

He satisfied himself with a rather formal bow, which he supposed looked ridiculous to the Biloxi men. Fleur accepted his courtesy with a shy smile and a gesture for him to join her. Folding his legs under him, he sat on the ground in front of the hut with her sleeping babe between them.

He handed Fleur his gift.

"And what kind of eggs are these?"

"Chicken," he said. "You have seen chickens at the market, on some of the farmsteads?"

"Very pretty birds. Also very strange. They don't fly away."

"No. They're not good flyers, though they can get themselves into a tree if they want to badly enough."

"I shall cook them for you."

"For us, Fleur."

"Yes. For us."

Laroux looked around wondering what he could do for her. Even though she had no husband, the villagers took care of each other. She would not want for a share of the hunting and fishing. Yet there was a damp spot just inside the doorway of the hut.

"Your thatch is leaking?"

"A little. I will fix it one day."

"I will do it."

"You do not have to."

"I want to."

He pulled off his shirt and folded it. With his knife in hand, he found a large stand of palmettos and long leafed palms on the edge of the village. His arms full, he carried them back to the hut, aware some of the men smirked as he passed. Thatching was women's work, he deduced, but it didn't bother him.

At the hut, Fleur held Mahkee's hands so he could try walking a few steps. As soon as Mahkee saw Laroux, his drooling mouth opened in delight. Whose heart could resist a welcome like that?

Laroux tossed the fronds down, squatted, and held his arms out. With Fleur's help, Mahkee tottered over, a grin on his face.

When Laroux could reach him, he grabbed Mahkee up and threw him in the air to a cascade of giggles. Had there ever been a moment in his life as perfect as this? He bent and gave Fleur a quick kiss, which made her face turn a dusky rose.

"I will cook for you now," she said, dipping her head.

He grinned, loving how shy she was with him even after she had slept in his bed three nights ago.

Laroux worked on the thatch while Fleur prepared corn meal cakes and the eggs. When dinner was ready, he sat down with Mahkee in his lap and ate with his fingers, a large leaf his plate.

Two old women bustled in and out of several of the huts, small gourds in their hands.

"The children are sick over there. The grandmothers make the fever brew for them."

Laroux's hands stilled. Sickness spread rapidly when people lived close together like this. And it was known the Indians who caught diseases from the French did not do well.

"Has there been a Frenchman in the village?"

Fleur laughed. "There was only you, and the wound in your shoulder was not catching."

She made light of it, but Laroux caught the look in her eye when she looked at Mahkee. She would know about fevers.

He spread his fingers out across Mahkee's tummy. There was no fever in the child. But the youngest were often the first to fall to disease.

"What kind of fever?" he asked.

Fleur shrugged. "There are many kinds of fever."

Laroux handed Mahkee to her and walked to the doorway of the hut where the coughing was strongest. One of the old women pushed him out, scolding him in her own language.

He looked over his shoulder for Fleur to come to him, Mahkee in her arms. "Ask her, Fleur. What's wrong with the children?"

While the women spoke, Laroux stepped back to the doorway and stuck his head in. The interior was dim and if it had not been for a small beam of light arrowing through a gap in the thatch overhead, he would not have seen the red bumps covering the child's face and neck.

Laroux backed out. Measles. A terrible dread rose in him. He had had measles as a boy, and likely many of the villagers here had survived measles in years past. But not the children. They would have no immunity whatsoever.

He interrupted the old woman and took Fleur by the elbow. "Come away," he told her quietly.

At her hut, he said, "Get what you need. You and Mahkee are coming home with me."

She pulled her arm from his grip, frowning at him.

"Fleur. I saw the child. He has red spots on his skin. Do you know what that means?"

He held her eyes as she read his face. She didn't know, he guessed.

"It's measles, Fleur. It's dangerous. Some people die of it." His throat worked until he could say the rest, his eyes on Mahkee. "Especially children."

All the color washed out of Fleur's face.

"You'll come with me, you and Mahkee."

Her voice breathy and strained, Fleur said, "My cousin's children. If they catch it, she'll need me."

"She will need help, yes. But the grandmothers will help her, and the other women. You cannot stay here."

She pressed her hand to her mouth, her eyes big and deep. "The children die?"

"Sometimes. Let's don't linger here."

On the way out of the village, they stopped to talk to Mato. "I'm taking Fleur and the baby with me. There's sickness here. Did you know it?"

Mato looked at his sister. "Yes, I know."

"I am afraid, Mato. Mahkee will be safe at Laroux's place."

"It's measles," Laroux said. "The fever with the red spots."

"I remember it. When I was a boy, I had it. It is a strong fever."

"Did Fleur have it?"

"She was not yet born, but our mother had it and survived."

"They'll have to come home with me."

"Laroux, I -- " Fleur said.

Mato shook his head. "You should go with him." He nodded toward the path leading out of the village. "Go."

Two days after Laroux and Fleur fled the village, Mahkee woke with a runny nose and a cough.

# Chapter Nineteen

## *Deceit*

If Colonel Blaise's estimate was correct, Catherine figured, a ship should arrive in the next two weeks. Catherine and Jean Paul would climb aboard, endure two months at sea, and then begin their new life in France. There would be plays and concerts and balls. There would be sweet cream, butter, white bread, pheasant cooked in wine, chocolate . . .

With Jean Paul's tanned skin, his deep dark eyes, his shoulders and hands evidence of a life they knew nothing about, Catherine's friends would find him fascinating. Her husband might not like being the fascination of the moment, but it would pass, and he would soon gravitate to friends of his own, men who, however nobly born, would recognize a noble man.

And Catherine would see Grandfather again, his kindly eyes full of love, his arms opened to her. She could hardly wait to step into his embrace.

Then why this feeling of unease? Catherine sat on the edge of the bed and leaned her head into her hands.

The first days after the letter from Grandfather arrived, Catherine had been so full of relief and elation, she had assumed Jean Paul felt the same. But after all these days, she had to face it. Something was wrong.

She found him, as she often did these days, at the bayou, standing with his arms across his chest, staring at nothing.

She touched his elbow, and he put his arm around her shoulders.

"Jean Paul," she said. "What is it?"

"I saw a big old bass splash just there. I was wondering if he'd let me catch him."

She stepped in front of him so she could see his face. "You know I don't mean that fish."

He pulled her to him and rested his chin on the top of her head. "Everything's fine."

She pulled back and searched his face. "What aren't you telling me?"

For the briefest moment, Jean Paul's face was utterly bleak. Catherine felt the ground shift beneath her feet.

He smiled. "I told you, everything's fine. You want to fish with me?"

"You're worried you'll be taken up once we're back in France. Is that it? I told you, Grandfather is a powerful man. He need only declare you are innocent, and there will be no charges, no trial, no prison. Ever. Truly, Jean Paul, you need not think of it."

He pulled her to him again and held her tight.

Why wasn't he reassured? Why was he so glum? "You don't believe me? I promise. Grandfather will take care of it."

He stroked her back. "I'm sure you're right." He whispered in her ear, his breath tickling her neck. "I don't think I want to fish right now. I think I want to take you to bed."

"Jean Paul, it's the middle of the day," she said, giving his chest a gentle push.

He scooped her up in his arms and strode toward the cabin.

"You're disgraceful," she cried. "You put me down right now. I have chores to do."

"Consider me a chore, then. I need tending more than that damned grist mill." He shouldered through the doorway with her, gave her a smacking great kiss, and dropped her on the bed.

"Oh, all right," she said, "but I'd rather be grinding corn."

"Is that so?" he said with a grin. "Let's see if I can change your mind."

~~~

Jean Paul lay with Catherine's head on his arm. She'd fallen asleep, and for these few minutes, he didn't have to school his face into a mask of good cheer. How much longer could he hide the truth from her? He was no actor, yet for a while, Catherine had seemed to believe all was well between them. Until today. But she'd thought the murder charge awaiting him in France was all that troubled him.

No doubt her Grandfather could save him from facing charges. After all, his name was often mentioned in the same sentence with the great comte de Orleans. But why would he want to? He wouldn't, Jean Paul believed. He wouldn't want his beloved granddaughter stuck with a man like him.

He hated deceiving her. But he had to. What if she refused to go home without him? How could he do that to her? She had to go home. Had to.

Catherine woke and stretched like a cat. He loved that about her, the way she had become at ease with him in this bed, no clothes, no inhibitions. God, how could he live without her?

She flopped herself across his chest and pulled his bottom lip down with her fingertip. "I love you," she said.

He clasped her hand in his. "And I love you." There was that much truth between them anyway.

She shifted to get comfortable. "Tell me something you miss."

This was her favorite conversation now, imagining what they would rediscover in Paris. Sometimes it was food, sometimes it was paper and ink, sometimes it was simply the way the light played in the chestnut trees.

"There was a bakery on the Rue Papin. Their croissants melted in your mouth. And their marzipan!" He sighed loudly.

"We will go to the Rue Papin and we will find this bakery. We will buy every croissant, every cake, every marzipan, and we will make ourselves sick eating them."

"Wait. I require café au lait with my croissant."

"Very well. A pot of café for you and a pot of chocolate for me."

"You know the best place for a feast like this?" he asked her.

"Well, the Tuileries have lovely picnic areas beneath the trees."

He shook his head.

"Not the Tuileries? A riverbank somewhere?"

He shook his head. His fingers played with her hair, then smoothed down her back to caress her bottom.

"Bed. That's the best place for a feast." He flipped her over and opened his mouth with a growl.

Catherine whooped with laughter, then grew quiet as they made a banquet of loving each other.

# Chapter Twenty

*Penance and Purpose*

Joelle, in the end, confessed to Father Xavier. She had not lied to him and Sister Bernadette, she explained, but later, curiosity had tempted her and she'd put the candy in her mouth.

"I see," he said.

She waited, hoping he would not tell Sister Bernadette.

"So you have tasted the forbidden fruit?"

Was that a note of amusement in Father Xavier's voice?

"What did it taste like?" he asked.

"Sweet. Sweeter than honey. And something else, maybe anise."

"You enjoyed it?"

"Yes, Father. I did."

"Hm," he said. She heard him draw in a breath. "Sister Joelle, I don't believe enjoying a piece of candy is a sin. Of course it is not. I am, however, troubled that you ate the candy when you knew Sister Bernadette disapproved."

"Yes, Father, I did."

"Do you regret your decision?"

She hesitated. "Sister Bernadette has always been good to me."

"Of course."

Joelle suppressed a groan. He was going to make her confess to Sister Bernadette.

"What do you think Sister Bernadette would say if she knew you had tasted the candy?"

"She would be angry with me."

"Yes, I imagine so."

Joelle sighed. "I suppose she would expect me to memorize the next chapter of the catechism."

"Memorize an entire chapter? Is that a task within your capabilities?"

"I have already memorized chapters one through three, Father."

"An impressive accomplishment, Sister. Very well. Then memorize chapter four and we may keep this penance between us two."

Joelle's shoulders slumped in relief.

"And," Father Xavier added, "you will remember you owe Sister Bernadette your obedience."

"Yes, Father. I will remember. Thank you."

"Go then, and behave yourself."

Joelle emerged from the chapel into the sunshine feeling wonderfully unburdened. She had not expected lenience, even humor, from Father Xavier.

In the following days, Joelle recommitted herself to piety and obedience. She attended Sister Bernadette when her feet were swollen and sore, she swept every inch of the chapel, the bedrooms behind the sanctuary, and the infirmary. She scrubbed down the cots and chased the spiders out. In quieter moments, she worked at memorizing chapter four. All this she tackled with smiling good will. This served the dual purpose, in Joelle's mind, of pleasing Sister Bernadette and willing discontent from her mind.

On wash day, Joelle whistled under her breath as she collected the laundry off the line. Tomorrow, the settlers would be coming into town for church and for market. All week she had considered her friendship with Monsieur Travert. He was a man, after all, and she was of course not meant to have dealings with men. Of course not. She had been taught that all her life.

And yet, she thought as she unpinned the sun-scented laundry, what harm did it do? Father Xavier was a man. Colonel Blaise was a man. *Jesus* had been a man. Oh, she thought with a start, was that blasphemous? She crossed herself quickly and concentrated on folding Father Xavier's linens into her basket.

Moments later, her mind crept back into contemplation of Monsieur Travert and sinfulness. He seemed a very good man. He loved his children. He treated her and Sister Bernadette with respect.

As for that moment between them, Joelle didn't understand what had happened. There certainly had been no sin. They hadn't even touched, nor spoken. Probably Joelle mis-remembered the whole thing. What did she know of men? But if catching a man's eye was the problem, then she simply would not look into Monsieur Travert's eyes. That should solve that.

And hadn't Father Xavier said telling Bible stories to the children was acceptable? Yes, Joelle would sit with the Traverts again. She would continue telling them about the days of the Creation. The sun, moon, and stars on the fourth, of course, but the fifth day when God created the birds and the creatures of the sea was much more exciting. Just here in this place, there were dozens of different birds, some of them with amazing pouches under their beaks to scoop up fish from the water. What a marvel that God had devised such a thing.

With a light heart, Joelle listened to the mockingbird trilling in the bushes. With her lips pursed, she did her best to imitate its song, then laughed at herself, as if she could reproduce the perfection of one of God's creatures.

She hefted the laundry basket to her hip and went inside to put Father Xavier's linens in his trunk, then continued to the small room she shared with Sister Bernadette.

Father Xavier stood in the center of the room, his hands behind his back and his jaw marble hard.

Joelle's step faltered. "You startled me, Father." Whatever was he doing in here?

Sister Bernadette stepped around him, grim faced and silent. Slowly, she held aloft a red ribbon. Joelle's red ribbon.

Joelle glanced at her chest, open, the contents spread out on the floor.

"You were in my chest?"

"What does this mean, Sister? Where did you get this ribbon?" Sister Bernadette said.

Joelle realized her mouth was open and closed it.

"Did a man give it to you? That Monsieur Travert?"

"No! Seraphina gave it to me. As a good-bye gift when she married."

On a hard swallow, Joelle looked from Sister Bernadette's accusing face to Father Xavier's. The line between his eyes and the set of his thin lips made him very grim. She had resolved to burn that ribbon, but in the end, she had not done it. And now --

Sister Bernadette waved the ribbon about as if to shake a multitude of sins from it.

"The fact she kept it hidden proves she knew it was wrong to have such a worldly piece of wickedness, Father."

Joelle felt the heat rise in her face. Did blushing prove guilt?

"Why did you keep it, Sister?" Father Xavier asked.

She tilted her chin up the littlest bit. "Because it was given to me in friendship, Father. And because it is beautiful."

He stared at her as if what she'd said was incomprehensible.

"I would keep a rose in my chest if it were possible, Father. Holy sisters may love beauty, may they not?"

"A rose and a red ribbon are hardly the same thing in God's eyes," Sister Bernadette huffed.

"Indeed they are not, child. A rose is God's own creation. A ribbon, however -- " Father Xavier sighed. "This is an object of frivolity, Sister. It is entirely inappropriate for you to cherish such a thing. I see now what Sister Bernadette has been telling me about your judgment."

He shook his head and sighed again. "I must insist you remain here in this room to contemplate what God requires of his loving sisters. You will pray, and you will reflect on your own sinful nature."

Joelle closed her eyes. Stay in this room, hours on end? No breeze, no light? She would suffocate.

"For how long?" she whispered.

"Until I say otherwise," the father replied. "Perhaps then we will discuss your becoming a nun. Let us leave her to her prayers, Sister Bernadette."

As her two elders left the room, Joelle's gaze followed the red ribbon trailing from Sister Bernadette's hand, the satiny red glowing in the light from the window.

She had often run the ribbon through her fingers when she opened her chest. If she were alone in the room. It was beautiful, that's all. But it was a forbidden pleasure. She should not have allowed herself to admire it again and again.

But was it so wrong?

Not for Seraphina, she supposed. But for a novice --

The day dragged on as Joelle sat at the window, examining her conscience as she was meant to do. Too often her attention snagged on that same mockingbird singing in the bush outside the chapel. Or on the dark cloud coming from the west to be replaced again by fluffy white ones.

And repeatedly she saw in her mind's eye the red ribbon catching the sunlight. A trivial, worldly thing, and yet she mourned its loss. Sister Bernadette would no doubt toss it in the fire.

That she wanted that ribbon so much was an indication that Sister Bernadette was right. Joelle had sinful tendencies, and she must be ever mindful of God's expectations.

She lowered herself to her knees and said the rosary three times over. When she rose, her back ached and her knees were stiff. The back of her habit was wet with sweat and her wimple was limp and damp.

She lay on her cot, her hands at her waist, and considered taking off her wimple. She was alone, and it was so dreadfully hot. But she did not risk it. Instead, she emptied her mind so that only Godliness filled her.

But her mind escaped her intentions. The smell of sage outside the window reminded her of the bundles of herbs she'd hung from the rafters back in the convent. She'd seen some of those same herbs, or something very similar, growing on the island. In particular, a five foot tall bush with wrinkled, toothed leaves and heads of lacy white blooms. It looked very much like the meadowsweet they dried in the autumn to make fever teas from.

Once she was released from this isolation, Joelle could take a close look around the island and see what else she recognized growing here. Soldiers were always acquiring scrapes and little cuts and the occasional burn. She could make salves, and maybe find more plants like feverwort to make infusions. She would like being of use in the infirmary, if Father Xavier allowed it.

Thinking of the infirmary, Joelle remembered the day Bridget's baby had been born. Sister Bernadette had scolded her for being there, for participating in such a bodily event, but it had been glorious. It had been wondrous. She could not believe it had been sinful to witness such a miracle.

And only a week later Bridget had given her baby to Marie Claude. An awful thing, in Joelle's mind, to give a baby away. But what a blessing it had been for Marie Claude.

And wasn't that the same day that Seraphina had given her the red ribbon? And just like that, her mind conjured up the strip of red satin again.

The hours dragged on. Joelle prayed until her mind felt enveloped in cotton wool. She reviewed her transgressions until a gray fog descended on her. She was exhausted, that was all. And disappointed in herself that she had let Father Xavier and Sister Bernadette down.

She suddenly realized what Father Xavier had said. *We will discuss your becoming a nun.* He could postpone that day for as long as he liked, for as long as Sister Bernadette liked. He could even deny it to her altogether.

Who was she if she were not to become a nun? Joelle bent her head over her knees. She knew nothing else, had never wanted anything else.

For the first time, she wondered if Sister Bernadette was right. Perhaps she was not meant to be a nun. Perhaps she was too frivolous. Impetuous. Lacking in judgment.

Because Joelle knew that if Sister Bernadette had not found the ribbon in her chest, she would have kept it in secret, forever.

~~~

Four days after the red ribbon's discovery, Joelle remained sequestered in the hot little bedroom. She prayed, she memorized half a page a day of the catechism, and she attained an intimate acquaintance with every tree, shrub, and blade of grass she could see out the window. She also became acquainted with a spider building a web big enough to catch a cat.

In other words, Joelle had a great deal of time to think. The ribbon itself no longer called to her, but she heard again and again Seraphina's voice: *God doesn't care if you have a red ribbon.*

Sister Bernadette would say that was devil's talk, but Joelle was not convinced. She believed her real transgression was against Sister Bernadette's cautions to resist her wayward nature. Red hair, red ribbon -- that's how Sister Bernadette would see it. Sisters were not meant to have fripperies to distract them from their purpose on this earth, and the ribbon was certainly a frippery.

Had the other novitiates in the convent been tempted by fripperies? Of course, there had been no fripperies in the convent, no red ribbons or hard candies. And no children. No fathers who needed mothers for their children.

Early Sunday morning, Sister Bernadette escorted her from the back bedroom into the chapel. "There are cobwebs in the corners again, Sister. Get them swept out and the altar ready for Father Xavier. Hurry now. "

A few soldiers had already come in to wait for mass to begin. Two of them had dreadful coughs, and that one, Paulie who used to flirt with Seraphina, looked ashen-faced.

"Are you sick?" she asked him.

He nodded. "I'll go to the infirmary after church, see if the corporal is there. Since the doc died, he's all the medic we got." With that, he gave a mighty series of coughs, and Joelle patted his back. Poor fellow. In Joelle's experience, there was nothing more miserable than a cold in hot weather.

While Joelle assaulted the cobwebs, Colonel Blaise marched up the center aisle. "We have sickness in the camp, Father," she heard him say. "We had a surgeon with us, and he had some skill with potions and pills, but he died some time back. Our corporal is good for sewing up wounds, but not much else. I wonder if one of you is familiar with medicinals. Something for coughs, for fevers?"

"Father?" Joelle said.

With a nod of his head, Father Xavier gave her permission to speak.

"I believe that is a meadowsweet bush behind the chapel. Or something very like it. At home, we brewed a fever tea from the leaves and flowers, and the bush is in flower right now."

"Whatever you can do will be most appreciated," Colonel Blaise said. "Sickness like this can spread from soldier to soldier so quickly. I fear we are in for a hard time of it."

Sister Bernadette frowned. "But Sister Joelle is to remain -- "

"You may see to this, Sister Joelle," Father Xavier said, "with Sister Bernadette's supervision."

Outside with Sister Bernadette, Joelle spotted Monsieur Travert and the children coming up from the landing. Colonel Blaise had said these fevers were contagious. Without a word to Sister Bernadette, Joelle rushed toward the Traverts.

Isabel and Felix ran to meet her and grabbed her around the hips. "We came to mass, but we really came to see you," Isabel said.

With an arm around Isabel and a hand on Felix's shoulder, Joelle greeted Giles with a head shake. "You must take the children home, Monsieur Travert. We have sickness on the island.

Coughing and sneezing and fever. Colonel Blaise says it's catching."

"Ah. I see."

His hair was mussed by the wind, and there was a nick on his jaw from shaving. She wished she had a salve to put on it.

Monsieur Travert looked toward the chapel where soldiers were entering for the service. On the other side of the grounds, a few Indians were setting up their market as they usually did. "I hope the Biloxi will go home as well. They're susceptible to our French diseases."

"I will tell them," she promised.

"I don't want to go home, Papa," Rosalie said. "I want to go to mass."

Joelle saw regret in Monsieur Travert's smile. Isabel had said they all came to see her. Was that true? Did Monsieur Travert, did the family, think of her as she did of them?

"Rosalie, I don't want you getting sick," Monsieur Travert said. "We'll come again when this fever has passed. Tell Sister Joelle good day."

Rosalie found a place between Isabel and Felix to hug Joelle, and Joelle bent to encompass the three of them in her arms. Again she felt that joy of connection, of loving, of being loved. Perhaps when she was very small, her mother or her father had loved her and hugged her, but Joelle couldn't remember those days. This was a love that filled her heart and made the day brilliant with sunshine.

She straightened and found Giles Travert's eyes on her. His face was serious, but his eyes were unreadable.

"Come along," he said to his brood. "We'll see if the fish are still biting at home. Goodbye, Sister."

Joelle raised her hand in farewell and watched them head for their dugout.

When she turned back, there stood Sister Bernadette, her arms crossed, her face full of disapproval. One might expect the sky to crack with thunder at such a look. Joelle decided to ignore it. She had done only what was right, seeing that the Travert family didn't catch this fever going around.

"I must tell the Biloxi about the fever before we collect the leaves, Sister Bernadette. It won't take but a moment."

She strode across the grounds to where several men were displaying baskets and leather goods. She spoke to the oldest among them, urging them to go home.

"We already have this sickness," the man said. "It comes to us through the trees, along the bayou, on the breeze."

"I'm sorry, sir," she said. "I will pray that all your people shall be well." And she would, she would pray very hard for the Biloxi and for the soldiers who lay sick in the infirmary.

With Sister Bernadette stomping along behind her, Joelle proceeded to the meadowsweet bush and stripped the leaves and flower heads from perhaps a fourth of the bush. She shredded them, packed them into the large wooden bowl, and poured boiling water over them. She did not know how long to steep the leaves, nor was she certain this plant was actually meadowsweet. Surely, though, a plant that looked so similar would have similar properties.

She and Sister Bernadette took the cooling brew to the infirmary where several soldiers lay listlessly on their cots.

Joelle helped Paulie sit up then held the cup to his mouth. "This should make you feel better," she told him. She and Sister Bernadette ministered to all the feverish young men, and then waited to see if the brew helped.

Within ten minutes, the soldiers broke into profuse sweating. Their foreheads cooled, and two of them shivered with chills. Sister Bernadette nodded with satisfaction. "That takes care of that."

After three hours of relief, however, the fevers came back and rashes broke out on their faces.

Joelle fetched Sister Bernadette from where she rested with her swollen feet propped up.

"They have rashes now, Sister," Joelle said.

Hastily, Sister Bernadette put her shoes back on and rushed out to the infirmary.

Paulie's forehead was dotted with red bumps. The soldier next to him had the rash all over his face and red dots had begun to break out on his chest.

Sister Bernadette blanched. "Measles," she said under her breath. "Go get the colonel and Father Xavier."

The men came promptly, Joelle close behind them. Father Xavier gestured for Sister Bernadette to join them outside.

"You've seen measles before, Sister?" Blaise asked.

"I had it myself, Colonel. When I was a child in the orphanage. Many of us did, at the same time. My friend Marie Theresa died from it."

"I understand you cannot get the disease twice?"

"That is so."

"And what about you, Sister Joelle? Have you had the measles?"

"I don't remember ever -- "

"You had measles when you were six years old," Sister Bernadette interrupted.

"And Father Xavier?"

"I have a vague memory of scratching at red bumps and swallowing my mother's foul fever concoction. What about you, Colonel?"

"I have the same memory. I suppose we four are safe. Sister Joelle, the men will be grateful for your fever tea and perhaps you will find something to relieve the itching?"

Joelle searched the island for other meadowsweet bushes, but there was only the one in back of the chapel. She found one small patch of what she thought was senna, harvested that, and returned to the infirmary. There were several coughing, sniffling soldiers leaning against the shady side of the wall, waiting their turn for whatever brew she and Sister Bernadette could concoct.

Colonel Blaise was back to tell them what Joelle already knew. Measles had broken out among the Biloxi, too.

Joelle held her basket up. "I found only these plants that I believe will be helpful, Colonel. There won't be enough."

"There are no doubt plenty of medicinal plants growing on the mainland. I will send some men with you if you will go to the village. Someone there will guide you, I'm sure. Take a keg of salt with you in trade."

"Sister Joelle cannot go off with soldiers! And she has no business in a heathen village," Sister Bernadette said, her voice high with indignation.

Colonel Blaise's back stiffened. His gaze might have cut glass. "The soldiers are for the sister's protection," he said.

"Sister Bernadette," Joelle said, "the soldiers will not hurt me. And I will learn the plants, learn how to use them."

Father Xavier looked from Joelle to Sister Bernadette. He sighed. "Sister Bernadette is right. You will stay here. The soldiers can find the plants without you."

Joelle had never known such anger. The blood seared her veins and swelled her heart. How could they worry about her going off with soldiers, who were meant to take care of her, not harm her, when people were sick? Did they think her so weak that she would allow the soldiers to flirt with her? Is that what they worried about?

This was not right. She knew what kinds of plants might be useful, and she would understand when the Indians told her how to use them.

"I will go, Colonel Blaise."

"Sister Joelle!" Sister Bernadette's entire body trembled in outrage.

"I must do what I can to help." Joelle glanced at Father Xavier, who only scowled silently.

"Thank you, Sister," the colonel said. "The Biloxi will welcome you. We have helped them in the past, and they will help us now."

Joelle left what she had gathered with the corporal and told him how to brew the leaves and twigs of the meadowsweet and how to make a poultice out of the senna plants.

She gathered all the baskets she could find and loaded them into the boat. It was selfish of her to be excited about leaving the island when so many were sick, but she couldn't help it. She was going to the mainland, would travel up the bayou deep into the forest. People lived in that jungle, French people and Indian people. What would an Indian village be like? She'd heard -- could it be true? -- that they were all naked, that they slept in trees, that they ate their meat raw. In a few hours, she would see for herself.

She would pay a penance for her defiance when she returned, but she would think about that later. For this moment, she was about to cross the water and become a truly useful person. Surely that's what God wanted from each of them, to be useful to one another.

# Chapter Twenty-One

*Tending the Sick*

Late in the afternoon, Joelle and the soldiers emerged from the forest trail into the Biloxi village. The stillness unnerved her, and then the sounds of coughing interrupted the quiet.

A group of men sat together while the eldest chanted. One man wafted a smoky torch in the air as he circled the group. With dawning understanding, Joelle realized the men were praying.

Nearer to where Joelle stood, an elderly woman tended a fire in front of her home, adding herbs to a pot of simmering water. This woman could tell Joelle what she needed to know.

"Bonjour," Joelle said softly.

The woman looked at her from a wrinkled brown face, her eyes deep and shadowed. She said nothing in return.

Joelle wouldn't be so easily dissuaded. She sat on the ground a few feet away. From several of the huts, she heard coughing and low voices. At length, she said, "Madame, do you speak French?"

The woman glanced at her.

"My name is Sister Joelle. I hope you will help me find the plants the soldiers need to make them well. Is that sweet grass you're adding to the pot?"

After a time, Joelle asked her the question that had worried her all the way across the sound. "Are there enough plants for all your people? Are there enough to share with the soldiers?"

The woman sighed deeply. She put her hands in her lap and looked directly at Joelle.

A shrill keening broke the stillness. The hair on the back of Joelle's neck stood up and she felt a bolt of fear.

"Someone died?" she whispered.

The old woman's eyes were closed, her body very still.

"I'm so sorry."

Was it a child? Would there be other deaths? Everyone knew the Indians were not as strong as the French when sickness came.

"How can I help?"

The Biloxi woman stared at her unblinking.

Joelle glanced at the soldiers. "We could start another fire, heat water for another brew while this one steeps."

The old woman nodded toward a cold fire pit. So she did understand French. With little interest in what Joelle did, she returned her attention to her pot.

Joelle organized the three men who'd accompanied her. They soon had a fire started while Joelle looked for a pot. Perhaps they should start two fires. No one seemed to be cooking any food, and those who were well needed to stay strong.

"Do you know how to cook, Corporal Denis?" she asked one of her escorts.

"I can boil mush if that's cooking."

"Will you see to that, please?"

Joelle found the same plant that looked so much like meadowsweet at the edge of the clearing. Half the leaves were stripped, so perhaps the Biloxi used it for a medicine, too. She gathered a small basket of leaves and added them to the simmering pot.

While her own brew simmered, Joelle watched the old woman fill a gourd and take the cooled tea into a hut. Once Joelle's tea was ready, she found a gourd and began on the other side of the village.

"May I come in?" she said at the doorway of the first hut.

It was dim inside, and cramped. The air smelled of sickness. A woman, kneeling beside two children lying on a pallet, looked up at her without interest.

Joelle crept in and knelt on the other side of the children. One child's eyes were swollen closed, the red bumps all over her face. The other child was covered with bumps from his hairline to his legs. She could feel the heat of his fever radiating from his small body.

Joelle said a silent prayer to God. Let them be well, Lord. Let me help them.

She held the gourd out to the mother. "To drink, for the fever," she said and pantomimed drinking.

The mother took the gourd and encouraged her children to swallow the bitter tea.

When Joelle emerged, she saw Jean Paul Dupre toting two buckets of water up from the spring.

"Hello, Sister. You'll find Catherine in that last hut, I believe."

Another gourd of fever brew in hand, Joelle entered the hut where Catherine was and found not illness but deepest misery. This was where the keening had arisen. This was where a child had died.

Catherine was bathing the child with a wet cloth. The mother rocked back and forth, a deep humming moan coming from her chest.

Joelle knelt beside the mother, her eyes on the child, a boy, perhaps the same age as Felix Travert. She had seen death before. Sister Emmanuelle had been laid out in a fresh habit and wimple and Joelle had sat with her sisters in vigil. But Sister Emmanuelle had been bent and withered with age, had been shrunken with long illness and suffering. This child's little hand was perfect, unlined, smooth and brown. Only days ago, he would have run and laughed, would have turned bright eyes on his mother and climbed into her lap.

Joelle closed her eyes. She couldn't breathe while she fought to control herself. How could the mother bear it?

Without disturbing the woman's trance-like grief, Joelle murmured her prayers to God to have mercy on this beloved child's soul, to take him into His loving heart.

The little hut was filled with the sound of the mother's droning hum, low and mournful. After a time, Catherine nodded toward the gourd of fever brew Joelle had brought. Joelle nodded. She was not needed here.

Again and again, Joelle refilled her gourd and visited another hut, and another. As night fell, two men entered camp with large baskets brimming with greenery. The first old woman and several others met them and took charge of the leaves and twigs. They fed their fires, simmered their brews, and turned the greenery into medicines.

Joelle tended her own pot, examining each leaf that went into the hot water. Her back ached and her head felt so heavy she wondered how much longer she could continue. Late into the night, Corporal Denis tapped her on the shoulder.

"Come on, Sister. You can't sit out here all night. We got you a hut to sleep in."

"But there are so many sick, and we need to keep the fevers --"

"Sister, Colonel Blaise said we're to see to you. We let you get down sick, he'll have us locked up in the stockade." He reached down and gently took her elbow. "You can start in again in the morning."

"But this pot needs --"

"Etienne's been watching you all afternoon. He'll take over. Come on."

"Go on, Sister," Etienne said. "I know what to do."

Joelle let the corporal lead her to a hut on the perimeter of the village. She lay down inside, her bones feeling brittle, her muscles tense. Overhead, the thatch was half gone, so this was an abandoned structure. She wasn't putting anyone out of their bed.

She heard Corporal Denis settling in just outside the door. Just as she closed her eyes, her last thought was how horrified Sister Bernadette would be to know she slept only inches from a young man.

~~~

Joelle woke instantly when Catherine placed a hand on her shoulder.

"I hated to wake you, Sister, but Kita is waiting for you."

Joelle shook her head to clear it. "Kita?"

"She is the oldest woman in the village. She knows the herbs you need and where to find them in the forest."

"Did she say -- are there enough for the soldiers as well as the villagers?"

"Kita says there are. She is willing to help you. I think because you helped them yesterday and last night."

Joelle blinked at the bright sun coming in the doorway. "How is everyone? Are the children getting better?"

Catherine sat back on her heels. "Kita's great granddaughter died in the night."

Joelle stared into Catherine's stricken eyes. The air, hot and still, seemed heavy with grief and fear. The sky itself seemed low and bleached of hope. Joelle made the sign of the cross and a silent prayer for this child's soul.

"How is it you're here, you and your husband?"

Catherine gestured toward the bayou. "Our home is not so far. We are neighbors." She let out a long sigh. "Whatever other problems there are in the world don't seem very important right now, do they?"

Joelle thought of her discontents, her doubts, her petty defiance with the candy and the ribbon. How trivial she was.

"Come on," Catherine said. "I have mush cooking. Eat something and then go with Kita into the woods."

Joelle and two soldiers followed Kita up the main pathway and then turned into a path so faint Joelle would never have noticed it.

From a slippery elm, they harvested a basket full of bark. For salves, Kita explained with gestures and broken French. A patch of yarrow with its creamy flower heads filled a tall sack made of rough cotton. For fever and poultices, Joelle learned.

A kind of cedar unfamiliar to Joelle yielded great quantities of leaves. They dug up the roots of another patch of low bushes, found another tree whose bark Kita acclaimed as the most valuable medicine in the woods.

All of them loaded down with baskets and bags of leaves, twigs, bark, and roots, they trudged back to the village, sweat stinging the mosquito bites they'd suffered.

Women in clusters around the village tended simmering pots, waiting for the herbs that would infuse their healing properties into the water.

In the late afternoon, Catherine brought Joelle a string of jerky and a cup of water. "You have to eat. And look at you, your wimple and your robe wet with sweat. Can you not at least take off your wimple?"

"I can't do that."

Catherine frowned but let it go. "Your corporal says it's time for you to go back to the fort."

Back to Sister Bernadette who would still be angry with her. But she had learned so much here, and she would bring back herbs -- and understanding -- that would help all the sick soldiers.

"Kita has given you half of today's harvest. She says you can come back in a few days. She knows where to find more."

Joelle looked around the quiet village. "They are a generous people to help us when they have trouble of their own."

"Yes. They are."

"Will you stay on?"

Catherine nodded. "Jean Paul and I together. As long as we can be useful."

Joelle helped the soldiers load the herbs into the boat and waved goodbye to Catherine.

She would talk to Father Xavier when she returned. She must be careful not to be disrespectful or impertinent, but she would like to know what prayers were appropriate for the souls of the Indian children. She knew God intended for the innocent unbaptized to inhabit limbo, but surely they could be granted the kindness of prayers.

Joelle shook her head. For all her wayward thinking the last weeks, she was merely a novitiate, and even if she were a nun, she had no business contemplating theology, for that is what she had just done. In all that she had been taught, there was no mention of relief for those in limbo. She must guard against the sin of arrogance. After all, obedience and compliance with Church teachings were central to taking her vows. Still, she might ask.

They were approaching a farmstead on the right bank of the bayou. "Corporal," Joelle said, "can we not stop, but stay in the stream, and hail them? We should warn people to stay home, shouldn't we?"

The corporal nodded to the other two soldiers to hold the boat steady with their oars. "Halloo!" he called.

After two more halloos, a tall black man came to the shore. Joelle recognized him as Thomas, the man who accompanied Marie Claude whenever she was at the fort.

Corporal Denis delivered the warning; Thomas nodded and raised a hand in acknowledgement. They stopped at several more farmsteads where they found people working in gardens or chopping wood or tanning hides, but at the next homestead, all was quiet and still.

There were pigs lazing in the afternoon heat, the sun beating down on the lush well-tended garden. A dog rushed down to the shore and barked furiously, and the stillness seemed all the deeper, for no one came from the cabin to investigate the disturbance.

Joelle and Corporal Denis looked at each other. "I think we'd better go ashore," she said.

When the soldiers paddled the boat up onto the landing, the dog quieted. Maybe he had been inviting them in instead of warning them off. He ran ahead toward the cabin, pausing to be sure they were following him.

At the open doorway, Corporal Denis motioned for her to stay back. As he leaned into the door, Joelle heard a raspy voice. "Don't come in here."

And then she heard a child's cough.

With chilling certainty, Joelle knew that was Giles Travert's voice. She moved around Corporal Denis and stepped into the gloomy cabin.

The children lay in the bed barely dressed, their bodies covered with the red eruptions. Monsieur Travert sat on the floor, his back against the bed.

Joelle was . . . stunned. He was unclothed. His chest was bare, his lower legs and his feet were bare.

She blinked. This was not important, neither the odd feeling in her chest at sight of Monsieur Travert's body nor the impropriety of his nakedness.

He held a hand up to stop her coming further, but she ignored it and rushed to his side.

The red bumps covered his face and chest, even his hands. She palmed his forehead, then touched Rosalie who lay closest to her.

"They're burning with fever," she told the corporal.

"Go, both of you," Giles said. "You'll catch it."

"Corporal Denis and I have already had measles, Monsieur Travert."

He gave a feeble laugh. "Good for you. A feat I never managed in all my thirty years."

Joelle took note that the water bucket was filled. She saw the remnants of dried yarrow, so Monsieur Travert had managed to dose his children at least once. But their fevers were back, and beneath the eruptions, their skin was too pale.

"We'll need the leaves from the boat, Corporal."

"I'll see to it."

Joelle stirred the dying fire and filled the kettle from the water bucket. While the water heated, she found what seemed to be Felix's shirt, wet it, and handed it to Giles. "For your head." With another cloth, she bathed the children's fevered limbs.

Within the hour, she and Corporal Denis had managed to get all four patients to drink a fever tea. After the cooling sweat, they were more alert and slightly more comfortable, yet they lay inert, indifferent to their surroundings. Even Isabel, such a busy child, hardly seemed to register that Joelle was there.

"We'll leave you some of these medicine herbs, Monsieur Travert," Corporal Denis said. "Sister, we best get on before it gets dark on us."

"You go on, Corporal. I'm staying here."

He gave her a hard look. "You already been gone one night, Sister. Father Xavier will be expecting you back." He hesitated, and added, "No other woman on the place, you know."

"Yes, I know. But the Traverts need help, and I'm going to take care of them."

"Joelle," Giles said. "You can't stay here. Thank you for the medicine, but you have to go."

The dark circles under his eyes testified that he had been too busy tending the children and fetching water to get any sleep.

"I'm staying, Monsieur Travert." She turned to Corporal Denis. "Etienne knows as much as I do about these herbs. He can help in the infirmary in my place."

"What am I supposed to tell Colonel Blaise? And Father Xavier?"

She couldn't worry about Father Xavier now. These children, their father, were struck down by this fever, and she was not going to let anyone here die. If Father Xavier didn't understand, God would.

She drew herself up. "Tell them I am doing my Christian duty, corporal. I am tending the sick, I am serving where I am needed."

"Etienne could stay instead."

Joelle looked at the three children, limp and glassy eyed. Rosalie, so grown up, so serious. Isabel, usually bubbling over with exuberance. Felix, his smiles so sweet. And now they lay weighted down by lassitude, fever, and pain. She couldn't leave them.

"The children know me, corporal."

His mouth quirked up on one side. "You're in for it when you get back to the fort, you know that."

Joelle huffed out a sigh. "Nevertheless, I'm staying."

"Good luck to you then, Sister."

# Chapter Twenty-Two

## *Fevered Babies*

When Mahkee's fever first spiked, Laroux wanted to fall to his knees and wail. How could God be so cruel? He'd brought him and Fleur to his own cabin so they would be safe from the sickness, and now Mahkee lay limply, his eyes glazed with fever, his skin hot and dry. Laroux had never touched a fevered skin so hot as this. Swallowing hard, he dismissed his own fears. Fleur needed him. Mahkee needed him.

"Bring the blanket," he told Fleur and tenderly lifted Mahkee into his arms.

At the landing, he stepped into the shallows and gently knelt to cradle the boy in the water.

At the first shiver, Laroux handed him to Fleur and the waiting blanket.

Fleur laid Mahkee in the bed, nestled in the blanket. "It will soon be dark," she said. "I must see what grows here that I can use."

Mahkee was sleeping for the moment, his skin noticeably cooler though still over-warm.

"I will stay with him," Laroux said and climbed onto the bed next to the child.

Fleur rose from her knees, hesitated, then leant over and kissed Laroux on the forehead before she took up the basket.

Laroux had not prayed in years. He doubted he remembered the rosary anymore. No doubt God had forgotten him, but he leaned over his knees, gripped his hands tightly, and prayed that God spare this child. All the children. Mahkee. And Fleur.

Fleur returned at twilight, her basket filled with blooms and leaves and twigs.

"The water in the kettle is hot. What can I do to help?"

"Shred these leaves. Break the twigs into small bits."

She set the basket on the table and walked to the bed where Mahkee slept. With a gentle hand, she smoothed the black hair from his forehead.

"He's cool for the moment," Laroux said.

"Yes. But it will come again. And then the red spots will appear."

Laroux left the herbs on the table and went to her. He knew her well enough now. She seemed calm, even resigned, but he'd heard the note of fear in her voice. This child was her world. Her heart.

He wrapped his arms around her from behind and held her, the two of them gazing at Mahkee lying so still on the bed.

~~~

Half a mile up the bayou, Marie Claude kept the same vigil. Matthew had begun to cough two days before, and now fever had him. Simon had come home from visiting the Biloxi widow he was smitten with and said this fever had struck the children in the village, too.

"Her two boys," Simon said, "had red bumps all over their faces and necks, down onto their chests and bellies."

Marie Claude's blood chilled. She and her brother had been stricken with the measles when they were children. It seemed every child in France had taken sick with these red bumps and high fever. She and her brother had survived, but two children in the village had not.

And now Matthew. How small he looked lying there in the bed, hardly strong enough to cough anymore. The first bumps had appeared that morning, on his forehead, now down to his chin.

"Simon, go to the village. Find out what they use to bring the fever down. There must be something growing here they use, something like feverwort or meadowsweet."

"I'll be back before noon."

When Simon returned with a basket full of leaves and bark, Edda made an infusion which they fed Matthew in tiny sips. It seemed to help, bringing on a sweat, but in a few hours, the fever was back.

Edda held him to her breast, but he did not suckle. She expressed milk into a gourd and tried to slip droplets into his mouth, but she had to gently massage his throat to get him to swallow.

Thomas insisted the women eat something in the middle of the day and fixed them each a plate. Then he sat on the stoop, ready to help. Ready to comfort Marie Claude if it came to that.

# Chapter Twenty-Three

*A House of Sickness*

The night was stifling, the air so still the single candle in the cabin burned without a flicker.

If Felix slept more peacefully, Isabel fretted and panted with fever and congestion. If Joelle had Isabel cooled off and calmer, Rosalie's fever would soar.

Joelle could not get Monsieur Travert to rest as he should. Even fevered, he would take the bucket out and haul it back with fresh water. He bathed Rosalie's face and chest as Joelle spooned fever tea into Felix's mouth.

"You have to rest," she said. "You have to sleep."

"I will. I will."

But he continued to nurse his children laid out in his own larger bed so that he could tend them more easily. At last, sitting on the floor and leaning against the bed, he nodded off, a damp cloth in his hand. While he slept, Joelle brewed salves and teas and tended to the children.

By daybreak, Joelle was exhausted, but there had not been a moment all night when one of her patients didn't need her. As the sun rose, all four of the Traverts fell into a quiet slumber. Joelle lay down on Rosalie's bed and promptly fell asleep.

A bright beam of sun on her face woke her. She raised herself to her elbow -- the children were still in the big bed, Isabel awake, the other two sleeping.

Monsieur Travert stumbled into the cabin with a bucket of water, still bare-chested. The muscles in his left arm stood out in relief, and his flat belly was tensed at the strain of the bucket's weight. Joelle averted her gaze and reached for the bucket.

"Let me have that. You shouldn't be up, Monsieur Travert."

His body was slick with sweat, so at least for the moment, he was not so feverish. "I've got it," he said, and hefted the bucket to pour water into the kettle over the fire.

"Please. Sit down. If you'll tell me what to do, I'll make some breakfast."

He sat on the floor and leaned against the bed, panting for breath. She handed him a cup of cool water and then stepped back.

"We might be able to get some mush down, Sister. Get the water boiling, then scoop a few handfuls of corn meal in with a pinch of salt. Just stir until it's thickened, and you're done."

"I can do that."

He smiled a little and closed his eyes.

~~~

The day seemed endless. A blacksmith pounded a hammer on the anvil in his head. His throat ached. His skin ached. When the fever spiked, he could hardly think straight. When it waned, he shivered so he could hardly hold a cup to Felix's mouth. But his children needed him. He made himself stay awake, stay up, but he didn't see how he could have managed without Joelle. They worked as a team so that each child was tended to no matter if Giles himself faltered.

The sun baked the earth, steamed the bayou. No hint of a breeze. Breathing alone was arduous, and his poor babes suffered.

Rosalie cried in her sleep and that broke Giles's heart. He bathed her heated skin and spoke softly to soothe her, but she was desperately ill, worse than either Isabel or Felix. In the worst of her fever, she would toss her head back and forth, her chest heaving in little pants.

Giles looked at Joelle seated on the other side of the bed with a damp cloth pressed to Felix's chest. What if he lost Rosalie? he asked her silently.

She leaned over the three children to take his hand and squeeze.

He was grateful she said nothing. He needed *her*, not promises, not prayers.

"You aren't taking care of yourself, Sister. Your head thing, your neck -- they're soaked with sweat. You can't help us if you're prostrate with the heat."

She released his hand as her eyes swept across his bare chest and skittered away. He had not until now appreciated how shocking it must be for her, seeing a man's naked skin. She should be used to it by now, though.

"You've been scratching your bumps," she said.

He nodded. "I got sick first. My bumps are further along than the children's."

"I made salve for when the itching starts."

"Later," he said. "Let's get some more of your fever tea in these three first."

Working together, they held the gourd for each child, dosing, cooling, comforting. The tea always helped, but the fever returned only an hour or two later. But they would keep trying. What else could they do?

After a bout of sweating, Isabel felt well enough to sit up and take some mush. Felix climbed into Giles's lap and sweat from the two of them mingled until they were both slick with it.

Joelle propped Rosalie up against her own chest and spooned tea into her mouth.

"Every little bit helps," she told Giles.

He eyed Rosalie's face, her eyes closed, her skin very pale beneath the red dots. "Yes. Every little bit."

Later in the afternoon, Giles breathed in the stale, still air in the cabin. Surely this heat had to break. It had been two days since the wind died and the sun blasted the earth like a furnace. Without thinking, he scratched at his chest till it bled.

"Oh! Look what you've done." Joelle jumped up and handed him the gourd of salve she'd made. "I should have put this on you earlier."

"Thank you, Sister." He rubbed the concoction into the rash on his face, neck, chest, arms. He reached behind him to cover the itch spots on his back, but of course could not reach most of them. He wouldn't ask for help though. Touching him, that would be too much for a novitiate to manage, he was sure.

She surprised him, though. She took the gourd from him and sat behind him. He could almost feel her hesitation, but her fingers lightly touched the middle of his back, spreading the cool relief over his shoulder blades, down his sides, down to his waistband.

Later, he would take care of the hated bumps on his groin and his buttocks. For now, it was a blessed relief to have the rest of his skin soothed. But it was disturbing, too. This lovely young woman's hands on him, skin to skin. He closed his eyes and concentrated on how much he itched.

"Do me, too," Isabel said. She was feeling a little better then, because none of the children had felt like talking for nearly three days.

Joelle slathered ointment on Isabel and Felix. Giles kept Rosalie's skin damp with cotton cloths.

Another long, desperate day. By late afternoon, Giles's headache ebbed into that blacksmith taking only taps on the anvil instead of mighty blows. He hadn't had fever since early in the morning. He was on the mend.

But not Rosalie. Her little body with the coltish long legs lay limp in the bed. She hardly answered him when he spoke to her. "Please, baby," he whispered in her ear. "Please don't leave me, my precious girl." He choked back tears, and smoothed the sweat-soaked hair off her face.

"Should we cut her hair?" Joelle asked. "That's what we did in the convent when there was fever."

Giles nodded. He should have done it yesterday, only his head was too full of heat and ache to think of it. Joelle handed him the knife, the one he kept sheathed on his belt when he was out of doors.

The blade was sharp, and he made easy work of cutting off Rosalie's long curling hair. Carefully, he smoothed the cut locks, coiled them in his palm, and placed them on the shelf above the bed.

Unaware she was now shorn, Rosalie seemed to rest easier without the heavy hair trapping the heat at her neck and on her head.

Giles stretched out on the floor while the children were quiet. He couldn't sleep, not with the headache and the itching and the muscle aches and the worry, but he rested.

Joelle knelt at the side of the bed to pray, her fingers working the black rosary beads. Her face was greasy with sweat, her natural color tinged with gray. Before his eyes, she swayed, and managed to catch herself before she fell.

"Damn it, Joelle!" he said, coming up off the floor.

Without asking permission, he yanked at the tie holding her neck piece in place, unwound it with swift sure motions, then slipped the wimple off -- "No," she whimpered -- and then he lifted off the linen cap.

"This is ridiculous, Joelle. You'll collapse in this heat, just to keep me from seeing your hair. I've seen your hair."

He ran his fingers quickly through the matted curls, pulling them up from her scalp. "It's a wonder you haven't fainted before now."

She leaned her face into the mattress, hiding from him. He could not find a shred of sympathy for her modesty. After what they'd been through together the last days, after he'd been half naked in front of her all this time -- it was absurd.

He squeezed the water out of a cloth and laid it on the back of Joelle's neck. Her hands covered the top of her head, but he shoved them aside and dripped water over her hair.

"That has to feel better."

Instead of a sigh of relief, Joelle erupted into sobs.

He stood behind her, stunned. Should he apologize? Or argue with her? Surely she couldn't think God would rather she collapse in the heat than take off that damned wimple.

"Papa?" Isabel whispered. "Did you make Sister Joelle cry?"

He ran a hand through his hair. "Apparently so."

Joelle straightened up, but she wouldn't look at him, or at Isabel either.

At least she'd stopped crying.

Giles crouched beside her. "Sister?" Hearing himself call her that made him realize he'd called her Joelle, without the Sister in front of it. That wasn't respectful, and he regretted it.

"Sister Joelle, will you look at me?"

On a shuddering breath, she lowered her hands to her lap and turned her face to him, swollen eyes and all. She'd already lost the gray tinge to her skin now she was cooler.

"I shouldn't have been so abrupt. But you've been heat sick before, and we need you, Sister. You know that."

She reached a hand up to her hair.

"Surely," he said, "there is no need for modesty between you and me."

~~~

There was every need for modesty between them, Joelle thought. He'd been sick and had not realized how improper it was for her to see him without his shirt. Even his bare feet had riveted her attention. Strong feet, the sinews showing beneath the skin. A man's foot.

And now she was stripped of the torturous garment that reminded her of who she was, what she was. With the wimple gone, the strap no longer cutting into her chin, it would be harder not to look at Monsieur Travert's naked chest, at the muscles moving in his arms when he shifted Rosalie on the bed. She had closed her eyes more than once, hating herself for noticing this man's body when his children were lying sick between them.

"You're exhausted, Sister. I should have been gentler. But you cannot put that thing back on."

"You look pretty without it," Isabel said.

Felix crawled to the edge of the bed and slid off. Without invitation, he climbed into Joelle's lap.

She wrapped her arms around him, accepting his comfort. The children did not care if her hair were uncovered. And Monsieur Travert was right. She would be of no use to any of them if she collapsed. Already, she felt better, her neck and throat exposed to the open air.

"It's only until the heat breaks," he said. "It has to break soon. Maybe tonight."

They needed her well. She understood that. "All right," she murmured and pressed her face into Felix's blond curls.

Behind her she heard Monsieur Travert rummaging in the chest at the end of the bed. When she looked up a few minutes later, he wore a shirt. The neck was open and she could see a triangle of sun-darkened skin at his throat, but the rest of his chest and belly was covered.

He did try, didn't he? To be respectful, to honor her position as a novice. Ever since Seraphina had said *God doesn't care if you have a red ribbon*, that phrase, *God doesn't care . . .* , came to mind over and over. Did God mind if she did not wear her wimple in front of this man, in this heat? Sister Bernadette would care, but would God?

Monsieur Travert did forget sometimes to call her Sister Joelle, but he did not touch her unnecessarily or look at her the way Seraphina's husband had looked at his new wife. He was merely concerned that she not suffer from the heat again.

No, she could not fault Monsieur Travert. But she could fault herself for the way her gaze, a glance here, a glance there, returned to his body, marked with red dots as it was. God would care about that. It was her sinful nature, as Sister Bernadette had always said.

For though Monsieur Travert did not touch her unnecessarily, Joelle longed to touch him. When she had smoothed the salve over his back, her breath had hitched. She'd spread her palm out flat on the broad plane beneath his shoulder blades, working the salve into his skin.

She had never touched anyone as she had touched him. And she wanted to do it again.

Did Monsieur Travert see, as Sister Bernadette did, that temptation to sin when he looked at her, her hair uncovered?

~~~

Giles placed a hand on Felix's leg and Isabel's arm where they lay sprawled and tangled on the bed.

"They're still feverish, but -- "

Joelle offered a small smile and finished the thought. "But they're not so hot as they were."

He nodded at Joelle, his partner, his savior. His gaze shifted to Rosalie.

"Are you awake, darling?" Giles leaned over her, speaking softly. "How's my girl? You think you can sit up, drink some water?"

Her eyes were glazed, and she didn't seem to notice him. He pressed his hand to her forehead. The fever was reasserting itself. Giles fisted his hands to keep the fear from taking over.

Joelle brought damp cloths and bathed her scorching skin as Giles dribbled fever tea in her mouth. Eventually, sweat broke out on her forehead and neck, and she lapsed back into sleep.

Giles wiped his forehead. The shirt he'd put on a short while ago was sodden with sweat, and the air, heavy and hot, brought no relief.

Surely this heat had to break, there had to be an end to this torment. Sweat stung the raw welts as it rolled down the sides of his face, his neck, his torso. He needed sleep, he needed this terrible headache to go away.

He made up his mind to hurry down to the bayou and plunge in while Rosalie slept. At the stream's edge, Giles didn't hesitate. He stepped in up to his knees and launched himself into the water. He surfaced, gasping for air, and dove again. Nothing had ever felt so good as pushing himself through the cooling water. But he mustn't linger. He strode through the shallows up onto the landing, water streaming from his hair, from his limbs, from his shirt and pants. He'd smell like bayou, but that was better than sweat and sickness.

He rung out his shirt and put it back on before he entered the cabin. Sister Joelle stared at him, startled, when he came in. She'd probably thought he'd gone to the privy, but here he was dripping on the floor, his shirt transparently wet.

"I wish you'd go down to the bayou before it gets dark, Sister. You'd feel better for it."

She shook her head briefly and looked away from him.

Giles walked over to the bed to look at his children. Felix seemed alert, though quiet, and his limbs were relaxed. Isabel was leaning against the wall on the other side of the bed, her eyes about to close. If she could sleep sitting up, that was a good sign.

Rosalie's fever had her tossing her head back and forth again. He climbed onto the bed and held her against his wet body. She muttered, her chapped lips barely moving. Giles bent to hear her, and was certain he heard *maman*. He closed his eyes, the pain too much to bear for a moment.

"Tea?" he asked Joelle.

She brought a cup and a spoon and managed to get half the cup down her throat while Giles wiped her body with the cooling cloth.

"She's so hot," he said, his voice breaking.

Joelle held his gaze, never flinching, never betraying a hint of fear. Only calm hope. Only that.

Such comfort she was. He swallowed and nodded. Rosalie would be well. She would.

The tea lowered the fever enough so that Rosalie could sleep peacefully, but Giles held her still. He wouldn't let her go, he'd never let her go.

He opened his eyes to see Joelle kneeling on the floor next to the bed, her gaze on Rosalie. The children wanted to love her. He wanted to love her, but it was not to be. *Sister* Joelle didn't want to be anyone's mother. His wanting her, needing her, the children wanting and needing her, that didn't matter. She had chosen a life with God. He couldn't have her. *They* couldn't have her.

When Joelle lit a candle, even that small flame seemed too much in the stifling heat, but she needed to see to crush more leaves and twigs. They'd need more of her tea, more of her salve during the night.

As dusk approached, the air carried a charge, a hint of violence just over the horizon. The candle flickered. A rustling in the trees promised wind.

Giles lay Rosalie on her back, picked up Isabel and took her to the door.

"Rain," she said on a sigh. "It's going to rain, Papa."

The wind picked up, thrashing the tree tops. Lightning streaked across the sky. Giles turned to Joelle, smiling. With Felix in her arms, she came to the doorway and looked out.

Thunder boomed up the bayou, and Felix crowed, "Thunder, Papa!"

Giles set Isabel on her feet and went to gather Rosalie in his arms.

At the open door, he let the wind whip around her, let the first raindrops fall on her heated skin.

Rosalie shivered violently. It was too much. Giles took her inside and wrapped the quilt around her and held her close.

"It's raining, Rosalie. You like the rain."

Her teeth chattered for a moment and he was terrified he had done the wrong thing, exposing her to the wind and rain.

He rewrapped the quilt so that his body was encased with her, and that seemed to be all she needed. The shivering stopped and she laid her head against his chest.

"Rosalie, my sweet girl," he murmured.

The rain pattered on the thatched roof, splatted onto the parched earth, rattled onto the bayou. Thunder shook the cabin.

Joelle wrapped herself and Felix and Isabel in the other blanket and they all huddled together on the bed, watching the storm out the open door.

With a long sighing breath, Rosalie shifted in his arms. "Papa?"

"Yes, sweetheart."

With that she fell asleep, her body cool and relaxed.

Giles closed his eyes and swallowed hard.

"Fever?" Joelle asked.

Joy welled up in his chest, and he smiled. "No fever."

"Hooray," Felix said. Isabel clapped her hands under the quilt and echoed Felix's cheer.

On a laugh, Giles leaned over and smacked a kiss on Isabel's cheek, on Felix's forehead, and without thinking, he kissed Joelle right on the mouth.

Before his mind realized what he had done, his body reacted, a thrilling sense of soft, plump lips, a moment's taste of salt and sweetness -- and then the startled look on her face recalled him to himself. He had kissed Sister Joelle.

Surely she understood it was simply a friendly, happiness-shared kiss. Or maybe she didn't.

He looked at her, unable to read what she felt, but she didn't look away from him. He held his breath, dreading her reaction. She would have every right to be indignant, angry, disappointed in him.

Isabel's giggle broke the tension. "Papa kissed Sister Joelle," she said and poked Felix.

"I'm sorry," Giles whispered.

He saw her throat work as she looked away from him.

"It was just . . ." she said.

"Yes. It was just . . . relief," he said.

# Chapter Twenty-Four

## *The Village*

In the Biloxi village, Catherine huddled with Débile in a hut, his wet fur not particularly pleasant, and watched the rain sheet down, the white light flashing over the sodden ground before the thunder boomed.

Jean Paul was out there somewhere with Mato, the two of them having gone further into the woods to look for herbs. She told herself not to worry. They were competent men. They'd have made themselves a shelter before the storm started.

At the next lightning burst, she saw Jean Paul and Mato trudging into the village, their backs bent under sacks of leaves and twigs. They'd traveled through the woods in this storm, in the dark? Were they mad?

The two of them took their burdens into Kita's hut where she kept a fire going to brew the fever tea and concoct the salves the afflicted needed. Catherine had labored with her until an hour ago when Kita had sent her away for a few hours' rest.

In a moment, Jean Paul dashed across the open ground and crawled into the hut, wet and shivering.

"I hope that's you," he said in the dark.

She laughed and reached for him. "It's me. Is that your teeth chattering?"

"Yeah."

"I always thought that was an exaggeration. Get those wet clothes off."

She helped him strip, then insisted he lay between her and Débile to get warm.

"I'll get you wet."

"And I'll get you warm. Why didn't you wait out the storm somewhere?"

"In a nice dry cave? That would have been welcome, but there are no dry caves in this country. And the wind blew down the lean-to we made. We were wet anyway, we figured we might as well come back."

She wrapped her arms around him and pulled him close, her legs twined with his. With Débile at his back, snuffling in his sleep, he'd warm up soon enough.

"How did you find your way in the dark?"

"I'd have probably walked into the bayou by myself, but Mato has the eyes of a cat. I just followed him."

After a few moments, Jean Paul said, "This isn't working. I need to get closer to you."

"You can't get any closer to me, Jean Paul."

"I can't? You sure?"

He shifted and his erection pushed against her thigh. He turned his head and nuzzled her breast.

"Oh."

"Hm." He ran his hand under her skirts, trailing cold fingers up her thigh. "I'm just doing this to get warm, you understand."

"Of course, and I'm happy to help."

Though his hands were cold, his kiss seared her mouth and her enthusiasm quickly matched his. With lightning piercing the walls, trees thrashing in the wind, she couldn't hear his growled moans, but she felt them rumble through his body and into hers.

In those moments before sensation swept away all thought, Catherine breathed in such a wonderful sense of well-being, her husband's body pressing against hers. He had not been himself since the letter came. He was worried and uncertain, she knew that. But like this, his body inside hers, her arms around him, his mouth on her, she was certain. He belonged to her and she to him, always, and there was nothing they couldn't do as long as they were together.

When they lay in each other's arms, listening to the storm and to Débile's snoring, Catherine played with his wet hair.

"Another child died while you were gone," she said.

Jean Paul pressed a hand over his eyes. "Who was it?"

"Ake, Mato's nephew. The one whose foot you sewed up that time."

"Ah, no."

"That makes three children and one young woman," she said.

160

"Maybe this storm will make a difference, cool everybody off."
"I don't know."

~ ~ ~

Jean Paul didn't know either. What if Catherine and he had a child and lost him to measles. How would they bear it?

At least, someday, when Catherine had a child in her new life back in France, that child would be safe, or far safer than here anyway. She wouldn't have to face the heartbreak these people were going through.

Maybe seeing what it meant to live here, to lose a child to illness, to imagine losing one to drowning or snake bite -- perhaps it would make it easier for Catherine to leave him when the time came. God knows there were no guarantees in life. Children died in France, too. But here, this was a dangerous land.

She and any children she might have someday would be far safer in a chalet in France than in a cabin in Louisiana. She deserved a life with a man of her own world, one unburdened by a charge of murder and a peasant's roots. And as for himself, once Catherine was where she belonged, well, it didn't much matter what became of him.

# Chapter Twenty-Five

*Fever's End*

The storm raged outside Laroux's cabin, the rain beating on the thatch, the wind billowing the leather window coverings.

The break in the heat had not brought Mahkee's fever down. Fleur had him at the breast, but the child wouldn't latch on.

"It's the sores in his mouth," Fleur said. "I think they hurt too much for him to suckle."

Laroux held the candle close. "Let me see."

Fleur opened Mahkee's jaw to show him a blister-like rash covering the back and upper tissues of the boy's mouth.

"It likely does hurt," he said.

They dribbled fever tea in his mouth and a concoction against coughing . . . Laroux hesitated. "Can you get some of your milk into a cup?"

He needn't have worried he would embarrass Fleur. Without self-consciousness, she expressed her milk into a tin cup. When she was ready, she held Mahkee, and in spite of the child's fussing, Laroux spooned milk into his mouth.

When Mahkee's eyes drifted closed, Laroux took him from Fleur. "Sleep now, while you can. I'll wake you if he needs you."

Fleur gazed at her sleeping child in his arms. "You are a good man, Laroux."

He kissed her cheek. "I try to be. Go to sleep."

While Fleur slept, he sat at the foot of the bed, his back against the wall, Mahkee in his arms. Laroux would give anything to spare Mahkee this pain. To spare Fleur this awful fear. She didn't say she was frightened, not his Fleur, but it was in her eyes and in her hands as she tended to her child.

When Laroux was a boy, his mother lost his little sister to a fever. It might have been the measles he and his brothers had had, but he couldn't remember. Maman had not been herself for a long time after that. He would find her in the back of the garden, weeping, or in the bedroom, fingering one of Gisele's little stockings.

If Fleur had to endure that kind of grief . . . He would help her, if holding her and loving her could help.

At dawn, a cock's crow in the distance roused him from a light doze. Mahkee was so still in his arms, Laroux panicked, his heart pounding into his throat, but Mahkee's bare chest moved gently up and down with easy breaths. God, he thought . . . What would Fleur . . .

The child slept peacefully in his arms. He passed his fingers over Mahkee's neck and found it cool. He ran his hands all over his belly, his forehead, his legs. No fever.

The boy had not had a drink of fever brew in hours, and yet his skin was cool. Could this be the end of it?

Mahkee woke at being handled, his eyes looking right into Laroux's. His gaze was clear and alert, and when Laroux touched the swollen lips, Mahkee smiled at him.

"Fleur," Laroux said. "Fleur."

She blinked and sat up, alarmed, ready.

"It's all right," he said, grinning at her. "Mahkee's all right."

His stalwart Fleur held her child close, her big eyes full of hope. "He is well?"

"Yes. It's over."

~~~

While thunder and lightning pulsed along the bayou, Marie Claude bathed Matthew's sweet face and crooned softly to him in his misery. Nothing she and Edda tried broke his fever, nothing kept the red dots from invading his nose, his eyes, his mouth. With a sick thud of her heart, doubt pushed through her veins. Matthew might not make it.

As she dribbled fever tea into his mouth, she offered God all manner of bargains if only He let Matthew live. But maybe God couldn't hear her over the storm. Maybe He was busy taking care of other sick babies. Maybe He had nothing to say to a woman who had killed her husband.

Over the sound of rain beating on the thatch, she crooned to him and whispered promises in his ear. "When you're old enough, I'll get you your very own puppy. And Thomas will teach you how to hunt and fish. We'll swim in the bayou on hot days and count the stars at night." On a swallowed sob, she promised him, "You're going to be a big fine man, my precious boy."

Hours later, Matthew did not even try to open his swollen eyes, did not turn to the sound of her voice. His small body threw off such heat that his skin was flushed beneath the rash.

Edda woke and came to the bed. "You sleep now, Marie Claude. I will bathe him and see if he will feed."

"I can't sleep, but he needs to nurse, if he will."

The last time Edda had offered him the breast, Matthew had latched onto the nipple, grimaced, and turned his face from her. This time, he simply did not respond. Edda expressed milk into his mouth and it simply puddled there. He didn't even swallow.

"Madame?" Edda said, fear in her eyes.

Marie Claude took him in her arms, his body burning hot against her cheek. "Matthew? Wake up, baby." His plump body had turned frail and thin. There was no resilience in his hot dry skin.

The storm had passed, the rain had stopped. She walked to the door and stepped out into the cool air. "It's almost morning, see? The rooster over at Agnes's place is crowing. 'Wake up, Matthew,' he says. Hear that?"

Matthew's breathing rattled and stopped. Marie Claude clutched him to her. He gasped, took in a labored breath, and in one agonizing moment, his body stiffened, his arm flailed -- and he was gone.

A vise squeezed her heart and closed off her lungs. Her mind reeled into darkness. Eons later, on her first gulping inhale, the vise let go and yet she was sure her heart lay stopped in her chest.

Edda's wailing penetrated the fog in her head. Marie Claude wondered how she had the strength to wail, for she herself could barely breathe. Heavy, aching pain throbbed through her body with each pulse. How could she live now?

When awareness of her surroundings returned, Marie Claude stood on the bank of the bayou, her boy cradled against her shoulder, close to her heart. There would never be another sunrise for Matthew. No puppy. No climbing, no running, no -- She lost her breath and blinked away the image of a gangly, snaggle-toothed boy holding up a handful of wriggly worms.

And for her, never another toothless, happy smile beaming up at her when she tickled her baby's chin and sang silly songs to him.

She stood there a long time, not hearing the dawn's birdsong nor seeing the streaks of orange in the morning sky. Thomas came to her, but she didn't turn to him.

Thomas placed his hand on Matthew's back, and she heard the deep breath he exhaled. He wrapped his arm around her shoulder, she leaned into him, and they stood quietly together as the sun rose.

When the rain started up, Thomas took her into the cabin and had her sit on the edge of the bed while he fetched a bucket of water. When he returned, he cleared off the table and covered it with a quilt.

Matthew was still in her arms, his skin cold, his sweet face gone gray. Thomas held his arms out to take him, but she shook her head.

"I'll do it."

Marie Claude washed her boy one last time, smoothing the hair from his forehead. When she was finished, she kissed the beloved cheek and placed her big hand over his tiny chest. Thomas stood at her shoulder and together they said farewell. Such joy he'd brought them.

"Edda will want to say goodbye," she said.

"Remy is taking care of her. I'll get her."

Marie Claude gazed down on Matthew, her hand clasping his foot. When Edda came in, Remy behind her, she shifted to make room for her. Edda loved him, too.

She and Edda together wrapped Matthew's little body in a length of new cotton, a creamy print with tiny red flowers. Marie Claude watched her hands smooth the creases of the shroud as if they were someone else's hands. Heard her own measured breaths as if they were someone else's breaths.

Outside, she heard the shciss of Simon's shovel as he dug deep into the loamy soil. When it was time, Marie Claude carried Matthew to the grave Simon had lined with rough planks of pine. She took comfort that her baby boy would be cradled even in death, and that he would lie next to their friend Pierre's grave. Matthew wouldn't be alone in the dark, cold earth.

She laid her child in the rude cradle and stood back. Simon and Remy sang a song full of mourning, and when it was time to fill in the grave, Marie Claude turned away.

Thomas took her hand and walked her down to the bayou where they sat on the bank in the drizzle and watched the water slowly flow towards the Gulf. Birds twittered above, happy last night's storm was over.

Marie Claude laid her head on Thomas's shoulder, and they silently grieved together.

# Chapter Twenty-Six

## *Recovery*

In spite of thunder cracking and wind rattling the shudders, everyone in the cabin slept soundly through the storm. Giles woke to a gray dawn and the occasional spat of rain drops outside. Rosalie lay cuddled next to him on the floor, her skin cool to the touch. At last, it was over.

His mind still reeled from those hours he'd feared he might lose her, and he trembled with the strain of fear and fatigue. He felt limp, weariness pressing down on him, but he would be better tomorrow and better yet the next day.

The lump in the bed that was Joelle and his children didn't stir. Giles eased out from under Rosalie. The pigs and chickens, the dogs and the turtle had been fending for themselves for days.

He stepped outside, closing the door behind him, and wondered if, between the storm and hungry foxes, he had any chickens left.

The dogs emerged from under the cabin and after a good ear scratch, they followed Giles down to the bayou. Stepping over fallen branches and puddles, he stood at the water's edge and watched the sun rise over the misty tree tops. Fog covered the surface of the bayou and snagged on the low-hanging branches. In the distance, an alligator grunted.

First time he saw one of those monsters, his friend Laroux was paddling him and Bella up the bayou in search of a good place to homestead. Giles had grabbed for his musket, his heart thudding hard in his chest. Before he could fire, it had slithered off the bank and submerged itself in the water.

"They don't bother people much," Laroux had said. "But don't go bathing in the river without a good look around first."

Giles had looked over his shoulder to see how Bella had taken to seeing such a creature. Baby Rosalie was asleep in her arms, and Bella raised wide eyes to him, but she didn't say a word. A strong woman, his Bella.

Grief washed over him. He supposed he would never stop missing her.

Just in front of him, a blue heron lifted off from the shallows and flapped into the air. The beauty of it, the unexpected pleasure, squeezed his heart. He'd nearly lost his girl, they'd all been in danger. And what would have become of them if he'd died?

Swallowing the awful fear, he closed his eyes. If it hadn't been for Sister Joelle's careful nursing, things might have been different -- perhaps horribly, dreadfully different.

And he'd paid her back with that entirely inappropriate kiss. He shook his head against the shame of it. He had forgotten, that's all, that she was a novice. She was so much more than that to him. To them. But they would have to go back to thinking of her as *novice*, not friend, not woman.

Felix's soft steps came up behind him. Giles held out his arm and Felix leaned against his papa's leg. Together they watched the sun lighting up the world little by little.

The gator grunted again. With perfect calm, Felix said, "There's a gator out there."

"Hm hmm."

"But he's not here."

"No. He's a ways off."

The sky was gray with streaks of yellow and peach. When the rain finally stopped and the sun did its work, the ground would steam and they'd yearn for the rain again.

"Let's go see about our chickens," Giles said. "How many were there?"

"Eleven. And I can count to twelve."

They found all the chickens, and the rooster, none the worse for wear. The pigs were coated in mud, but as Felix said, they liked mud.

Even with the sun shining, rain started to spit, and Felix gave a little shiver. "We better get you inside, my boy. You haven't been well but about a minute and a half."

They stomped their feet on the little porch and opened the door to find a homey scene. Rosalie sat in the bed, her back propped against the log wall, a cup in her hand, and Isabel stood next to a kneeling Sister, attempting to untangle the length of linen that would go around Joelle's throat. An errant sunbeam came through the door behind them to catch the fire in her copper ringlets.

"I'm helping Sister Joelle. She said I could," Isabel said.

"So I see." He had to force his gaze from that glorious hair, but then Isabel called his attention back to it.

"Look, Papa." She lifted a curl and let it spring back. "Isn't that funny, Papa?"

Joelle ducked her head and Giles was glad she couldn't see him stare. She was beautiful. Beautiful, and kind and loving and practical and strong. He wanted her, not just in his bed, but in his life.

These last weeks trying to find a wife had wakened him to desires, for companionship, love, sex. He was tired of being lonely, and just because he had three children with him every minute of every day, children whom he adored, it didn't mean he wasn't lonely.

But his needs were not Sister Joelle's problem.

He turned away. "Who's hungry? Felix found eggs already washed clean in the rain, and I found ears of corn plump and ripe, ready for the picking."

Giles checked that Rosalie's forehead was still cool. "Try not to scratch your bumps, sweetheart. Joelle has some salve for you to stop the itching." *Sister* Joelle, he reminded himself.

When he turned back, Joelle was again wimpled and tied up so that only her hands and her face showed. Her sleeve slipped back as she adjusted the chin band, and Giles wondered what had become of the red ribbon she'd once worn on her wrist.

She looked at him, shy again.

"Your hair is beautiful, Sister. You don't have to be ashamed of it."

She laughed, her color rising. "Sister Bernadette says --" She broke off and ran her hands down her black smock.

"She says what?"

She glanced up and away. "She says it is the mark of a sinner."

Giles barked a laugh. "What nonsense. Are your beautiful eyes also the marks of a sinner?"

She stilled and held his gaze.

"Listen, Sister, I'm as good a Catholic as anyone, and is there anything in our religion that says gorgeous red curls are the mark of sin? Sister Bernadette is not the final authority. She is merely the one who has you under her thumb."

He saw confusion in her eyes, and perhaps there was a glint of hope, as well.

Giles glanced at the children. Their attention was on the eggs. Felix was cracking them in the wooden bowl, Isabel fishing out the bits of shell with her fingers.

"I know you're to be a nun," Giles said, "but please don't think you have committed some kind of awful sin because I saw your hair."

"Of course not." Her voice was so low he barely heard her. He couldn't stand it if she doubted herself about this, not after all she had done for them.

"And what Sister Bernadette doesn't know . . . " he said with a grin.

She gave him a weak smile, but there was a gleam of mischief in her eye, too.

He felt caught in her lovely eyes, but he didn't forget who she was, not this time. "Sister," he said gently, "you have done a great service for this family. You should be proud of yourself. God is proud of you. Why else are any of us on this earth if not to help one another?"

"Thank you, Monsieur Travert."

Giles paused, and then he took her hand anyway. "No, Sister, I thank you." He gave her hand a little squeeze and let go.

"How are those eggs coming?" he said. "Felix, you can help me shuck corn."

~~~

After breakfast, Joelle made another pot of salve from the last of the succulent leaves and slathered it over the children's itching bumps. She finished up with Felix and swallowed hard. Monsieur Travert, Giles, had the bumps, too, all over his back and chest, neck and face. She didn't know how she could touch him again. It made her skin go hot remembering how her palm had smoothed the salve over his back, how her skin had felt against his. But she was here to nurse, to heal. She had to do it.

She turned from the bed. "Monsieur Travert, if you'll take your shirt off -- " He had left the cabin.

He didn't want her hands on his skin. Of course not. She was to become a nun. Why would any man want her touch?

The family was well now. She should return to the fort. But how was she to do that today? Monsieur Travert could not take the children out on the bay, not so soon after their fevers. It might bring on a relapse. And he himself, perhaps he was not yet strong enough after his own fever to paddle all the way down the bayou, across the sound, and back again.

She would have to stay a few more days. She should laugh at herself, at how distressed she was, at how glad she was, all at the same time. Instead, she felt like crying. How foolish. There was still work to be done, and Monsieur Travert needed to rest as much as possible.

Joelle found the broom and set to tidying the cabin. With all the rain, there were muddy prints all over the floor. The grate needed cleaning out. Perhaps the garden would yield fresh beans and squash for dinner.

When Monsieur Travert came back in, his face was pale and his steps were heavy. She'd heard him at the woodpile, chopping kindling in the hot sun.

"You've over done it," she scolded.

He sat on the edge of the bed and leaned his face in his hands. "Maybe I did."

He lay back across the mattress, his feet still on the floor, and within moments he was asleep.

"Poor Papa," Isabel said. "He needs a nap."

Joelle eyed the muddy boots and the uncomfortable sprawl of his body.

He might roll onto the bed with those boots and ruin the clean sheet she had laid down. And it was still hot. He was still recovering. "Those shoes have to come off," she muttered. Could she do that?

"All right then," she said and bent to her task. The laces were knotted tight and smeared with muck.

"Papa says I'm the best knot picker in the family," Isabel said. "I can do it."

Between the two of them, they got the boots off. Monsieur Travert's socks were filthy and his big toe stuck through the wool. Those were going straight into the wash pot. But now he was barefooted. And she had to touch him to get his legs on the bed.

She stood there staring at his bare feet. She'd seen them every day. It was nothing. Everybody had feet. She had feet. Father Xavier had feet. They were just feet.

But Monsieur Travert's feet -- they were beautiful. She could see the fine bones under the skin, see the strong veins branching from his ankles.

Joelle raised her hand to her wimple. Her fingers traced the edge, remembering the shape of it. The meaning of it.

What a foolish woman she was. Monsieur Travert was tired and sick, worn out. And she was the nurse here. She grabbed hold of his ankles and slewed his body onto the bed.

There. Done. He didn't even know she'd touched him. And she wouldn't think of it. The phantom feeling still in her hands, the warmth of his flesh, the bone and muscle of his leg, she would forget it.

Joelle wiped her hands on her habit. There. Forgotten.

# Chapter Twenty-Seven

## *Sequestration*

The third day without fever, without fear and worry, ended with a brilliant sunset. Fall had not presented itself, but the storm had broken the worst of the summer heat. Giles built a smoky fire of damp pine needles and twigs to discourage the mosquitoes, and invited Sister Joelle and the children to sit and watch the sun dip below the treetops.

Isabel sat between Giles's knees, Felix cuddled in Sister Joelle's lap, and Rosalie enjoyed her place sandwiched between the adults. The cicadas sang lustily, and when twilight came, bats whirred overhead to search out mosquitoes and moths.

"What's the name of that star, Papa?" Isabel asked.

"That one? That's Venus. Not really a star. It's a planet, like earth."

"It looks like a star. A big one."

"Yes, it does."

"Is the moon a star?"

"It's a moon, Isabel," Rosalie told her, displaying her superior knowledge.

Sister Joelle seemed content to simply gaze at the stars emerging through the twilight, and Giles wondered what she knew about the sky. The Church surely did not teach the nuns that the earth revolved around the sun, not even ninety years after Copernicus.

He had been careful of her, since that brief kiss, and she had relaxed in his company. He was glad of that, but he himself did not feel comfortable. He was too aware of her as a woman for that. He didn't want her to go, and he feared that in the morning, she would decide it was time for her to leave them.

They would miss her, all of them. Such a needy crew they'd become. He supposed his own loneliness infected his children.

Did she really want to return to the fort? What would she do with herself all day? Since the children had been well, she'd been busy helping with the chickens, the cooking, the wash. Best of all, she had told stories to the children, sang songs while she worked, and sat up in the evenings to talk to Giles. About the convent, about the lane below the convent. Her life had been circumscribed, but her mind was curious and eager to know about the world.

What if he asked her to stay? To marry him? She might be offended. But she might not be.

"When did you decide to take your vows, Sister?" he asked.

Isabel and Rosalie continued to discuss the moon while Joelle considered.

"I don't remember. I suppose I've always known I was to be a nun."

Did she realize she had other choices? Was it his place to raise the question? Would it be blasphemy to tempt a woman away from taking her vows?

Who was he to gainsay her decision? He was presuming he knew better than she did. If God called her, of course she must take the vow.

But what if He had not called her? What if she only assumed He had because everyone she knew was a nun?

"Papa, the moon is not a planet, is it?" Rosalie demanded.

"Not a planet. A satellite that goes around a planet, around us."

"See?" she said to Isabel.

"Felix is asleep," Joelle said quietly. "I'll put him to bed."

"And I'll see to these two budding astronomers. Come along, you two, get your faces washed and your nightgowns on."

Once they had the children in their beds, Giles touched Joelle's arm. "Come outside and sit awhile. The fire's still smoky enough to keep the mosquitoes away."

They sat on the stoop, simply listening to the night sounds and gazing at the stars.

"That's the Milky Way," he said and swept his hand to indicate the swath of starry cloud.

"Made of stars?"

"Millions of stars."

"'Where is He who has been born King of the Jews,'" she murmured, "'for we have seen His star in the East and have come to worship Him.'"

He looked down at her pretty face shining in the starlight. "Maybe they saw Venus high in the sky."

She turned to him and smiled, and he gulped. What would she do if he kissed her?

He turned away. She trusted him. That was not a treasure to be squandered.

He should take her back to the fort tomorrow. The children would find it all the harder to lose her the longer she stayed.

"We're getting accustomed to having you here, Sister."

She clasped her hands in her lap. "I must go back."

"What is it you want in this life, Joelle?" He knew he shouldn't turn this into an argument, but . . . "If you wanted to stay -- "

She cut him off. "I can't."

He clamped his jaw shut. He had his answer.

After a while, he said, "Tomorrow, then."

"Yes. Thank you."

Giles inhaled slowly. He took her hand, knowing it was against all propriety, but it was dark, and even if she wouldn't be his, he needed her to understand. "I thank you, Joelle. I don't know how I'd have managed without you."

She did not withdraw her hand, and he held it as they watched the moon rise.

~~~

Joelle woke early, everyone around her still sleeping. She lay quietly, taking in the gray glow coming through the eastern window and the soft sounds of Rosalie's breathing in the bed next to her. Giles put Rosalie into her own bed every night, kissed her forehead, and then tucked Felix and Isabel too. But Rosalie continued to slip into bed with Joelle during the night and snuggle up next to her.

Monsieur Travert lay on the floor where Felix slept with his nose pressed into his father's back. Isabel slept in her little bed, her arms and legs splayed out in perfect ease after a typical day of joyous abandon.

Felix had insisted his turtle be allowed to spend the night in the cabin with them, and she listened to its claws scratching on the floor as it explored.

Since everyone had been well, Joelle had washed and mended all the clothes the family owned, hardly a seam that didn't need reinforcing or a hem that had not torn. She had played barber to Felix and washed Isabel's and Rosalie's hair. She had cleaned the cabin from corner to corner, roof to floor. She had collected eggs and cooked and told stories and sung songs.

She had fallen in love with everyone in this family.

Temptation had been such a small part of Joelle's life, but since she'd been in Louisiana, she had yielded to temptation both times it presented itself. She had eaten the candy. She had kept the red ribbon. And a third time -- she had stayed to nurse the family. Of course they truly needed her nursing, but her heart had beat with quick, hard determination when she realized she could be useful, be needed, be . . . with them.

And now she was tempted to stay, to become part of this family. Monsieur Travert would let her stay. He would marry her, she thought.

Rosalie needed her so that she could remember how to be a child, how to be carefree and at ease. Isabel needed Joelle to laugh with her, to teach her how to be high spirited but not wild. And little Felix, he didn't remember his mother, but he needed Joelle to hold him when he was tired or hurt.

And Monsieur Travert. Giles. Joelle was not so ignorant of men and women that she didn't see his loneliness.

Oh, how seductive to be needed. This was a test of her commitment to God. Of how strong her calling to become a nun was.

Sister Bernadette would say she must resist her weaker self. Put away selfish thoughts. She was not put on this earth to be personally involved with other people, to love individuals or be loved by them. She was to find her joy in serving God, and if occasionally that meant serving particular people, one still must remember that a nun's life is committed to the holy, not the needs of the flesh. But Sister Bernadette did not understand what it felt like to love someone.

Rosalie shifted beside her and opened her eyes.

"Good morning," Joelle whispered.

Rosalie's smile -- how was Joelle to give up seeing that smile of a morning? When would she ever see such joy on another person's face meant just for her.

Rosalie pulled at one of Joelle's curls peeking out from her cap and giggled when it sprang back. Before Monsieur Travert woke, Joelle would have to put her wimple on, but for now, she grinned as Rosalie played with her hair. It was good to see this serious child be silly.

"Papa!" Felix said. "Wake up."

Giles grabbed him and growled, making Felix shriek with laughter. And so Joelle's last day with the family began.

~~~

Over breakfast, Giles reminded the children that Joelle had been here only to visit and help them all get well. It was time for her to go back to the fort.

Rosalie put her spoon down and stared into her lap. Isabel burst into great gulping sobs. And Felix, he stared at Joelle with his big brown eyes.

Giles had an unkind moment when he saw Joelle's eyes fill with tears. Good, he thought, she needed to know how much she was wanted here. What she was giving up to go back to the fort, back to her life as an almost-nun.

Ashamed of himself, he took Isabel into his arms. "Hush, baby. It's not as if you won't see Sister Joelle ever again as long as you live, is it? We can see her every Sunday. We can take her a treat. What do you think we could give her next week?"

"She likes those purple flowers that grow in the water," Isabel snuffled.

"Then we'll take her purple flowers."

Everyone fed and dressed, the chickens and pigs, the turtle and the dogs all seen to, Giles led the way to the dugout. Isabel clung to Joelle as they walked. Rosalie followed behind with her head down. No one was happy about this, including, Giles thought, Joelle herself.

For the fortieth time he asked himself if she would stay if only he pressed her. But that couldn't be right, to push at her when she had chosen her path.

At the dugout, he turned back and looked her in the eye. You could stay, Joelle. She didn't speak, either, but she swallowed hard and ducked her head.

~~~

An hour later, Joelle took a deep breath. They were here.

Giles pulled the dugout ashore and helped her out. Quickly, while the children were still in the boat, Joelle turned a bright smile on him. "Thank you for bringing me back. I'll see you all on Sunday," she said, gave a wave to the children, and strode away.

"Sister Joelle."

She knew she was being rude, but she couldn't bear it if the children cried. She couldn't bear if it he touched her.

She turned around.

The children were ashore now, staring at her.

"We'll come to the chapel with you," he said.

"It isn't necessary, Monsieur Travert."

"I believe it is, Sister. Father Xavier and Sister Bernadette need to know the service you've done us."

At her continued silence, he added, "You can't believe Sister Bernadette won't question your decision to stay with us."

"No. I'm sure she will."

Giles . . . no, she must call him Monsieur Travert even in her own mind. He didn't understand. She was likely to be scolded like a child. She was likely to be confined to the back room again. She did not want him to witness that humiliation.

He was about to insist. "Please," she said. "I need to do this alone."

He waited, then he nodded.

"Sister?" Isabel said.

She couldn't just walk away from them. What an awful idea. She knelt to Isabel. "I hope you won't cry, sweetheart. I would be so sad. You're to come on a Sunday, aren't you? And bring me purple flowers?"

Felix gave her a hug and then stepped over to lean against his father's leg. Rosalie quietly climbed back into the dugout.

Joelle walked back to the boat and stretched out a hand to touch Rosalie's cheek. "I will see you again, Rosalie."

Joelle had to breathe past the tightness in her throat at Rosalie's closed face. She wouldn't cry in front of the children. She would see them again.

Giles's eyes were on her, but she said nothing more. The skirt of her habit brushed his legs as she left them.

At the chapel, she walked through the quiet, dim interior to the back where the bedrooms were. She paused and wiped her hands on her skirt. She was going to be berated, probably punished. No use in postponing the moment. She opened the door.

Sister Bernadette lay on her bed, her feet propped up. As soon as she saw Joelle, she swung her legs to the floor.

"There you are," Sister Bernadette accused.

"Yes, I am back."

"Seven days you've been gone! Seven days spent with a man, in the forest, in the jungle." Sister Bernadette's eyes glared, her nostrils flared. "And then you come back here expecting to be treated with respect, with honor! Indeed not!"

Sister Bernadette huffed past her and rapped on Father Xavier's door.

He opened the door, the Bible in his hand.

"She's here."

"So I see," he said. He looked at her curiously, mildly. "The Travert family is well?"

"Yes, Father. All of them. We were quite worried for Rosalie, the eldest, but the night of the storm, her fever finally broke and did not return."

"We? We! She means her and that man."

"Yes. Monsieur Travert and I. He was very ill himself, Sister, but he recovered first."

"Recovered, you say. See, Father? The man was recovered and still she stayed."

"Monsieur Travert was weak, Father. With three sick children. He needed help."

Father Xavier nodded thoughtfully. "There are still soldiers in the infirmary who -- "

He broke off at Sister Bernadette's scowl.

He cleared his throat. "There is the matter of your disobedience, Sister."

"I told you not to go. Father Xavier told you not to go. And yet you went off with those men to a heathen village. And you did not come back!"

"I decided the Traverts needed me, Sister Bernadette."

"You decided! You don't get to decide anything! You're nothing but a ... a ... novitiate, and a very poor one at that."

Joelle should have been chastened, even frightened, at Sister Bernadette's tirade. Instead, she felt calm. She had done the right thing, she was certain of that.

"Shall I go to the infirmary now?"

"To nurse those men? Absolutely not. They have done well enough without you all these days. You will sit on that bed," Sister Bernadette said, her straight arm pointing at Joelle's cot, "and you will sit there and sit there and sit there until I say otherwise."

Joelle glanced at Father Xavier who preferred to study his shoes.

"Yes, Sister." Joelle stepped over to her bed and sat down, her heels together, her hands in her lap.

They left her alone. Joelle emptied her mind, and she sat and she sat as the hours wore on. What else could she do?

# Chapter Twenty-Eight

*Estranged*

Catherine was exhausted when she and Jean Paul returned home from the village. She had slept very little, helping tend the sick, keeping cook fires going, feeding and nursing and consoling. Jean Paul had helped scour the woods for medicinal plants, chopped firewood, and repaired thatch after the big storm.

The fever had burned itself out among the Biloxis, but someday, it might return, and perhaps more children would succumb. She worried about whether any of the French children along the bayou had died. With a tightness in her chest, she thought of Marie Claude and little Matthew. But Jean Paul had told her Indian people were harder hit than the French, and Marie Claude would be an excellent nurse if Matthew became ill.

She dozed again, and when she woke, she lay abed, feeling lazy. The sun was well up, but there seemed little point in rushing about, tending the garden, patching the patches on their clothing, tending to all the myriad chores that had filled her days. It wouldn't be long before the ship to take them home came in.

There would be nothing to pack, really. Not much more than the clothes on their backs. She eyed the ratty blue silk dress hanging on its peg. She had been wearing it the night she was abducted, drugged, and spirited on board the *New Hope*. She had worn that gown every single day for months! Unbelievable. She, a woman who had had so great a wardrobe that an entire room had been relegated to house it. How many times in a day had she changed her clothing? Easily six changes a day. It was a lot of work to maintain the splendor expected of her.

Still, she would take the ruined dress home with her. Someday when she and Jean Paul were old and gray, she might rediscover it in an old trunk. How they would marvel over it, recalling these months in the wilderness. How unhappy they had been. And then how happy they had become in their cabin along the bayou.

And she would take the good wool cloak Jean Paul had bought her. It was a good cloak. Not fine enough for Paris, but she would not part with it, not when he had given it to her.

Where was he anyway?

She got up and dressed. Outside, no sign of Jean Paul. Débile was here, though, nosing around the woodpile, so he hadn't gone far.

She wandered over to the bird's nest where she had watched babies hatch and grow. When she was back on Grandfather's estate, she would walk in the woods next spring and find another nest to watch.

The first days in this wilderness, Catherine had been sick with longing for home, for Grandfather, for all she had lost. She had gotten over it. Homesickness was a waste of energy. She had work to do, a new life to learn how to live. But now, with home almost within reach, the yearnings had come back. To be truly clean. To sleep in a feather bed on lilac-scented sheets. To dine in company and discuss art and philosophy. To sing to the accompaniment of a string quartet.

Oh, yes, she missed her old life.

Even so, as hard as life was here, she would never regret these months. She gazed over the garden. With her own two hands, she had broken the soil with her hoe, tilled and planted and weeded. Now there were rows of beans and corn and squash and peppers. She had done that.

Not so long ago, she had never even built a fire. She'd thought it would be easy. It wasn't. But she had learned. She knew how to do many things now that she had never dreamed of doing. She was not a good cook, but she could cook. She could chop wood. She could make soap.

No, Catherine was not the same woman who had danced at Versailles and dined with European royalty. She smiled to herself. She liked her new self better than the one who had lived for fashion and gossip and pleasure. She had become a woman worthy of a man like Jean Paul Dupre.

And where was he this morning? She wandered down to the bayou and found him sitting in the dugout, his bare feet in the water. No fishing pole, though. Those days in the village, both of them busy taking care of their friends, he had lost the gloom that had shadowed their days. They'd been good together again.

She picked up her skirts and waded into the water to lean into him, easing between his legs and putting her arms around his neck. "Good morning, husband," she murmured and kissed him.

He put his hands on her waist, but he didn't kiss her back. She looked at him. "What's wrong?"

She caught the hitch in his breath. "What?"

"We have to talk."

"All right," she said. "I like to talk."

That almost got her a smile, but not quite. "I've noticed," he said and pecked her on the end of her nose. "Come on."

He set her back so he could get up and walked her to the cabin, hand in hand.

"You haven't found a buyer for the farm?" she guessed.

He shook his head.

"It doesn't really matter, Jean Paul. The price you get for it won't equal even one of the bank drafts Grandfather sent us."

He sat her down at the table and took the seat on the other side.

"I want you to listen to me."

She set her hands together on top of the table.

"Catherine, you will go back to your grandfather. To your life. I will stay here."

She jerked her hand back and stood up so fast she knocked her stool over.

"What are you talking about? We're going home together."

He shook his head. "I'm staying here."

"No!" She wanted to beat him on the chest with her fists. She wanted to slap him. She wanted to press her lips against his to stop the hateful words. "We are going together."

"You belong with your grandfather."

"I belong with you!"

"Your old life, dances, music, books, luxury -- that's the life you are meant for, Catherine. Not . . . this." He swept his hand to indicate the crude cabin, the farm, the bayou.

"Then we'll have those things together, Jean Paul. You too are meant for music and books and all the things Paris has to offer." She whirled away from him and then turned back with her hands on her hips. "You're being ridiculous."

He shook his head, his eyes on the table top.

"Look at me, Jean Paul," she demanded. "Are you too proud to be the husband of a rich woman, is that what this is about?"

His mouth tightened. He didn't answer her.

"You don't have to be an idle rich socialite, Jean Paul. You can have a farm if that's what you want. You can chop down trees from morning to night if that's what you want." She sat down across from him and leaned toward him. "You can spend your evenings with literary people, other poets. You can share your poems. You could write essays or plays -- You could meet Montesquieu! I know him. You could --"

She sat back from the table. "You aren't even listening."

"That's your world, Catherine. It's not mine." He got up and gathered his musket, powder and shot. "I'm going hunting."

And he left her, fuming, trembling, terrified.

When he returned, Catherine did not ask him if he'd shot anything. She didn't ask him if he were hungry. She didn't trust herself to speak. What would issue from her mouth would be pleading, crying, or angry argument; she didn't know which, but she knew she would not be able to control herself if once she began.

He took his musket apart to clean it, so apparently he had shot at something. He didn't speak to her either.

Catherine left the cabin to fill the water bucket and saw a big cat laid out on the ground. So this was a puma. Its gaping mouth revealed big fangs. Its claws were as long as her finger. With sudden urgency she ran back into the cabin -- he could have been mauled, bitten -- but he sat there calmly wiping the musket down with oil. No bloody shirt, no torn flesh. She turned on her heel and went back to her water bucket.

Jean Paul spent the afternoon skinning the puma and stretching the hide on a frame.

When she passed by with a basket of corn over her arm, he straightened up.

"You've been crying?"

She didn't answer him. It was childish to not speak, but she just couldn't. If she let out the rage and hurt, she'd disgrace herself. Later, maybe tomorrow, she could reason with him.

They went to bed early, having nothing to stay up for, no conversation, no comfort from one another's company. After an hour of silent tension, Jean Paul rolled over and touched her shoulder. She flinched and shifted away from him.

"Catherine," he said softly. "You know I'm right about this."

"You are not," she said and turned her back on him.

The next day, Catherine could hardly stop crying. She avoided Jean Paul. She didn't want his comfort. She couldn't let him tell her again he was right and she was not. A long miserable day ended with headache and heartache, and still they didn't talk.

The third day, she broke their silence.

"We're going to have a good life together, Jean Paul. In France." There. She spoke calmly, reasonably. No tears, no anger.

He set aside the hoe he was sharpening. "You know it won't work, Catherine."

"Of course it will. You're worried that you'll be arrested. You won't. Grandfather will not allow it."

"You assume your grandfather will wish to defend me. Catherine, there is no place in the life of a count's granddaughter for the son of a farmer, even if he was a musketeer. You know that, and your grandfather will know that."

"You're wrong, Jean Paul. Grandfather loves me. And I love you. He'll see that you are given a title and estate so that we may live independently from him. We need not be part of society if that's not what you want."

"It won't work."

"It will work!" She tried, but she couldn't hold it back any longer. She sobbed and reached for him. "Don't leave me, Jean Paul, don't ever leave me."

He held her while she cried, but he remained unmoved. How could he care so little?

He merely reasoned with her, over and over throughout the day. She didn't belong in worn calico. She wasn't meant to have calluses on her hands and feet. She was next thing to a princess and here she was toiling on a hardscrabble little farm in the middle of nowhere. With a nobody, he reminded her.

The next day she raged at him again, and again ended up in tears, Jean Paul resolute and distant, and she was left with Débile's big head resting in her lap, his big sad eyes on her.

Then Sunday morning. "I need more salt," he said. "Are you coming?"

All her breaths the last two days had seemed shallow and strained. They had spoken only to argue. They had not touched. They certainly had not loved each other. And yet that's all she wanted, to be touched, to be loved. For him to tell her he was sorry, he was wrong, he loved her and he would never let her go without him.

Instead, he asked if she was going to the fort.

"Yes. I'll come."

Throughout the mass, sitting next to each other on the bench, Catherine kept her distance so that her elbow did not brush his. When mass was over and everyone filed out, she stepped away so that Jean Paul could not take her arm.

Outside, he said, "We'll talk to the colonel before we go to the store." He didn't try to touch her again, and she walked behind him with her arms crossed at her waist.

Yes, Colonel Blaise said. He still expected the ship in the next week or two. Yes, he was sure Catherine would be taken aboard for the return voyage to France.

"Two passages," Catherine said.

"One," Jean Paul said.

Colonel Blaise raised his brows and looked from Catherine to Jean Paul. It would be unseemly to argue in front of the colonel, so Catherine said nothing more.

"I'll send word when it arrives," the colonel said.

They walked back into the sunshine. Did Jean Paul not understand how he hurt her? After what they had come to mean to each other, he would send her away?

"Why?" she said under her breath, her chest too tight to speak. Perhaps he didn't even hear her.

"Because you are the granddaughter of a count," he said, his voice flat. He had said this and said this. "You will be the wife of a count, or even a prince."

"I'm already married," she hissed at him.

"Your grandfather will annul our marriage."

She didn't want to cry here, in public. She didn't want to cry anymore at all.

"You are impossible." She strode off to join her friends in their usual Sunday gathering under the trees.

She approached Marie Claude and Agnes standing apart from the others with their back to her. When she walked around to greet them, she stopped.

"What's wrong?"

Marie Claude's eyes were red. She'd been crying.

And then Catherine knew.

"Matthew?" she whispered.

Agnes nodded. "The measles."

Catherine gripped Marie Claude's hands. "Oh, God, Marie Claude. I'm so sorry."

"We're going to skip the school today, Catherine," Agnes said. "Will you come walk with us?"

There didn't seem much to say as they walked the length of the island. How do you comfort a woman who's lost a child? And only months after miscarrying another? Maybe the best thing she and Agnes could do for Marie Claude was simply to be with her.

They skirted upwind of the pig sties, reminding Catherine of Suzette, the huge sow Jean Paul had been so fond of before the renegades had slaughtered her.

When they were back in France, she would buy Jean Paul all the pigs he could want. No, she chided herself. That was what he feared. Her buying things for him. He would have his own fortune, and he could raise pigs or cattle or bunny rabbits, whatever he wanted.

Agnes slipped her little hand into Marie Claude's and Catherine remembered how Agnes had once comforted her the same way. Not with words, just her reassuring presence. How could Catherine be thinking of pigs when Marie Claude's world had been shattered once again.

# Chapter Twenty-Nine

## *Life Goes On*

Laroux lay on the bed next to Mahkee, tickling his foot to make him giggle as Fleur smoothed salve over his itchy bumps.

His Fleur smiled. Since Mahkee's fever broke, she smiled all the time. She was happy here with him.

He breathed out a deep sigh of contentment. They were a family now. He would take care of Fleur and Mahkee. He would see she had everything she needed, everything she wanted. Candles, steel needles, thread, cloth, a new pot. Laroux had plenty of cash saved up from selling the dugouts he crafted. He was making a good living, accruing orders for boats faster than he could make them. They would want for nothing.

Fleur put Mahkee to the breast and he suckled like a boy with growing to do. Laroux kissed Fleur on the forehead. "I'm going outside to work."

He picked up the plane he'd made from a hatchet blade and a carved cage of oak. A crude tool, but he'd refined it until it did a decent job smoothing the rough chiseling inside a boat.

After an hour's labor, he ran his hand over the smoothed cypress. Such a beautiful wood, reddish yellow when it was fresh, turning to silvery gray when it was aged. This would be a handsome dugout when he was finished with it.

"I'm ready to go."

He turned to find Fleur with Mahkee asleep on her shoulder, a leather bag over her other shoulder.

"Go?" She had said nothing about leaving the day after the storm, nor the next day nor the next. He had thought that she was here to stay. That she was . . . his, now.

She smiled. "Will you paddle me across the bayou? I'll walk home from there."

"But this is your . . . This can be your home, Fleur. You and Mahkee."

She tilted her head to look at him.

"I've ordered a cradle, a bed, for Mahkee. It'll be ready any day."

He set the plane in the dugout and put his hands on her arms. "There's no need to go, Fleur."

She studied him, her dark eyes bottomless.

He dropped his hands. Of course. She missed her mother, her sisters, her friends. She'd want to see them, to visit, to catch up.

"I'll paddle you up the bayou and we can pull in at the north landing."

When they arrived at the village, all was quiet. Laroux was sure some people had died from the measles, mostly children. They were a tribe in mourning.

Fleur walked swiftly ahead of him, directly to her sister's hut. He waited outside, but Fleur did not emerge. He walked through the village, finding some people at work, grinding meal, cutting venison into strips to dry, but everyone was subdued. No idle chatter, no laughter.

He found Mato with his father the chief sitting in front of a hut. Mato had strips of leather in his lap braiding a rope. Akecheta sat with straight back and closed eyes.

Mato nodded at him and said "Laroux." He gestured for him to sit with them.

"How many?" Laroux asked quietly.

"Three children and a young mother."

Akecheta opened his eyes. "How is my grandson?"

"Mahkee is well, Akecheta. He had the sickness, but he is well."

The old man closed his eyes again.

"The big woman lost her baby," Mato said.

"Marie Claude?"

Mato nodded toward the black man coming out of a hut across the way. "Her man Simon sees a woman here. He said the baby had the measles. And died."

"I'm sorry to hear that." Marie Claude would be devastated. Any mother would be. He and Fleur could stop by and visit her on the way home. Or would that be hard for Marie Claude, to see Mahkee in Fleur's arms? Fleur might know what was best.

"Fever comes to your people as well as mine," Mato said. "Even soldiers can die."

They sat together awhile, listening to the small noises of squirrels chattering and rustling in the trees.

"I am making a dugout," Mato said. "Come. We will work together."

Laroux followed Mato into the woods where he'd felled a cypress and picked up a stone hammer and a steel chisel.

"It will be a good boat," Laroux said after they had worked through the afternoon. "It is smaller than the other boats in the village."

"I have taken a wife. It is for her."

"For her?"

Mato smiled. "My father, my brothers, they laugh at me. But yes, it is for her."

He should make one for Fleur. She could come back here to visit whenever she wanted to. He thought she'd like that, especially if her brother's wife had her own dugout.

Laroux went back to the hut of Fleur's sister, but she wasn't there. He found her in her own hut.

"Are you ready to go home?"

Mahkee slept on his back against the far wall of the hut. Fleur stepped outside.

She looked at him a long time, her eyes unreadable. At last she gestured with her hand to include her hut, the village. "This is my home, Laroux."

Hurt. Disappointed. Even argumentative. Even angry. All these feelings flooded his senses. But she made it clear. His home was not hers.

"You will not come back with me?"

She shook her head. "But I will come to you again."

So she was not his, not yet. *When? When will you come?* he wanted to ask. But he must not rush her. He could wait.

He leant over and kissed her softly on the cheek. "Until you come to me then," he said.

He paddled down the bayou and stopped at Marie Claude's place. She was his friend, and maybe she would be glad of a chance to share her heartbreak.

Unlike the village, this farmstead was full of noisy activity. Two men were splitting and sawing rough planks. Marie Claude and the slave woman were bent over in the garden picking beans.

"Bonjour," he called as he walked into the garden.

Marie Claude straightened and raised a hand in greeting. She made her way down the row and came to him.

She held a hand out to him to shake, but he took her in his arms. "Marie Claude. I'm so sorry."

Her body trembled, but she didn't sob. He let her go when she stepped back.

"You heard then."

"Yes. I've been to the village where Simon was visiting."

She drew in a shuddering breath. "Can you stay for supper?"

He would gladly stay. He did not look forward to his lonely cabin.

They sat on the stoop and talked about the garden. About the dugouts he was building. About the weather.

"Remy have time to make that bed?"

"It's finished. Remy decided it should rock like a cradle, so he rounded the bottom some."

Laroux grinned. "That's a good idea." When Fleur came back to him, the bed would be there for Mahkee. She would understand then that he would take care of her and the baby.

After supper, Remy and Thomas helped him wrestle the heavy bed down to his dugout. He borrowed a length of rope to secure the bed to his dugout, then stepped back on shore. He took Marie Claude into his arms again and squeezed her hard. Then he climbed into his boat and paddled home before dark fell.

~~~

What a kind friend, Marie Claude thought as Laroux paddled into the dusk.

He had hugged her, to comfort her. He had even squeezed her. She had not been hugged since her father and brother told her goodbye, the day she left the farm for Paris. What a dear thing, for Laroux to hug her.

She headed up to the cabin, the fireflies coming out, the cicadas tuning up for their nightly chorus.

She stood inside the cabin, only the fireplace giving off any light. She didn't need a candle lit. It would just attract the moths. She'd once seen her husband catch a moth in his fingers and set it alight in the candle flame. Joubert was a bad man and she was glad he was dead. She didn't even have dreams about killing him, that's how glad she was.

But it was lonely here in the cabin. Edda had already started sleeping with Remy in the half-finished cabin he was building for the two of them. Simon and Thomas slept in the shed. She was the only one alone in the night.

Before the fever came, Matthew had still not slept through the night. He would wake and be hungry, and then the last week or two, he was grown up enough he wanted to play, too. Edda wanted only to go back to sleep after she fed him, but Marie Claude had stayed awake to sing to him and cradle him safely in her arms. She'd shown him the moon and stars, and talked to him about being a grown up boy someday.

Standing in the middle of the darkening cabin, she closed her eyes. She could hear his gurgling laugh, feel his body warm and sleepy in her arms.

Matthew.

She covered her face and great gulping sobs wracked her body. She might never stop crying for him, aching for him, never in her life.

# Chapter Thirty

## *Wildflowers*

Giles and the children arrived too late for mass due to the catastrophic calamity of the morning. Isabel had swept the floor and had a nice pile of sand and leaves ready to scoop up when Felix knocked the bin of corn meal right on top of the dirt. After all the drama and recriminations, after kisses, hugs, and reassurances, they had fed the mess to the pigs, who very much appreciated it.

Climbing out of the dugout at the fort, Isabel said, "I'll carry the flowers."

"No. I will." Felix was still indignant that Isabel had yelled at him for ruining her nicely swept-up pile of dirt.

"We can all carry the flowers," Rosalie decreed.

Giles helped them divide the purple flowers from the bucket where they'd been kept fresh all morning. "All right. Let's see if we can find our Sister Joelle."

The grounds were crowded today. Giles spotted many of the young women who had come over on the same ship Joelle had. There was pretty Emmeline looking happy, her husband at her side. No sign of the wild-haired, disagreeable Harriet -- it amused him to think of her in a canoe in the depths of the American wilderness, happy in her peripatetic life.

"Felix!" Rosalie rushed over and took his wrist. "I told you to stay close," she complained. "See, Papa? He still wanders off."

Because Felix had declared, quite hotly, that he was A Big Boy, Giles had stopped stringing the children together.

"Don't worry, sweetheart. I've got him. Can you find Sister Joelle?"

They didn't see her anywhere. Finally, Giles took the children with their bouquets of purple flags to the chapel where Father Xavier and Sister Bernadette stood talking with people.

"Good morning, Sister, Father," Giles said.

"Good morning, Monsieur Travert," Father Xavier replied. "What lovely flowers, children. Are they for the chapel?"

Isabel shook her head. "They're for Sister Joelle."

Sister Bernadette's spine stiffened and her mouth drew down. Tipping her head to Father Xavier, she said in a low, but quite audible, voice, "You see. As I told you. Entirely too familiar."

Father Xavier looked uncomfortable, but he yielded to Sister Bernadette's scowl. "Sister Joelle is in seclusion, Monsieur Travert."

Giles felt a surge of anger. They were punishing her? As if she were a child?

"She's in seclusion?" the young woman with a blue ribbon in her hair asked. "Whatever for?"

Sister Bernadette turned the scowl on her. "That does not concern you, Seraphina."

This was the pretty girl Giles had noticed back in June, the bold one. Joelle seemed to like her; he'd seen them together several times.

"Never say Sister Joelle has been wicked and must be chained to the wall," she laughed.

"Seraphina, that's enough," Father Xavier said.

"Papa?" Rosalie turned her face up to him, worry lines on her forehead. "Where is she?"

"She is spending her days in contemplation and prayer, child," Father Xavier said.

"But we brought her flowers."

"Perhaps another time." Father Xavier turned to speak to Colonel Blaise when he approached, ending the conversation. Sister Bernadette gave Giles his own personal glare and huffed off toward the picnic area.

Clenching his jaw to keep from cursing, Giles saw himself demanding to see her. Which was ridiculous. He had no right to any such demand.

But the children had looked forward to seeing her. They'd be disappointed. He shook his head. *He* was disappointed.

"Monsieur Travert, isn't it?" Seraphina said. "I'm Seraphina Elliot. I think I know where Sister Joelle is. Shall I take her your beautiful flowers? She'll be so pleased you thought of her."

"We can't see her?" Rosalie said.

"Not today, I think. You must be Rosalie," Seraphina said. "Sister Joelle told me all about you. You," she said looking right at Felix, "must be Isabel, and you," she said looking at Isabel, "must be Felix."

Felix chortled, Isabel grinned. Giles hoped Rosalie would not correct her, missing the fun, but she smiled, too.

Isabel thrust her flowers toward Seraphina. "Tell her they're from us."

Felix and Rosalie handed theirs over, too. "Tell her we miss her," Rosalie said.

"I will do that. Shall I take her your kisses, too?" Seraphina bent down for each child to kiss her cheek. "She'll be so happy you kissed her," she laughed.

Her husband, Monsieur Elliot, who had been waiting quietly, gave Giles a smile that broke into a grin. *That's my Seraphina*, he seemed to be telling him, affection and pride in his eyes.

"Thank you, Madame Elliot. You've saved the day."

Giles watched Seraphina round the chapel and knock on the side door. In a moment, she was inside.

He had to force himself to relax his jaw. It would do no one any good if he ground his teeth to nothing, and Rosalie was looking at him, unease in her eyes. He touched her shoulder to reassure her that her father was not about to turn into a howling beast.

Father Xavier had strolled off with the colonel or Giles would have taken him aside and voiced his objections. In a civil manner, of course. He would simply remind the priest that Sister Joelle had done an important, necessary deed when she stayed to nurse his family. That he was grateful God had seen fit to send her to them. And perhaps, he would suggest, it was unfair to punish a grown woman for acting in charity to people in need.

That sounded very civil to Giles's mind. He would find Father Xavier after lunch and remember to be mild, persuasive, but polite. One did not harangue a priest, after all, and expect to accomplish anything.

~~~

Fully dressed, Joelle sat on the edge of her bed, her mind wandering, when a knock came on the side door. Who on earth could that be? No one ever came to that door but she and Sister Bernadette, and Sister would not knock.

She supposed she should ignore the knock. She wasn't supposed to talk to anyone.

The knock came again. This was ridiculous. She was not imprisoned, after all. Joelle got up and answered the door.

There stood Seraphina, a big smile on her face. "For you!" she said and thrust a bouquet of purple flowers at her. If Joelle hadn't stepped aside, Seraphina would have bowled her over coming in.

Her guest looked around at the bare room, the two neatly made beds, a small shelf with the Bible on it, and two small chests.

"So this is where you live," Seraphina said.

"Seraphina, I am glad to see you, but I am in seclusion."

Seraphina waved her hand. "Yes, I know. Don't you want to know who the flowers are from?"

"They're not from you?"

"No indeed. They are from Monsieur Travert and his three little waifs. Sadder looking children I've never seen."

"Oh, no, were they?"

"They wanted their Sister Joelle. And to tell you the truth, Monsieur Travert looked more than a little disappointed himself."

Joelle felt the heat rise in her face and turned away. "I spent several days with them, when they all had the fever."

"Yes, I know. Everyone knows. Quite scandalous behavior, Sister."

"But they were sick . . ."

Seraphina laughed. "I'm teasing, Joelle. Of course they were sick. But you're stuck back here in this little room just the same. I assume that's why, to punish you for taking care of sick people? No, I can be more precise than that. For taking care of a sick man."

"It's not supposed to be punishment. It's supposed to give me time to think on my transgressions."

"Oh. I see. The transgression of nursing people burning up with fever. Of course."

"Seraphina."

Seraphina held a hand up. "I won't say another word. So what do you think about in here all alone?"

Joelle smiled. "My transgressions."

Seraphina rolled her eyes. "That must take a minute and a half. Then what?"

Joelle nodded toward the window. "There's a bush the birds especially like. Has purple berries all over it. And the squirrels play all day long."

Seraphina plopped down on a bed. Unfortunately it was Sister Bernadette's bed. No matter. Joelle would straighten it afterwards.

"Enough about your sinful life. Would you like to know about married life?" With a wicked gleam in her eye, Seraphina said, "It's wonderful. Better than I dreamed."

Joelle sat on her own bed and smiled. "So you're happy with Monsieur Elliot. The work isn't too hard?"

"Ah well. Work. Yes, it's hard. Takes all day to feed us and keep us clean and keep the garden going and on and on and on. But at the end of the day, we go to bed."

Even Seraphina could blush!

"I know, you're a novice and not supposed to know anything about men and women, but Sister, if making love isn't God's gift, I don't know what is. How can it be anything but perfect when a man's body and a woman's body are made for each other? Did you know that? We fit together, our bodies do, and Joelle, it's glorious."

Joelle swallowed. It hurt to see the joy in Seraphina's face and know she would never feel it.

They sat quietly together, the sounds of the fort coming through the window.

Finally, Seraphina cleared her throat. "I guess I shouldn't ask this again, but I will, because I care about you, Sister Joelle, and I want you to be happy. Are you sure you can give up love, a husband, children? That family out there wants you. They need you. Did you never, in those days you spent with the Traverts, wish for that life? Wish for his touch?"

Joelle threw her hands over her face. "Oh Seraphina, of course I did."

Seraphina left Bernadette's bed and came to sit beside her.

"Sister Bernadette would say I'm the veriest demon, trying to tempt you away from God. But I'm not, Joelle. Truly. I love God, too. I just think . . . I wonder . . . I just want you to be sure this is what you really want. This life. This -- " Seraphina shook her head. "I don't want you to be lonely. And bored. And someday wish you'd made a different choice."

Joelle took Seraphina's hand and squeezed it. "I know you're not a demon," she said with a laugh.

"You are allowed to change your mind, you know," Seraphina said softly. "That's why you serve a novitiate first. So you have time to think."

They sat listening to squirrels fussing at each other outside the window.

"I better go before Sister Bernadette catches me back here. Oh. I almost forgot." She leaned over and gave Joelle three quick pecks on the cheek. "From Rosalie, Isabel, and Felix."

~~~

Giles saw Seraphina emerge from the back of the chapel.

He knew where Joelle was. He knew where Father Xavier and Sister Bernadette were.

He could see Joelle, just for a moment. He would tell her that he would have Father Xavier release her from her confinement. He could at least save her from days of penance, boredom, frustration. How she would hate being shut up and idle.

He caught Seraphina's eye and she sashayed over to them, a brilliant smile on her face. "I delivered the flowers, and the kisses. And you know what? Sister Joelle has sent kisses to you, too!"

She bent over and smacked big kisses on each little cheek, Rosalie smiling sweetly at the gift, Isabel giggling, and Felix looking embarrassed.

"Madame Elliot," Giles began. "I wonder if . . ." He glanced at his children and back to Seraphina.

Seraphina gave him a searching look, the playfulness gone from her face. "Are you sure that's wise?"

She could read his mind, could she? "Only for a moment. I won't go inside."

A moment's consideration, and Seraphina nodded. She turned to Rosalie. "I wonder if you three would join Monsieur Elliot and me for a picnic. I brought mulberry jam I made all by myself."

Isabel, of course, was first to accept. She took Seraphina's hand and without even a look back at her father, said, "Come on, Rosalie. Felix, take Rosalie's hand." Such bossy girls he had.

He watched for a moment as his children went happily off with Monsieur and Madame Elliot. Then he turned toward the door at the side of the chapel.

He knocked, too loudly. Sister Joelle opened the door and stood there gaping at him.

God, he was glad to see her. She looked as though she had not been sleeping well, but she was beautiful just the same.

"Hello," he said.

"I'm in seclusion," she blurted.

"I know, but --"

"I can't talk to you." She looked behind him. "Where are the children?"

"They're with Madame Elliot. Look, Joelle. Sister Joelle. This is most unjust. And all because of my family. I'm going to talk to Father Xavier and put an end to this seclusion. You'll be free to come out and enjoy the day --"

She was shaking her head.

"I'm sure he will come around once I talk to him."

"No, Monsieur Travert. You must not."

He ran his hand through his hair. "Sister Joelle, I can't abide seeing you shut up like this. You don't deserve it, and there's no point in it."

"There is a point to it, Monsieur Travert. I am a novice. Father Xavier is my guide in this life, and he believes I must contemplate my actions. And I am doing that."

"Contemplate your actions. You mean you must come around to his opinion that you have done something wrong."

Her hand was on the door. He stood two feet away, willing her to step out into the sunshine with him.

"Have you decided that?" he asked softly. "Did you do wrong staying with me and my children?"

"No," she whispered. "That was not wrong." She lifted her chin. "But I was willful, Monsieur Travert. That is what I must contemplate."

She looked stubborn with her chin tilted like that. He wanted to take her face in his hands, tell her to leave this place, to come home with him and the children.

Joelle glanced over his shoulder. "It would be better if you were not seen here, Giles. You must go." She stepped back and gently closed the door in his face.

# Chapter Thirty-One

*Merely a Convenience*

Laroux had waited days for Fleur to come to him, his senses alert for every splash of water that might mean a dugout on the bayou, for every sound of the wind that might be Fleur's voice hailing him. But she didn't come.

The cypress crib lay near his own bed, lined with a new mattress of smoked moss. Laroux caught himself staring at it while he ate his breakfast, wishing Mahkee were in it.

When the day was over, he went to bed and felt the emptiness of the cabin as if it were a tangible thing pressing on him. He'd been lonely before, but now that Fleur and Mahkee had been here, slept here, eaten here, been loved here in this cabin -- What was he going to do about this awful loneliness?

And why did Fleur not come?

He tortured himself with every possible reason. She had merely been curious about him, that's why she'd come before, and now she was curious no longer. She had decided she didn't care for him after all. He was too strange. Too needy. Too skinny.

She didn't like living in a cabin, up off the ground.

She didn't like the food he had on hand.

She didn't like it that he was not a great hunter. Nor a great warrior -- he'd gotten himself wounded and nearly killed in that fight with the renegades.

In calmer moments, he rejected all those reasons. Fleur had chosen to come home with him, had chosen to make love with him. He had not seduced her. She cared for him, and she damned sure knew he cared for her.

Throughout another long day of solitude, Laroux chipped and planed the dugout Monsieur Flaubert had ordered. Might finish it by nightfall if he kept at it.

Shaping and smoothing the cypress, his mind continued to go round and round. Why was Fleur not here with him?

She didn't need him as he needed her. He had always known that.

It was just too quiet for her here. Too lonesome. Fleur lived in a close community. She had family and friends around her all the time. She had her chores, her routine, her comforts. Her people.

She might never choose him over the life she led in the village.

The next morning was Sunday. Fleur would likely be at the fort with her family. He could see her and hold Mahkee close, his little arms tight around his neck. He could toss the boy in the air and make him laugh. And maybe Fleur would come home with him.

He tied his own dugout to the one he'd made for Flaubert and paddled across the sound to Fort Louis.

Maybe he expected too much. Why should she come to him when she already had more than he could give her?

Maybe he should let her go. He had work to do, dugouts to sell. The harder he worked, the faster he would earn enough money to go home and resume the life that was meant to be his. He'd regain the old home, marry one of the neighbor girls, start a family. There would be an end to this endless solitude, this gnawing loneliness.

The wind kicked up and made the water slap against the side of his boat, and the second boat continually pulled and dragged. He was glad to finally reach the landing and stretch his back out.

"Laroux!"

He straightened up to greet Flaubert.

Flaubert held out his hand. "Well met. And I see you are a man of your word -- that's my boat?"

"That's her. You want to take her out and give her a trial?"

"Absolutely. You will come with me?"

Laroux looked down the length of the open ground to where the Biloxi congregated.

"I have business," Laroux said and nodded toward the market. Without waiting for Flaubert's response, he crossed the distance, his eyes on the people moving among the trees.

There! There she was! And Mahkee on her hip. He hastened his steps, his chest feeling tight. He wanted to march right up to her and claim her, grab her and Mahkee both in front of her father, brothers, uncles, before everyone.

He did no such thing, of course. Instead, Fleur stepped forward to meet him, her shy smile all the welcome he needed. He breathed in, hugely relieved she was glad to see him.

Mahkee held his arms out for him and shouted, "Roo!"

"Come here, you rascal." Laroux hugged the boy to his chest and inhaled the scent of his hair and skin. How he had missed having this child in his arms.

Laroux blew a noisy kiss against Mahkee's neck and the boy's giggle was the happiest sound he'd ever heard.

He would like to lean over and kiss Fleur, just a gentle hello kind of kiss, but her father, her brothers -- he did not believe such a gesture would be welcome. Instead, he took her hand and squeezed it.

"I have missed you," he said.

"I have missed you, too, Laroux."

"Up!" Mahkee demanded.

Laroux tossed him high in the air, Mahkee's shrieks filling the sky.

"Oh, no!" Fleur said. "He has just eaten!"

And just like that, Mahkee lost all the milk he'd just drunk. Laroux closed his eyes just in time, but the mess hit him full in the face and all down his front.

Fleur covered her mouth, laughing at him. Laroux looked into Mahkee's delighted face and laughed, too.

"Come," Fleur said. "I will wash you off."

At the water's edge, Laroux took off his boots and socks and followed Fleur into the shallows. They knelt together, Mahkee between them, heedless of wet clothes and stares from settlers and soldiers.

Fleur cupped water in her hands and gently washed Laroux's face. He stared at the smile on her face, mesmerized by the gentleness of her hands, stroking his cheeks, his chin, his chest.

"Come home with me," he said.

Fleur's hands stilled on his chest. Her gaze shifted to someone behind him.

Laroux turned to see why her smile had slipped away and there stood her brother Mato, his arms crossed, his jaw hard.

Fleur took Mahkee from him and waded ashore, leaving him with her brother.

Laroux stood in the water and looked his friend in the eye.

"I hear a thing about you, Laroux," Mato said.

"What is this thing?" he said as he stepped ashore.

"You will return to France."

"Yes."

Mato stared at him for the length of a long breath. "When my sister lost her husband, she did not speak for many days. We feared she would lose the child in her belly. We feared the light in her eyes would not come back. We will not have her suffer again."

"I love her. I love the child."

Mato shook his head.

"You doubt me?"

"I have learned a word in your language. *Convenient*. Fleur is merely convenient for you. She will not be your for-now wife."

Laroux clenched his fists. "What does Fleur want?"

Mato's face and body revealed an implacable stance. "My sister wants what all women want. But you do not offer what she needs. She will not come to you again."

Fleur stood twenty yards away, watching them. He held her gaze, asking her, *Is this what you want?*

She dropped her eyes and when Mato strode past her, she followed him.

# Chapter Thirty-Two

*Broken Dreams*

Thomas worked at his forge making nails throughout the day, but he kept an eye on Marie Claude too as she flitted from one chore to another, repairing the chicken coop or skinning a rabbit. It wasn't necessary for her to work the live long day. There were enough of them on the place to do all that needed doing without her exhausting herself, but she wouldn't sit still. He could understand that. If she sat still, grief over Matthew would catch up to her. It was better to keep moving, that's what she'd think.

She wasn't accustomed to being comforted, his Marie Claude, but that's what he longed to do. He wanted to hold her while she cried, hold her while she slept. But that could not be.

So he kept an eye on her whatever she was about. If she faltered, if she found herself overcome, he would be there for her. Meanwhile, he made nails on his small forge.

He pounded out a strip of iron, his mind invariably finding its way back to Matthew. A beautiful child, Matthew was. Full of smiles, his little hands waving in the air, gripping the blue jay feather he'd brought in for him. Thomas had never had a child of his own, never thought he would once he was taken from Martinique, but he'd let himself feel like Matthew was a little bit his. And so he grieved, too, the pressure behind his eyes warning he would be shedding tears in a minute if he didn't get hold of himself.

However much he wished for that little body in his arms, it had to be harder for Marie Claude. He glanced over to where she was laying strips of venison across a frame to dry. She bumped the fragile frame and half a dozen strips fell into the dirt. She stood there, staring at the ground as if she didn't know what to do. He picked up the bucket of water he kept next to the forge and strode over to her.

"We'll just wash them off a little bit, they'll be fine," he said.

He picked them out of the dirt and rinsed them off, handing them to her one at a time to drape over the rack. She moved slowly and deliberately, like a woman dead on her feet, but it wasn't fatigue, he knew that.

"Let's go sit a while down by the bayou," he said. "Maybe we see some of those pink birds you like so much."

She looked at him like she didn't understand a word of that nor much cared to either. He lifted a strand of blond hair falling over her face and tucked it behind her ear.

"I got too much to do," she said and turned away.

He could insist. She had always listened to him before. But maybe it was too soon. She just wasn't ready yet to let herself grieve.

Marie Claude's friend Catherine emerged from the cabin carrying a bucket of wash water. "Let me have that," he said. She was the one used to belong to some kind of royalty back in France, yet here she was, lugging a heavy bucket of dirty water.

Marie Claude had good friends, this lady and Agnes from just up the trail keeping her company. He didn't see that Marie Claude paid them any more mind than she did him though.

"Thank you, Thomas." She looked at Marie Claude striding for the garden. "She's still at it, I see. Working herself to the bone, isn't she?"

"She doesn't know what else to do but work." His gaze followed Marie Claude to the garden where she picked up a hoe and started chopping down dried corn stalks.

~~~

Catherine had always admired Marie Claude from the earliest days of the Atlantic crossing in the *New Hope*. She had never known anyone so kind and calm and capable. It hurt to see her suffering. So much heartbreak in so short a time, but Marie Claude did not yield to it. She kept herself moving from sunrise to sunset, building a chicken coop, grinding corn, cracking nuts.

As they had done months ago when Marie Claude was so badly beaten that she'd miscarried, Agnes and Catherine stayed with her. Their friend didn't need nursing this time, but her loss of Matthew was a grievous blow. She needed her friends.

Agnes lived close by, so every morning Valery walked her to Marie Claude's farmstead and came back for her in the afternoon. Catherine had moved in for now, sleeping in the bed with Marie Claude at night, making herself useful during the day while keeping an eye out that Marie Claude took care of herself.

"I'll do that," Catherine said, reaching for Marie Claude's hoe. "You rest a while."

Marie Claude absent-mindedly handed her the hoe, her thoughts elsewhere. Without speaking, she walked off to find another chore.

Thomas left off what he was doing at his smithy and intercepted her. He said something, she shook her head no. He touched her arm, looking into her face. She shook her head no again. He tilted his head as if to say, well come on then. In a few minutes they were heading for the woods with machetes.

Agnes arrived. "Bonjour. Where's our friend?"

"She's with Thomas. She said something yesterday about rethatching the cabin, so they're probably cutting palmettos."

"She's going to wear herself out."

"I think that's the idea," Catherine said. "As soon as her head hits the pillow, she's asleep." Unlike herself. She lay awake every night stewing over Jean Paul and his obstinacy.

Agnes took up the second hoe.

"Should you be hoeing in your condition?"

"I don't use my belly to wield a hoe, silly."

"I'd feel better if you picked the last of the beans instead."

Agnes straightened up with her hand on her back. "Do you insist?"

Catherine grinned. "I absolutely insist."

Agnes yielded with a smile. "Very well."

Catherine finished up the corn rows and sat in the shade with Agnes to shell the dried beans.

By now, Marie Claude was handing palmetto palms up to Thomas to lay across the high beam.

Agnes gestured toward the pair on the roof. "I don't know that Marie Claude really needs us here. Not like she did after the miscarriage."

"No, she has Thomas now. And Edda. Marie Claude is made of rock, she is," Catherine said.

"She isn't, you know," Agnes said. "Her heart is as big and as kind and soft as any woman's, but she is tough." Agnes ran her thumb down the seam of a pea pod. "Tougher than I am. I don't know how I'd survive that much heartache."

"You would. You'd survive, Agnes. We do what we have to."

Agnes nodded toward Thomas crawling across the roof. "He loves her, I think."

Catherine nodded. "And she loves him."

"Valery says it would be dangerous for them to be together. White men don't like it when a black man takes up with a white woman."

"Who would have to know?"

Agnes shook her head. "People would know. And if there were a baby?"

Hardly anyone found happiness, Catherine thought. Seemed like everyone she knew was lonely. Marie Claude. Laurent Laroux. Giles Travert. Sister Joelle. Only Agnes and her Valery were happy.

Catherine had thought she and Jean Paul would be happy together the rest of their days, but she would never be happy again if he didn't come home with her. And he would be a lonely man without her. He was so stubborn. And stupid.

"You know what he said to me?" Catherine said as if they had been in the middle of a conversation about him.

"Hm," Agnes answered.

"I told him, remember that little theater on Rue d'Artois, the one with the small, intimate performances? We can go there together and then have a late supper. You know what he said?"

"Hm."

"'That's something you can look forward to with your friends.' That's what he said."

Agnes seemed intent on the beans in her lap and didn't answer.

"'You,' he said. Not 'we,'" Catherine added.

"I see," Agnes said.

"And I reminded him how hot it is here, even in autumn. Remember how summertime in Paris was cooled by breezes off the Seine, I said, how you could walk among the wooded parks, enjoy picnics in shady arbors?"

"Did that tempt him?" Agnes asked, her hands busy zipping open a pod.

"He said, 'Picnics attended by three footmen to pour your wine, to slice your ham and peel your apples? That was your life, Catherine, not mine.'

"'It'll be ours, Jean Paul,' I told him. And then you know what he said? 'I want that life for you, Catherine. I want you to enjoy your old life again.'"

"He wants what makes you happy," Agnes said.

Catherine snorted. "Then he rhapsodized about food at this imaginary picnic. 'Foie gras,' he says, 'fresh white bread, soft fragrant cheese. Wine.' As if all I miss from home is a picnic."

To the extent that he made her pine for a glass of wine or a crisp wafer topped with caviar, he succeeded in making her homesick. She had put away all her yearnings for that life, for clean clothes, music, poetry -- but now that it could all be hers again, she *wanted* again.

And she was furious with him for making her want it when he would not want it with her.

It didn't matter. He absolutely would be going back to France with her. She insisted.

Agnes said. "When we're finished with these beans, I'm going to ask Simon to walk me home. Are you going home today?"

Catherine shook her head.

"Oh, my. Catherine, look at you. You could shrivel the leaves on the trees with those eyes."

Catherine's shoulders sagged. All the fight in her drained away. She had been insisting, but he had been resisting just as hard.

"He doesn't listen to me, Agnes."

Agnes's arm came around her. "He won't change his mind? He won't go back to France?"

Catherine gulped, swallowing sobs. "He says he will not."

"Do you want to go home so very much?"

"Of course I do," she said, wiping her eyes. "Grandfather needs me. And, oh Agnes, don't you miss it? The comforts, the ease and pleasures of . . . everything. Art, music, gaiety, dancing . . . cleanliness!"

"I miss reading. Terribly. And the food here is . . . well, sometimes I think if I have to eat one more bowl of mush --"

Catherine managed a laugh. "But there are so many ways to eat it. Mush with possum. Mush with rabbit. Even mush with venison. You're such a fussbudget, Agnes."

"He'll come around, Catherine. You'll see. He won't let you leave him here."

Catherine gripped Agnes's hand. "He will, won't he? He'll come around. He has to."

"But not unless you go home and convince him." Agnes looked at Marie Claude and Thomas on the roof. "We're not really needed here, Catherine. Let Simon walk both of us to my house and Valery will take you home in his dugout."

Catherine nodded and took in a deep breath. She couldn't solve her problems here at Marie Claude's place. She had a job to do at home, persuading Jean Paul he could not live without her.

"Agnes." Catherine hesitated. "I am very rich. I can take you with me. You could go home to France and be my companion. Or if you wanted to, I would set you and Valery up in a bookstore of your own. Do you want to go home?"

"My dear friend." Agnes took her hands. "Valery and I, we have made this bayou our home."

Catherine nodded, her throat working.

Marie Claude's man Simon delivered them to Agnes's homestead where they found her handsome husband whittling one of his cunning little animals. He rose and wrapped an arm around his wife and with his other hand blatantly caressed her rounding tummy. "You did not make yourself tired, *mon chou*?"

"I am tired, Valery, but don't fuss."

"My lady Catherine," he said and bent over her hand. Thousands of miles from Paris, and Agnes's husband still practiced the most gallant manners. Catherine adored it. "Lovely as ever, my dear. Come, sit in the shade. It is autumn, yet we are still blessed with this insistent sun."

They enjoyed cups of spring water while Valery continued to refine the palm-sized alligator made of cypress.

"What is his name?" Agnes asked.

"My little alligator? He is Alvin, of course."

"And is Alvin a friendly alligator?" Catherine asked.

"Alvin is the most charming, courteous alligator in all the bayou. Do you not see the sweet smile he bestows on you?"

"But I see tiny little alligator teeth, too."

"Well, even charming alligators must eat, Catherine." He put aside his knife. "See my lovely wife, nodding where she sits. Come, my dearest, to bed with you."

"But I must go with you when you take Catherine home."

Valery raised his brows and looked at Catherine. Were they in France, it would be most improper for him to take her down the bayou unaccompanied by another woman. But Catherine could not see the sense of that here, not when Agnes needed her rest.

"Agnes, you lie down. Valery and I will be intrepid *voyageurs* down the mighty bayou and when he returns he will regale you with our adventures."

"Just so. To bed with you, darling."

Valery whistled as he paddled them down the bayou. A happy man. Born happy, Catherine thought. Not the same sort of man as her Jean Paul with his broody ways.

"Valery," she said.

"Hm?"

"If you had the chance to go back to France, would you go?"

"No, madam, I would not."

"But we're all so poor here. You work hard. You have no books, no music --"

He feigned indignation. "Have I not just serenaded you, Catherine Dupre? How you insult me."

She laughed. "I apologize most profusely. Your sonata was lovely."

With a gracious bow, he accepted her apology.

"Of course I miss many things," he said. "Wine, for instance." He gave her a wicked grin. "A nice Bordeaux would go well with my possum and mush. Like everyone else here, I'm sure I could list many things I wish for. But they are only things."

"Not just things, Valery. Music, art, conversation. These are not things."

"No, I suppose not."

"But you are happy without them."

"Do you not find the most interesting conversations take place in your own head? Do you not find art in the beauty all around you? No, I tell you, Catherine, I am a man who has found joy in the peace of this place."

Catherine thought about that for a while. "What if Agnes wanted to go home?"

"I don't believe Agnes would leave me here, but you would have to ask her."

"But would you let her go without you?"

"*Ma chère*," Valery said. "Do not put such puzzles into my head. This is a conundrum only you and Jean Paul can solve."

They were quiet until they came within sight of Catherine's own homestead. Valery stilled the dugout in the stream and said her name quietly.

"Catherine, it is not my place to say anything to you, but if you will allow it of our friendship, I would wish to pose you a question."

Catherine smiled at him. "Our friendship will allow it."

"Before this infamous letter arrived from France, were you so unhappy?"

Catherine clutched her hands in her lap and did not answer. Valery paddled on to the landing where Jean Paul stood waiting for her.

A few weeks ago, he would have greeted her with a smile that made his face glow. Not today. Not any day since he'd finally told her he had no intention of going home with her. His face was grim, and he only glanced at her before he greeted Valery.

"Come and sit awhile," Jean Paul said.

"*Non, mon ami.* My Agnes is asleep and will not hear the big bad wolf coming to get her. I must go home."

Catherine stretched up to kiss Valery's cheek. "*Merci,* my friend," she whispered.

She followed Jean Paul back to the cabin. He kept going to the woodpile. She went inside to start supper.

They ate in silence. After supper, Jean Paul sharpened his knife, Catherine watched dusk fall. Later, Jean Paul went to bed, and they still had not spoken since she came home.

She sat up, listening to the rain begin to patter on the roof. She had grown to love the sound of rain on the thatch, the coziness of the cabin lit only by a dying fire. But she took no pleasure in those comforts tonight. She supposed she had come to love this home because she loved Jean Paul.

He was not asleep, she was sure of it. "I want you to come home with me, Jean Paul. Everything will be all right. I promise."

She knew he heard her because his breath stopped for a moment, but he did not speak.

She pressed her fingers to her mouth. What more was there to say?

He didn't love her enough to trust her to protect him. He didn't love her. He couldn't if he meant for her to leave him.

The next day, a couple of soldiers pulled a rowboat into the landing. Jean Paul went down to greet them, but Catherine stayed back, her stomach roiling. What could they want except to tell them the ship had come in.

She would be going back to France.

She would be leaving Jean Paul behind.

It was just as well. He didn't want her here anymore.

She tipped her chin up. She would learn to live without him. When she was back at Versailles, all these months with a man who had no conversation, no graces, who didn't even love her -- they would be like a long-ago dream. She would forget Jean Paul Dupre quick as a finger snap.

She twisted her fingers together. Maybe the soldiers were here for something else. There had been talk of exploring further up the river, looking for an easier way to get to the new settlement named after Catherine's godfather, le duc d'Orléans. Maybe Colonel Blaise was just asking for volunteer explorers.

The soldiers left. Jean Paul stood at water's edge for a few moments, his arms crossed, staring at nothing. Finally he turned and caught her gaze. They stared at each other, the twenty yards between them as broad as an ocean.

He broke their gaze and walked toward her without looking at her again. "You sail on Sunday," he said and walked on by.

Two days passed. Catherine did not cry, or argue, or plead. She felt numb and heavy -- she felt unwanted and unloved. Jean Paul didn't touch her, even in their narrow bed. He didn't talk to her. He didn't do anything but make himself scarce, hunting or trapping or fishing or whatever he could find to do that meant he didn't have to be with her.

She washed all his clothes. She mended and strengthened seams in his shirts and pants. She cleaned the cabin till not a single spider sheltered in the corners.

When all that was done, she walked the homestead. When she arrived last winter, this plot was hard packed and covered with weeds. And now it was a garden. She visited the empty wren's nest. In the spring there would be another clutch of eggs, another three baby birds chirping in the early morning.

If he wanted her to stay, she would. If he asked her to stay, she would.

But he wanted her to go. As if she meant nothing to him.

Their last night together was like their first. Catherine lay pressed against the wall. He lay on the far edge of the bed, his back to her, his arms crossed.

And so their last hours together were to be like this. She couldn't bear it. She put her hand on his shoulder. He didn't flinch as he had the first time she'd touched him in this bed. She moved closer and wrapped her arm around his waist, her nose pressed into his back.

Jean Paul turned over abruptly. He gripped her chin and kissed her like a man starving for the taste of her. He pushed his way into her mouth, pressed his length on top of her, his hands on her breasts, her hips, then on her head, holding her steady as he plundered her mouth.

Catherine wrapped herself around him, her legs clamped around his hips, her hands gripping his long hair.

There was no tenderness in their touch, no sweetness. Only frantic need. He yanked at her nightgown, she arched her back, helping drag it from underneath her. She tore at the string of his underdrawers. Too impatient to pull them down, Jean Paul plunged into her, his hot length pinning her to the bed, his hips pummeling hers.

Catherine met every thrust, digging her nails into his back, mindless with urgent hunger.

Behind her closed eyes, bright flashes of red stunned her. Her battered heart thundered. Her body caught fire, every nerve aflame with yearning and need. "Jean Paul," she cried, her senses dragging her into a swirling maelstrom of deep purple and blue and love and grief.

Jean Paul's body thrust hard, and again, and again, filling her with all that he was, all that he dreamed, all that he had.

He collapsed on top of her, gasping, needing her and wanting her and broken inside that he couldn't have her.

He kissed her one more time, her beloved face cupped in his hands, his mouth gentle on hers, telling her what he couldn't say in words. He loved her. He loved her. He loved her.

He rose from the bed, dressed in the dark, and left the cabin. If he stayed, he might speak. He might beg her to stay. Beg her never to leave him. And that would be wrong.

# Chapter Thirty-Three

*A Proposal*
*September*

Edda slept in the new cabin with Remy now, and Marie Claude found her own cabin an empty, hollow place, like the cavity where her heart used to be. She knew someday the grief would not crush her so, but that someday was long in the future.

She grieved for her unborn baby who died the day she killed its father. She grieved for Matthew whom she'd held in her arms and laughed with and sang to. And she grieved for the future she had envisioned, herself a mother with a dozen youngsters running in and out of this cabin.

Last evening, as she and Thomas sat on her stoop and watched the fireflies come out, she'd nearly said what she'd been thinking. *You could give me a baby, Thomas.*

She blushed even this morning, thinking of it. Brazen. Scandalous. Immodest. She had never thought she could be so shameless. Why would Thomas want to lie with her, a big ugly woman like she was? He was kind to her, that's all. They were friends, that's all. Just because she thought of him in that way didn't mean he thought of her that way.

Besides, for a black man to lie with a white woman, that could cause trouble. It probably wouldn't, they being out in the wilds of Louisiana. Who cared what anybody else did out here? But it could. It wouldn't be fair to Thomas to put him in danger of a beating, or worse.

Marie Claude went about her chores, aware of everyone else on the place busy with theirs. Edda was washing clothes. Simon and Remy were clearing out the bushes from behind the new cabin, and Thomas was down at the bayou fishing for their noon-day meal.

She put her broom aside and walked down to the landing to join him. He nodded toward the second cane pole. "Got worms in that tin cup there."

She baited a hook and tossed her line out over the bayou. Together they sat, quietly companionable, enjoying the birdsong and the breeze blowing up from the Gulf.

"Smell the salt from here," he said.

"Un huh."

They weren't catching anything. They might as well talk.

"I been thinking, Thomas."

He lifted his pole and saw his bait was gone. "Well hell on it. I didn't feel a single nibble."

"We got smart fish in this bayou," she said. "Don't you want to know what I been thinking?"

"What you been thinking?"

She drew a big breath to prepare herself. "I been wondering if you'd marry me."

Thomas's body went very still, but he turned his head and stared into her eyes.

"See, if we were married, we could have babies of our own. We could be a family."

Thomas gently touched her cheek. "There you go again. You forgetting my skin is black."

"No, I'm not forgetting. That's why we have to get married, so nobody, none of those white men, can say nothing to us. Cause we'd be married."

Thomas passed a hand over his face and looked away.

"You aren't saying anything," Marie Claude said.

He breathed deeply and shook his head.

Feeling every drop of her blood heating her face, feeling shame burning holes in her belly, Marie Claude set the fishing pole down and made to get up. "Well, if you don't want to marry me, that's all right. We get along pretty good the way we are."

Thomas grabbed her hand to keep her. "Sit, Marie Claude."

She folded herself back to the ground.

"I don't want you going off from me thinking I don't want you," he said. "I do." He looked her straight in the face. "I do want you."

Now it was her heart that wanted to flip over. She gripped his hand hard and didn't let go.

Thomas looked back at the bobber on his fishing line. "But you're talking from all that hurt inside you. Taking up with me won't make all that grief go away."

"No, it won't do that. But Thomas, if we had a baby, you and me, well, there wouldn't be anything under the sun better than that. We could have a baby."

"It'd be a black baby, you know that?"

Marie Claude smiled. He was coming around.

"That's why we got to get married. So people can't say nothing to us."

Thomas got up and walked a few paces off. After a few moments, he said, "I'm a slave. You keep forgetting that, too, Marie Claude." And he walked away.

Marie Claude rebaited her hook and tossed it out into the bayou. She would sit here awhile and calm herself down. He said he wanted her. He just thought his skin, his being a slave, was enough to stymie them. She didn't believe that. He was hers, at least as far as the law went, and if she said he wasn't a slave, then who was to say he was?

She'd think about it. Now there was a glimmer of hope in her life, she would find a way.

# Chapter Thirty-Four

*A Sunday of Consequence: A Missing Child*

Joelle contemplated carving marks on the rough cabin wall, one for each day of her seclusion. Sunday again, so it had been eight days since Giles knocked on her door. And five days before that, he had brought her back to the fort from his homestead. So it had been thirteen days of seclusion. She might go mad at any moment, but likely, she thought with bitter humor, she could hold it off for two or three more minutes.

At least Sister Bernadette allowed her to attend mass every morning. Father Xavier, bless his heart, seemed to forget about her if she were not right in front of him.

She straightened her habit and wimple and stepped into the chapel. There were already a few people seated on the benches. People who talked, who touched each other! How lonely she had been in that bedroom with only Sister Bernadette for company. Sister Bernadette, Joelle believed, had come to enjoy the scolding and having Joelle all to herself. Thirteen days -- Joelle had long ago ceased to regret having defied her elders during the epidemic.

Joelle sat on the front bench next to Sister Bernadette. She turned around once to see who was coming in, but Sister Bernadette hissed at her and she turned her face back toward the altar.

At the final amen, Joelle heaved a breath, prepared to return to the bedroom for the rest of the day. To compensate for the hours of boredom ahead of her, she indulged herself in another look over her shoulder to see if Giles and the children were here.

There they were, way in the back. Rosalie, standing on the bench, grinned and waved at her, and Joelle felt all the tension in her shoulders release. They were here. They were happy.

Giles was leading the children up the aisle, against the tide of people exiting the chapel. His eyes were on her, happy, intent -- she wanted to go to him, to let him take her hands in his.

Sister Bernadette followed her gaze and whirled to stop Giles where he stood ten feet away.

"Monsieur," she said. "Mass is over. You have no business in this part of the chapel."

"Good Morning, Sister. As a matter of fact, our business is simply to greet our friend Sister Joelle."

"That is not possible. Sister Joelle returns to sequestration at this very moment."

Giles's face darkened. His jaw tightened. "Sister Joelle is not a child to be -- "

She caught his eye and shook her head. *Don't. Don't make a fuss.*

Isabel and Rosalie clung to his hands, Isabel biting her lower lip, Rosalie looking up to her father, a line between her eyes.

"You're punishing her for doing a Christian act of charity," he said. "Where is Father Xavier? Does he approve of this, this isolation you're imposing?"

Felix had slipped around everyone's legs and tugged on Joelle's skirt. "Come with us to the dugout, Sister, and I'll give you this many flowers," he said, his arms held wide.

"More purple flowers?" she said. "I love those purple flowers." She looked at Giles, insisting he listen to her. "I must stay in my room today, Felix, but if you give the flowers to Sister Bernadette, she will bring them to me and we will both enjoy them." *You must leave this to me,* she was telling him.

Joelle leant down and kissed Felix on the forehead. With a little wave, she cast a loving look at Rosalie and Isabel. Then she walked to the back of the chapel and closed the door behind her.

She sat on the edge of her cot and stared out the window. At least she had seen them, all of the Traverts. The measles spots had all faded. How she had missed them these last days, missed their arms around her neck, their fusses that ended in giggles, and their total confidence that between her and their father, they were safe and at ease.

She wondered if Rosalie had mastered the art of cooking over a spit. Had Isabel remembered how to sew on a button as Joelle had shown her? And little Felix, did he still like to sleep with his nose pressed against his father's back?

Those days in the cabin, nursing, worrying, loving -- there had been nothing like it in her life, the connection, the closeness and ... She had trouble putting the feeling into words. She had mattered, she, Joelle, all those days at the cabin.

They all seemed well. Not happy, however. Giles didn't understand that she couldn't be his friend. Joelle had thought for a time that she could be, but Sister Bernadette had made it clear. Nuns did not have friends, not outside the Order.

But what a lonely life it would be without friends. She would have no one but Sister Bernadette.

Ah. That was the problem.

The years growing up in the convent, Sister Bernadette had been in charge of Joelle and the other young women. She had been strict, humorless, impatient at times, but she had not been mean. But if Joelle would have no one but Sister Bernadette, Sister Bernadette would have no one but her. And she feared Joelle would fail her, would never be ready to take her vows, and that would leave Sister Bernadette all alone. Father Xavier, though present, was not interested in either of them. He would not be a companion to a mere nun.

And so Sister Bernadette acted out of fear.

Joelle could see the years stretching into the future. She and Sister Bernadette, in this bedroom, each other's sole companion, day after day, month after month, year after year. Making themselves useful to Father Xavier, to whomever might need them. But alone.

This is what God expected of her? No more than this?

Joelle stripped off her wimple and the under-cap. It was still hot even if it were late September. A few weeks ago, she wouldn't have done such a thing, bare her head even in the privacy of her quarters, but the days of contemplation alone in this room had brought her a newfound sense of her self. She ran her fingers through the damp curls, confident God would have no quarrel with her for it.

Depressed at the vision of a useless, lonely life ahead of her, she lay down on her bed and closed her eyes.

She woke with a start to pounding on the back door.

"Joelle! Open up!" That was Giles's voice. He pounded on the door again. "Joelle!"

The panic in his voice had her rushing to the door and flinging it open. "What is it? What's happened?"

"Is Rosalie with you?"

"No."

"Christ," he said, both hands in his hair. "She's missing. I can't find her anywhere."

"We'll find her, Giles. I promise."

Joelle rushed past him into the sunlight just as Laurent Laroux trotted up. "She's not in the general store," he reported.

"Where are Isabel and Felix?" she asked.

"Marie Claude has them."

"The soldiers are looking over all the construction sites, the saw pit, the log piles," Laroux said. "I'll go back to the landing, see if she's shown up there, if she's in any of the dugouts."

Giles seemed frozen for a moment, lost, terrified.

"She likes the pigs," Joelle reminded him. "Come on." He shook off his fear and grabbed her hand. Together, they hurried down the length of the island to the pig sties.

"Rosalie!" they called over and over. The pig man, Monsieur Porcher, woke from his nap at their cries. No, he hadn't seen any children down here the whole day.

Joelle and Giles continued to the end of the island, calling her name over and over. At the shoreline, a span of water ahead of them where the bay met the gulf, they stopped.

Giles thrashed around in the bushes, frantic to do something even if it was obvious Rosalie could not hide in this sparse vegetation.

He stopped, defeated, and looked up at the sky. "Where could she be?"

"We'll go back the other way. Come on," Joelle said. "We'll find her. We will."

As they approached the other end of the island where the fort lay, they heard cries of *Rosalie* from all directions. Colonel Blaise stood among a knot of soldiers. "The dugouts are all accounted for, sir," one of them reported.

"I looked through every barrack, every shed, every outhouse, Colonel. She's not in the stockade."

"You checked the store?"

"Yes, sir."

"All right. Fan out. I want every inch of shoreline covered. *Bientôt!*"

Giles stopped cold when he heard the last. Joelle took his hand. "She didn't drown. The water is shallow all around here. She didn't drown, Giles."

He squeezed her hand. "No. No, she didn't drown," he said, but his eyes followed the soldiers as they trotted toward the beaches.

"Why do you think she slipped away from you? It isn't like her to be thoughtless like this."

"No." He hesitated, and then he told her. "She wanted to show you her new front tooth."

"Oh." And Joelle had let Sister Bernadette keep them away. She pressed fingers to her lips. She had not done the right thing, after all. The children should have come ahead of Joelle's need to be compliant, to prove she could be the perfect novice. And now Rosalie was missing.

"Let's look behind . . . maybe she's . . . Come on," Joelle said.

She strode, Giles at her side, to the chapel, around the side, and to the back. And there, under the window, between the bush and the wall, was Rosalie.

"Rosalie, sweetheart," Giles said and knelt to her. Her face crumpled up as she cried and reached for her daddy. He enveloped her in his arms and she hid her face in his chest.

"I wanted to show Sister my tooth," she wailed.

"Oh, has your tooth come in?" Joelle said. "Can you let me see it?"

Rosalie wiped her face on Giles's shirt front and opened up for Joelle to see the budding incisor.

"A very fine tooth, Rosalie. You'll soon have one to match it on the other side, I think."

Rosalie nodded, sniffling but satisfied. Giles said nothing more, but settled on the ground with his back against the wall, Rosalie in his lap. The look he gave Joelle was so full of gratitude and relief, she felt swept away. That was love in his face. Was it love she felt, too?

He reached an arm up for her, and Joelle sat beside him on the ground, her hand in Giles's.

He kissed the top of Rosalie's head and they waited her out. When her sniffles turned into quiet breathing, Joelle realized she was asleep.

She grinned at Giles. All the drama and the fear and worry, and the cause of it all slept peacefully.

Laurent Laroux, Fleur at his side, strode around the building, still searching, and discovered the three of them sitting quietly.

"Ah," he said softly. "All is well then. I'm glad, Giles."

He took Fleur's hand and left them to enjoy their hard-won peace. Joelle heard him in the distance calling the search off.

Giles smiled. "Let's just sit here a moment, shall we? I think my heart is worn out."

So still they were that a mockingbird perched nearby and began singing out its pleasure in being alive.

With Rosalie safe in his arms, Giles felt the earth shift back on its axis. He leaned his head back and said a silent prayer of thanks.

For this moment, if only for this moment, he felt peace and happiness welling from deep inside. His beloved child nestled at his heart, and Joelle's hand curled into his.

"I'm glad you are here, with me." He flicked his gaze over Joelle's bare head.

"Oh!" She clapped a hand to her head. "I came out without my wimple!"

He grinned. "And yet the sky has sent no thunderbolts."

"Oh, Giles," she whispered. "If Sister Bernadette sees me . . ."

"Hush. It's only you and me. And in a minute, I'll shove you through this window and no one will know."

She giggled like a girl at the image of herself being bustled, skirts and all, through a window.

"I like to hear you laugh," he said. He brought her hand to his lips. "I've missed you, Joelle."

Her gaze on his mouth, her mind emptied of thought until she merely felt. His hand holding hers was rough, yet gentle. She closed her eyes. Was this what Seraphina meant? Between a man and a woman, there could be this breathless, wondrous connection?

She felt his lips on hers, just a brushing, a hint of a kiss, and he withdrew. She opened her eyes and looked into his.

"What do you want, Joelle?"

# Chapter Thirty-Five

*The Same Sunday: The Parting*

Jean Paul got Catherine to the fort in the early afternoon, plenty of time for her to be ferried out to the ship on a rowboat. The ship would sail on the evening tide, and Catherine would begin the voyage home to France, to her beloved grandfather. She would resume her life as the daughter of a grand comte, the life she was intended for.

Jean Paul could not tell whether his hands trembled without looking at them, for his entire being seemed to quake. He drew deep breaths, trying to hide from Catherine how close he was to breaking.

She got out of the dugout by herself, not waiting for his helping hand, not looking at him.

They'd loved each other last night. A mistake. She might have thought he'd changed his mind. So he'd not returned to their bed, and when she woke, he ignored her smile, answered her curtly when she asked if he were hungry, and avoided her the rest of the morning. He couldn't let her think he needed her. He couldn't let her sacrifice herself for him.

Catherine had packed her basket early this morning. Her comb, the ratty shawl, her ragged blue silk dress she'd arrived in, and the wool cloak he'd bought her in the winter. All her worldly goods. She walked beside him now, clad in the calico dress she and Marie Claude had sewn. On her feet, the leather shoes Jean Paul had made for her out of the boots he'd worn as a musketeer.

Six feet of cold space between them, they walked toward the people gathered under the trees so that Catherine could say goodbye to her friends. She gave him a disdainful look over her shoulder, telling him he was not needed here, so he strode on to the gulf shore and stood there with his hands tucked under his arms.

Valery found him there and quietly kept him company. In the distance, they could see the ship that would sail away on the tide, taking Catherine away from him, toward France and luxury and security.

On a sigh, Valery broke the silence. "You have not in all this time asked me for my advice. I do not understand why people do not do this, my being such a wise man."

"Evidenced by your being stuck in this god-forsaken wilderness?"

Valery stroked his moustache. "Stuck, no. For having found refuge and peace in this god-forsaken wilderness."

Jean Paul swallowed. "There was no need to ask, Valery. She has a chance to go home."

"Hm," Valery said coolly.

"For God's sake, she's next thing to a princess."

"Then you could be the consort of this woman who is next thing to a princess."

Jean Paul shook his head. "Of course I could not. Her grandfather would never allow it. He would annul the marriage and -- I'm a wanted man, Valery. I don't suppose you knew that. All the mighty comte de Villiers would have to do is allow the law to take me. Problem solved."

"And if Catherine were right, that her love would protect you?"

Jean Paul hung his head, a man defeated by class and expectations. "You must see it would never work. I am a farmer's son. A soldier."

"And she is next thing to a princess."

"Exactly."

Valery pursed his lips. "Hm. And she chooses not to stay?"

Jean Paul gave him a look. "I will not allow it. She must go back."

Tapping his lip, Valery mused. "So you have made the decision. Quite right. You are the man, after all, and -- "

Jean Paul whirled on him. "I will not argue this with you, Valery. You don't know her, you don't -- " He dragged his hands over his face. "You don't know her."

Valery indulged himself in one of those insufferably mysterious smirks of his and Jean Paul wanted to hit him.

"I rather think I do, my friend." Valery strolled away, leaving Jean Paul to suffer on his own.

~~~

"So you're really going?" Agnes said. "I don't know whether I'm crying because I'm happy for you or crying because I'm sorry for me."

"I think you're crying because you're pregnant!" Catherine said, trying to keep their farewells lighthearted. It wasn't going to work though.

Marie Claude had Giles Travert's boy in her arms, gently rocking him as he slept against her shoulder. Isabel sat nearby happily making a wreath out of pine needles. Their sister had gone missing, Marie Claude had explained, but all was well now. Rosalie was found, and the gossip going around was divided between speculation about why the child had been looking for Sister Joelle and why Sister Joelle had run through the entire camp bareheaded, those copper curls shining in the sun, Giles Travert's hand grasping hers.

"Are you sure this is what you want, Catherine?" Marie Claude said.

"It's what he wants," Catherine said, her heart feeling like hot lead.

In the weeks since Catherine had told her friends about this, they had listened to her rant about Jean Paul's stubbornness, about how she could make everything good for both of them back in France. They had never quarreled with her, but had only listened.

This time, Marie Claude quarreled. "You really believe that, that this is what he wants?" She shook her head.

Catherine stiffened. "He makes it clear with every breath he draws. He doesn't want me anymore."

Marie Claude stared at her, no expression on her face. She glanced at Agnes, and they shared a silent communication between them.

"You don't understand, either of you," Catherine said. "He insists I go. Alone. He doesn't talk to me unless he's insisting. It's over." How she managed to say the words aloud without falling to her knees she didn't know.

Sister Bernadette rushed up to her. "They're ready to go. They're waiting for you."

Marie Claude wrapped her free arm around Catherine and hugged her. "You still have a choice," she whispered.

Catherine turned to Agnes, who cried noisily on her shoulder. Agnes, who last winter had been so wounded she allowed herself to feel nothing, nothing at all. Valery, bless him, had somehow brought her around to this heart-whole woman unafraid to cry.

"Oh, Catherine, you won't be here when my baby is born," Agnes said between sobs. "I will miss you so much."

"Come now, Madame Dupre," Sister Bernadette insisted. "The tide, you know."

Panic rising, Catherine looked over the grounds. "Where's Jean Paul?"

"Your husband is already down there," Sister Bernadette said and gave Catherine's arm a tug.

So he was that eager for her to be gone, already at the boat, waiting to see the last of her.

Fury rushed back in full force. She could hardly see for the resentment flooding her mind, could not think, could not reason. This mindless anger had grown and grown with every passing day of Jean Paul's indifference. He wanted her gone. She would go.

At the water's edge, a sailor stepped forward to help her into the boat. Jean Paul pushed him aside and lifted her over the gunwale himself. He nearly dropped her and she darted a look at his face, but there was nothing to see there. Nothing at all.

He did not even say goodbye. Did not even look her in the eye. She settled herself on the bench, her basket in her lap. Wasn't this how it had been that first day, when he wouldn't look at her in the dugout on the way to the farmstead, and so she had looked her fill at him?

She stared at him, her jaw clamped tight, her fists clenched.

The biggest sailor shoved them off and then jumped aboard as the others began to row.

Her whole body shook. Rage, that's why. She hated him. He'd betrayed her, that's what he'd done. He had let her think he loved her and then he proved what a liar he was.

There he stood, his arms crossed on his chest, gazing at a spot over her head. For a moment, she feared the rage would desert her and she'd be left --

His shoulders heaved. Just once. Catherine blinked hard and stared at him. What had that been? Had Jean Paul just swallowed back a sob? She squinted her eyes. His cheeks glistened.

A shuddering breath filled her lungs. There he stood. There. God what a fool she was.

She scrambled past the sailor at the oar and tossed herself overboard. The water up to her chin, she started stroking and kicking. The waves pulled at her skirts, but she kicked harder, toward shore, toward Jean Paul.

He was striding into the surf, pushing the water aside to get to her. When he caught her up she wrapped herself around him, trying to breathe and sob at the same time.

She hugged him tight as his breath convulsed against her chest, holding her out of the water, squeezing her so she could hardly breathe. How had she let him convince her he didn't love her? How had she been so stupid?

She cradled his face in her hands and kissed his forehead, then as he let her body slide against his, she could reach his cheeks, his nose, his mouth. His shoulders still shook and he couldn't kiss her back, not for a moment, but when he could draw breath, his mouth took hers in the kiss of her dreams, the kiss she would remember until the day she died. *This kiss*, this kiss that promised a lifetime of being loved and cherished.

# Chapter Thirty-Six

*The Same Sunday: Lesson Learned*

Laroux went to the fort because it was Sunday, because the farmstead was quiet, because he was lonely. He saw Fleur and Mahkee under the trees with the other Biloxi where they had their marketplace. He stayed away.

Since Mato had warned him off, he had felled another cypress and begun yet another dugout. He had cut and carved and smoothed, day after day. He had tended the garden as it finished its season. And he had kept his mind blank. Numb. That was safer. That was easier.

If he let himself think of her, he'd simply curl up and ache. So he pretended that he did not think of her. He pretended he did not yearn to see Mahkee.

Laroux discovered he was not very good at pretense. Against his will, thinking seeped through his numbness, and he wandered through what felt like a heavy fog in his mind.

He was a Frenchman, wasn't he? He was meant to go home, regain the family estate, marry some blue-eyed girl, and live a dreary, over-long, French life. It is what he'd sworn to do.

But to whom had he sworn this? Himself only. His married sisters did not need him. They never expected to see him again. The blue-eyed girl would marry someone else. Who insisted that he return to France?

As he stood with his arms crossed, his back to the Biloxi at their market under the pines, he endeavored to keep his mind blank, but of course that didn't work. Fleur and Mahkee were fifty yards behind him. Did she see him standing here like a mute post?

Laroux's friend Valery clapped a hand on his shoulder. "Come down to the landing and watch our dear friends make fools of themselves."

Relieved to be brought out of the muddled thoughts in his head, Laroux laughed. "Which friends are these?"

"The two who think they can live without each other. The two who are too foolish to sit down and talk to each other. I expect a grand scene."

"You must mean Dupre and his wife."

"The very ones."

"Surely they don't still mean for her to get on that ship by herself," Laroux said.

"We shall see. Ah, a fine gathering. I believe we could sell tickets."

Marie Claude, holding one of Travert's girls by the hand and his boy in her arms, joined them, and Agnes slipped an arm through Valery's. Dupre stood a short distance off, alone, as if an invisible but very strong force encircled him to keep everyone away.

Catherine sat in the boat, stiff and unsmiling. Dupre crossed his arms and watched the sailor push the boat into the shallow surf.

"Valery, what if she doesn't -- ?" Agnes said.

Valery shook his head and patted her hand. "Have faith, *mon chou*."

At that moment, Catherine Dupre leapt out of the boat and into the water. Jean Paul churned into the surf to get to his wife.

"You see?" Valery smiled. "Do I not know all?"

Agnes wiped her eyes on her husband's sleeve, laughing and crying at once.

Laroux turned to Marie Claude. "You were expecting this?"

Her smile made her whole face glow. "We hoped it. We were all but sure." She looked right at him. "As if she would trade life with the man she loves for all the fripperies in France. Aren't folks foolish sometimes?"

He looked at her, and she held his eyes. Finally she raised her eyebrows as if to say, yes, you, Laurent Laroux, and turned away from him.

# Chapter Thirty-Seven

*The Same Momentous Sunday: The Decision*

Joelle stood calmly in the middle of the bedroom floor, her head still uncovered, hardly listening to Sister Bernadette's hysterical condemnation for having been outside, in front of all those people, without her wimple or even her cap.

"Disgrace . . . shame . . . ungodly . . . "

"Sister," Father Xavier began, but Sister Bernadette could not be over-ridden.

Joelle's mind teemed with images of this day, of Giles and the children in the chapel, Felix tugging at her skirt. Of Giles, both hands in his hair, frantic with worry about Rosalie.

He had held her hand as they rushed through the trees, down the island, past the pig sties. He hadn't let go of it until they found Rosalie under this very window.

How tender he'd been as he knelt to his sweet girl. No recriminations, no fussing, just loving reassurance. What a wonderful man he was. And funny, too. The very idea, stuffing her through the window to keep her from being seen bareheaded.

Too late for that. Everyone had seen her running through the grounds without her wimple. Her hand in his. She was well and truly disgraced. Sister Bernadette was right about that.

Somehow, it didn't seem important. Rosalie was what was important.

It seemed clear to Joelle now. There was a difference between doing what the Church expected of a nun and doing what God expected. For surely He would have expected her to help find Rosalie, without delay. How important could her hair be compared to a missing child?

Sister Bernadette didn't know about the kiss, of course. Joelle supposed she would have to reveal it to Father Xavier in confession, but it had not felt wrong.

230

It had felt right. It had made her feel only goodness. She examined her inmost self and could find no tinge of sin in her heart. She could think of no better word for her hand in his, for his lips caressing hers. It felt right.

Father Xavier interrupted the tirade. "Sister, you must calm yourself."

Sister Bernadette threw her hands over her face and burst into tears. "She doesn't even want to be a nun anymore. Can't you see it? She has succumbed to wickedness. He had her by the hand! Didn't you see?"

Joelle was stunned at Sister Bernadette's collapse. She took the older woman by the arm and sat next to her on the cot.

"Sister." She stroked Bernadette's arm. "Sister, I am not wicked. I'm not."

"That's just the way Satan works. You wouldn't know you were wicked!"

Joelle looked to Father Xavier. Surely he knew she was not wicked. He met her eyes and smiled slightly.

"Sister Bernadette, you will rest yourself now. Sister Joelle, you will come with me and we will discuss this wickedness."

Joelle followed Father Xavier out into the sunlight, the breeze through her curls reminding her she had forgotten to put her wimple on. She stopped and clapped a hand to her head.

"Don't fret, Sister. Let us walk down to the beach."

They were silent for a long while, the only sounds the sand squeaking under their shoes and the placid waves washing ashore. Father Xavier walked with his hands behind his back, his head bent. Joelle tipped her face to the sky to feel the sun on her face.

"Sister Bernadette is much attached to you," he said.

"And I to her, Father."

"She fears to lose you, I think. But she will be pleased when the next voyage of the *New Hope* brings more young women. She'll be like a hen with new chicks."

"Yes. I am glad for her. She needs someone to fuss over." They walked a few steps in silence until Joelle blurted what had always troubled her.

"Sister Bernadette worries that my hair is a sign I am likely to sin."

One side of Father Xavier's mouth quirked up. "What do you think, Sister Joelle? Are you likely to sin?"

Joelle took the question seriously. "Yes. But I don't believe I am more susceptible than anyone else."

"Tell me what God says to you, child. Have you sinned?"

"All these days of my seclusion, I have prayed and examined my heart and my conscience. Father, I cannot find God's displeasure with me."

He nodded.

"I feel God abides in me, even now, with my head bared to the sun, and even though -- Father, Giles Travert kissed me."

"Ah."

"And I . . . " How to explain this to him? "And I still feel God within me."

"Ah," he said again.

"I still belong to God. I feel it here," she said and touched her breast. "But Father, when Monsieur Travert held my hand and when he kissed me, I felt such a sense of belonging. To him. Do you know what I mean?"

"I am not without imagination, my dear."

"I believe you were right, that I should sequester myself, Father, for I have had much to think about. Before I left the Traverts', after the measles was over, he asked me what did I want. Such a confusing question. I have never thought to want anything but to be like Sister Bernadette. But I didn't know --"

Joelle breathed deeply. "Monsieur Travert asked me again today. What do I want?"

Father Xavier halted and faced her. "Have you found your answer, Sister?"

He examined her smiling face, gave her a decisive nod, and resumed their walk.

# Chapter Thirty-Eight

## *Old and New Dreams*

As soon as the sun was high enough, Laroux picked up the puppy and paddled to the Biloxis' village. Mato sat with his father the chief. They both looked at him narrowly, but they welcomed him at their fire.

Laroux didn't have the patience to go through all the civilities that preceded any real conversation around a Biloxi fire. He came to the point.

"I wish to marry Fleur and be a father to her son. I will marry her in the French church before God. I will bring three dugouts -- as many as you wish -- and I will marry her again as your people do here in the village. I will never leave her. I will not go to France."

"Only three dugouts?" Mato said, his mouth tipped up on one side. He looked at his father and said again, "Only three dugouts."

"How do we know you will not change your mind and return to your country?" the chief asked.

Laroux smoothed the sleepy puppy's ears before he answered. "Because I say I will not. Because I will marry Fleur in my church, and I will swear before my God: Here will I remain, all my life long."

Father and son looked at each other in silent communication. Laroux had hope. They had not turned him away yet.

Mato's father grimaced. "Three dugouts."

"As many as you wish."

The old man smiled and winked at his son. "Three is sufficient."

Mato shook his head. "Fleur has probably lost interest in you, Laroux. It's been two weeks since you spoke to one another. Likely she has her eye on Cheta now."

Laroux grinned. "I'll ask her, shall I?"

He found her at the stream letting Mahkee splash and chase minnows.

Her face lit for a moment, and then became guarded again. He sat on the bank next to her and watched the puppy splash into the water to play with Mahkee.

"You are here," she said softly.

He nodded. "Your father knows."

Fleur did not look at him when she spoke. "I will not be with a man who will leave me."

Mahkee threw his wet body around Laroux's legs and laughed before he tottered into the shallows again. Laroux let out a long breath, smiling, at ease now.

He got to his feet and pulled Fleur to hers. "I don't know how it is done among your people, Fleur, but this is how it's done in mine."

Holding her hand, he dropped to one knee and looked into her lovely face. "Fleur, will you do me the honor of becoming my wife?"

"Your wife, Laroux?"

"My wife. For as long as we both shall live."

Her hand still in his, Fleur looked at Mahkee shrieking and splashing. She looked off into the trees. Finally, she turned her gaze to him.

"You will not go to France?"

"I will not."

"You will live here with me, in the village?"

"If that's what you want."

A hint of mischief lit her eyes. "You will stay on your knees until I say yes or no?"

"Until you say yes."

She leant over and kissed his lips. "Then I say yes."

The world lit up with white and blue and palest gold; even the shadows seemed to glow. Laroux picked her up and whirled her around in circles.

Mahkee climbed onto the bank and held up his dripping arms for Laroux to whirl him around, too.

He set his boy down to wobble dizzily before he righted himself and splashed back into the stream. With Fleur back in his arms, Laroux pushed a stray lock of hair behind her ear and murmured, "I love you, Fleur. I will be by your side forevermore."

Laroux stayed with Fleur in the little hut that night, loving her, loving the boy. Never in his life had he known this feeling of peace. Heir to a fine estate, he had been a sophisticated Parisian who owned a stable of horses and wore an ostrich plume in his hat, yet in this thatched hut with a dirt floor, in the middle of a humid forest, he was home.

In the morning, he made love to his beloved before Mahkee woke, promising her with his body that he was hers, always and forever. When Mahkee roused, he grinned to find Laroux in his house and climbed over his mother to sit on his chest and giggle as he poked at him.

Such lightness Laroux felt. It had taken him too long to understand this was all a man needed in this world, a family to love and take care of. And he would take care of them. He had money saved, more than he would ever need living as the Biloxi lived. He could buy axes, cooking pots, whatever the tribe needed. He would talk to Mato about it.

Meanwhile, he had three dugouts to work on.

"You promised my father three dugouts?" Fleur said and laughed. "You will have a new name now."

"Why?"

"One dugout would have been very generous," she said. "Three? Hm. We will have to think of a good name for you, my sisters and I."

Mahkee scrambled off Laroux and toddled to his Uncle Mato in the hut's door.

"Come on, Three Boats. Time to get to work."

Fleur burst out laughing. "There is your name. You are now Three Boats."

He grinned at her, his fist gently bumping her chin. "Could be worse."

He joined Mato outside.

"My father Akecheta says you must learn to hunt as we do, which means you must use a bow and arrow. You will practice with mine this morning, but we will go far from the village so your arrows do not end up in someone's dog."

Laroux bit his lip to keep from grinning like a boy. This was going to work. He was going to be a husband and a father, and Mato was going to be his brother.

# Chapter Thirty-Nine

*Gathering Allies*

The week following such an eventful Sunday as her friends' dramatic reunion in the surf, after everyone's favorite, Sister Joelle, disgraced herself running bareheaded hand in hand with Giles Travert, Marie Claude set in motion her own moment of drama to come.

She began with her closest neighbors and friends, Agnes and Valery Villiers. She walked the path alone, scoffing at Thomas's nagging insistence that she needed a man's accompaniment in the woods.

She sat with her friends over the mid-day meal and told them what she wanted. Valery stroked his handsome moustache, as he liked to do when he was thinking. Agnes only beamed. She would not admit to any impediments to a marriage between Marie Claude and Thomas, but Agnes was nothing but smiles, and the occasional bout of tears, now that she was pregnant.

"You will be speaking to your other friends, Marie Claude?" Valery asked. "Because I don't believe that Father Xavier would be much swayed by my humble self alone."

"Valery snores during mass," Agnes whispered loudly.

"I've noticed," Marie Claude said with a grin.

"Elegant snores, I hope?" he said.

"The most elegant I have ever heard," Marie Claude said with a solemn face, but she couldn't help the laugh that followed. She was rather startled at herself. It had been a long time since she laughed.

Valery put a hand on her shoulder and squeezed. "That laugh is a most welcome sound, my friend." He looked at Agnes and nodded. "My lovely wife and I, we will be there at your side. We will see what can be done."

"And I will ask Laroux. I don't believe Father Xavier has any quarrel with him."

"I don't know. Laroux's interest in the Indian girl is well known."

Next she stopped at Catherine and Jean Paul's. As she expected, the two of them were going about the day as if they were joined at the hip. It embarrassed her a little to see them so happy with each other, constantly touching, catching the other's eye and smiling, but she was glad for them, too. They were good people.

"Of course," they both said. They would lend their weight to persuading Father Xavier to marry Marie Claude to Thomas.

"He might surprise us all, you know," Catherine said.

"You mean he might be happy to marry a white woman to a black slave?"

"Ever the optimist, my wife," Jean Paul said. "I expect you're right, Marie Claude. He will be shocked at the idea, but I never heard of any law against it, in the Church or out of it."

The two of them took her to the village where they found Laroux sitting with Mato and Akecheta. Jean Paul joined them, though of course Catherine and Marie Claude could not. They found Fleur and her friends shelling the season's first pecans.

"Oh, let me see if I can do it," Catherine said. She took two pecans from the basket and squeezed them together in her right hand.

Everyone knew how she had been trying to do this since last spring and had simply not been strong enough. They stilled their hands and watched her strain, the tendons in her wrist standing out, her mouth set in a grimace.

"Oh! Oh! I felt one of them crack!" She opened her hand and one of them did indeed have a hairline crack down its length.

"I did it!" she shouted.

Jean Paul and Laroux sauntered up to them. "Look what I did," she called.

She held up one intact pecan and one slightly cracked. Jean Paul leaned over and kissed her on the forehead. "My mighty woman," he said. He sat down with the others and looked to Marie Claude.

"Will you tell Laroux what you need?"

She looked at her friend sitting next to Fleur and explained what she wanted, what she needed from him to make it happen.

"Of course I will speak for you and stand with you, Marie Claude. And I will be asking Father Xavier's favor on my own account, too." He looked at Fleur and took her hand. "We married yesterday, here in the village, but I'm going to marry Fleur in the Christian church as well."

Marie Claude sat back among all the congratulations directed at her friend Laroux. Soon, maybe, she and Thomas would have the same friends celebrating their marriage, too.

The sun was getting low in the sky and Marie Claude headed home to talk to Thomas again. She hoped he wouldn't be mad because she went behind his back to talk to her friends. If he didn't really want to marry her, though, he needed to say so. But if he did want to marry her, then she'd done the right thing.

He was waiting for her at the landing and pulled the dugout ashore.

"You didn't have to worry," she said. "It's not dark yet."

"Near enough," he said.

She started up the path and he said, "Stay a minute."

She walked back to him and the two of them stood side by side, their arms crossed, and stared at the darkening water.

"When they took me from Martinique, I thought my life was over. Not that I was about to die, but that everything I loved was gone. My mother, my sisters, my sweetheart. Because my skin is black."

So he had had a sweetheart. Marie Claude had expected that, a fine looking man like he was.

"Then Monsieur Joubert made it clear he meant to work us to death and it wouldn't take long, either. Hardly seemed worth opening my eyes of a morning.

"But then you came. You made me, you made all of us, feel like human beings again. You took a terrible risk when you challenged your husband over the indigo vats. And he hurt you bad before . . . before he died."

He dropped his arms and turned to her. "You are a brave woman."

She gazed into his beloved face and held her breath. What was he trying to tell her? That he would . . . or that he wouldn't . . . ?

He took her hand in both of his. "If you have the courage to marry me, then I too will find such courage. I will be honored to be your husband, Marie Claude."

She filled her lungs and threw her arms around him. He squeezed her so that her body and his were pressed tight together, his hard chest against her breasts, his thighs warm against hers.

Thomas moved his hands up her back, one settling at her nape, the other in her hair, and kissed her.

Ah. So this was a kiss. Kind and gentle and sweet, his mouth moving over hers. Her hands moved into his hair and she tried to kiss him back, pressing her lips against his.

He reared his head back and smiled at her in the gloaming. "Not so hard. Not yet."

She dropped her arms. "Oh. I guess I don't know how to do this. Nobody ever --"

"You'll learn soon enough." He put her arms back around his neck and showed her again how to begin.

# Chapter Forty

*A Heart's Desire*

Sunday morning, the sky blazed a brilliant blue. There was a hint of crispness to the air, and Giles breathed it in. At last. Fall.

"Papa!" Isabel shouted from down at the landing. "There's a snake down here!"

"Does it have a skinny head?"

"Yes."

"Then stomp your foot and tell it shoo," he called.

Giles settled his brood in the dugout, then pushed off into the stream.

The days since he'd kissed Joelle under the window had been difficult. He thought of her constantly. He wanted her, as a woman, yes, of course. But he wanted her here, at home, in the cabin, at the table, in the garden, with the children. He wanted her to sit with him of an evening and watch the stars come out. To laugh with him when Isabel got up to her hijinks.

She had let him kiss her. He'd given her plenty of time to pull away. She had wanted him to kiss her.

Was she changing her mind about becoming a nun? Maybe not. Probably not. She was simply young, that's why she'd let him kiss her. She was curious. She probably had put herself in and out of hell ever since she accepted that kiss. She was probably tied up tight, wimpled, ashamed, sorry. She might not even look at him today.

She wouldn't be able to turn away from the children though. She loved them, he thought.

They sat through mass, Giles disappointed not to see Sister Joelle's wimple over the heads of the other congregants. He could see Sister Bernadette's stiff head covering, but no sign of Joelle. She'd probably confessed that kiss, that's why she was still sequestered.

241

He knew she didn't want him to interfere, but he'd have to. He'd simply explain that it was not her fault. Entirely his fault, all of it.

Maybe he would have to promise to stay away from her to get her out of that damned bedroom. Perhaps that was best, that he stay away from her. He would try harder next time a ship of potential wives came in. The children would learn to love some other woman.

"Where is she?" Rosalie whispered when services were over and everyone stood to file out.

"There she is," Isabel shouted and pushed through the crowd to get to the back of the chapel where Joelle stood watching them.

She wore a black dress, of course, but not the over-smock. And her glorious curls were bare for anyone to see.

His heart thumped hard, seeing that hair, hoping it meant what he thought it meant.

Isabel threw her arms about Joelle's waist and Joelle bent to hug her. Felix and Rosalie joined them, all three of them talking to her at once. Joelle laughed, trying to touch all of them, to listen to all of them.

By the time Giles reached them, nearly everyone else had left the chapel. He stopped five feet away, just looking at her. He felt as if he couldn't get enough air in his lungs, afraid to hope, unable not to.

"Hello, Monsieur Travert," she said, one arm around Rosalie, the other around Isabel.

"Hello, Sister Joelle," he said, his voice hoarse.

She shook her head. "It's just Joelle now."

The blood roared through his ears for a moment. "Is it?"

They moved outside, both of them stiff and quiet. Marie Claude marched up and announced, "I brought a pot of honey for lunch. You children come on with me."

They ran off with her, Isabel skipping, Felix marching manfully in step with Marie Claude, and Rosalie holding her hand.

"That was kind of Marie Claude," Joelle said.

Yes, it was, but Giles neglected to say that out loud. "Should we walk along the shore?"

Gulls flashed white in the sunshine and made the water glitter when they dove in for a fish. Not so very far off shore, dolphins cut through the low waves. Neither Joelle nor Giles spoke again until they'd walked to the far end of the beach.

By then, Giles had his courage up. He stopped her. He touched her hair.

"Does this mean you will not become a nun?"

She nodded.

He closed his eyes and let out all his breath. Thank God.

"Does that mean --"

She looked at him steadily, her hands in his.

"I am so in love with you," he blurted. He pulled her close and kissed her, not the barely-there kiss of last time. This kiss had all his heart behind it.

She held on to the front of his shirt, breathless, when he broke away.

"Will you marry me, Joelle? Marry me, Joelle."

The smile she gave him lit the last dark lonely corner of his being.

"I will marry you, Giles."

"You're sure? You don't need to convince Father Xavier or Sister Bernadette?"

"I'm sure."

He wrapped her in his arms and just held her. She leaned into him, warm and soft.

He adored this woman. He kissed the top of her head and then moved her back so he could kiss her face, her neck, her mouth.

Giles remembered himself. Joelle was a maiden. He mustn't rush her. He looked her in the eye. "Do you understand, Joelle? What it means to be a wife?"

Her lovely face flushed red. "I know it means more than kissing."

"I don't want you to . . . I want you to want to . . ."

She laughed. "Seraphina says it is wondrous."

Giles let out a breath. "Yes. Yes it is."

"And I will be a mother. Oh, Giles. I want this so much. "

"And so do I." He couldn't stop kissing her and within a few minutes, her mouth moved under his, learning to kiss him back. He had to stop or he'd ravish her right here on the beach. He pulled her in close and tucked her head under his chin while he got his body under control.

He cupped her face in his hands. "I love you, Joelle."

She didn't say the words back, but the tears in her eyes and the brilliant smile on her face were answer enough.

They walked back into the grounds where people were picnicking and visiting, Joelle's arm through his, Giles feeling like he was ten feet tall.

They found their friends near the chapel clustered around Father Xavier. Colonel Blaise stood with them in his characteristic stance with his arms across his chest, and beside him stood Marie Claude and Thomas.

"Papa," Isabel cried and came to him. Rosalie slipped her hand into Joelle's, and Felix sat on the ground playing with roly polys that had curled into little balls to escape his prodding fingers.

"We believe," Jean Paul was saying, "that there is no impediment to this marriage, Father. Thomas is a Catholic as much as I am, or Laroux here. A Catholic may marry another Catholic whatever else is between them."

"But he is her slave," Father Xavier said, a line between his brows.

"I have said he is not," Marie Claude declared. "I have said it to Colonel Blaise."

"Yes, she has, Father. She has asserted it more than once."

"And this makes him free?" Father Xavier asked.

Colonel Blaise shrugged. "We are a long way from magistrates and courts. I am satisfied with Marie Claude's declaration. A piece of paper with my signature on it should do."

Father Xavier turned to Thomas with narrowed eyes. "What makes you think you can take care of this woman as her husband?"

"I will take care of her."

"He is a valued member of this community, Father," Giles said. "I don't know what we would do without a smithy."

Father Xavier stared at the ground, thinking it over. He raised his head and again looked suspiciously at Thomas. "You have been baptized in the Faith?"

"Yes, Father."

"Can you recite your ten commandments?"

"No, Father."

"Neither can I," Marie Claude said.

Father Xavier looked troubled. He shook his head. "A Catholic should know the commandments. Even if not to recite, then at least to know them and affirm them before God."

Joelle stepped forward. "I will teach them, Father Xavier."

He eyed her shrewdly, and then looked beyond her to Giles. Giles merely smiled. He feared it was a smug smile, but he couldn't help it. Joelle was to be his, she was to live her life with him, not with Father Xavier.

The priest looked around at all Marie Claude's friends gathered round her, Catherine and Jean Paul Dupre, Agnes and Valery Villiers, Laurent Laroux and Fleur. Even Colonel Blaise. Giles did not believe the priest would go against all these good Catholics who wanted to see Marie Claude happy.

"Very well. But your bride, Monsieur Laroux. She is not Catholic. She will have to undergo a week of prayer and study with me before I can baptize her."

"I have explained this," Laroux said, looking down into Fleur's face. "She has agreed."

"Prepare for a third ceremony, Father Xavier, if you please." Giles looked into Joelle's smiling face. "Joelle and I will marry as well."

Giles grinned as Dupre and Villiers and Laroux shook his hand. Agnes clapped her hands together. Catherine leaned into her husband and said, "Didn't I tell you?"

~~~

Marie Claude was awash in feeling. All these good friends were here for her, to help see she got what she wanted with Thomas. Her heart thudded, almost sure now that Father Xavier would marry her and Thomas.

If that's what Thomas really wanted. She stepped past Colonel Blaise and tipped her head for Thomas to come talk to her.

"He will marry us, Thomas. Is it truly what you want? I don't want you to feel like you have to. I mean --"

He crossed his arms, his mouth set in a straight line. Oh. He really didn't want to marry her after all. She felt the heat rise in her face. She should have known, a big homely woman like her. He'd just felt sorry for her when he said he would marry her.

"Marie Claude, you will be hurt if you marry me," he said. "People will say ugly things about you. You will be shunned and scorned, and so will our children."

He didn't understand! "No, Thomas. It won't be like that. Some people will shun us, I know that, but they can't say anything -- they can't *do* anything -- because we'll be just as married, before God, as they are."

He studied her, his face impossible to read. She dropped her gaze and looked away. It was as well she had given him this chance to back out of it. "It's all right. You don't have to marry me. We can go on just like we have been. In fact, we can --"

He held his hand up to stop her babbling. "I only want you to be sure, Marie Claude. It will not be easy for you to be married to me."

She squeezed her hands together, joy surging through her. He wasn't saying no. "I am sure. I am so sure, Thomas."

"Then it will be as I told you. I will be proud to be your husband."

All the air seemed to suddenly be scented with cinnamon and vanilla and roses. Marie Claude grinned at him and took his hand, right there in front of everyone. "I'll be proud, too, Thomas."

# Chapter Forty-One

*Three Weddings*

Word traveled up and down the bayou. There were to be three weddings on Sunday, each one stranger than the last.

People were divided about which wedding would be the most scandalous: the white woman and her black slave, the white man and the Indian woman, or the widower and the almost-nun.

"Oh, pah," Seraphina was heard to exclaim. "There's no scandal to any of them. Father Xavier will marry them in the Church and they will all be as married as you or I."

The grounds of the fort were crowded. There were pumpkins for sale in the market, new gourds, nuts, early greens, and sweet potatoes. The recent ship had brought flour and cotton, salt and salt pork, and the day was bright and blessedly cool. A fine day for a trio of weddings.

So many people had come to mass that Father Xavier elected to have it outside under the open sky.

In the little room behind the chapel, Joelle sat on the edge of the bed so Sister Bernadette could comb out her drying curls. There had been tears and recriminations in the last week, accusations of abandoning the very woman who had raised her in the convent, of abandoning God.

Joelle had not been able to make Sister Bernadette understand, but she had brought her to an acceptance. This morning, Sister Bernadette had asked a soldier to bring buckets of warm water into the bedroom for Joelle to bathe and had even helped to wash her hair.

Sister Bernadette answered a knock on the door and Seraphina rushed in. "Today's the day!" She nearly squealed, she was so excited. "I knew it! You and Giles Travert belong together. Anyone can see it."

She whirled back to Sister Bernadette. "Good morning, dear Sister. Isn't this a glorious day?" It was just as well she didn't wait for an answer, for Joelle's glance at Sister Bernadette's down-turned mouth made it clear what Sister Bernadette thought.

"Look what I brought!" Seraphina pulled two shiny green ribbons from her pocket. "Green is the color for red hair, everyone knows that. Sit down again and let me see what I can do."

Seraphina wove the ribbons through Joelle's curls, anchoring them with a few pins. "Don't move. I'll be right back."

"Ribbons again," Sister Bernadette muttered in the moments Seraphina was gone. Joelle touched her hand to her hair, careful not to disturb the ribbon.

"Here," Seraphina said as she came back in with a handful of white wildflowers. "Sit still. It won't take a moment."

When Seraphina was finished, she stepped back to admire her creation of green satin and white flowers among the copper curls. "No mirrors in here, so you'll just have to take my word for it. You look beautiful, Joelle."

And Joelle felt beautiful. "Is it time yet?"

"Oh yes. The bridegrooms are huddled under a pine tree trying not to look impatient. Fleur's Biloxi family and all us girls from the *New Hope* have Fleur and Marie Claude surrounded so the grooms can't get a peek at them.

Sister Bernadette teared up. "Oh, my dear. I hope you're doing the right thing."

Joelle took her hands and kissed her dearest, oldest friend on the cheek. "I am, Sister."

The bayou community gathered around Father Xavier under a brilliant clear sky. Even the soldiers from the fort were mustered off to the side to observe the service.

First to marry were Laurent Laroux and Fleur, her people gathered to one side, Laroux's friends on the other. They knelt to receive the blessing, and when they were pronounced man and wife, Laroux took his bride into his arms and kissed her to loud hoots and whistles from the Frenchmen.

Fleur backed out of the kiss, laughing and blushing, her hand to her lips, and Laroux, his handsome face aglow, laughed. The next moment, he turned to Fleur's auntie and took his son Mahkee into his arms. With his other arm around Fleur, he turned to the crowd, grinning and accepting his friends' congratulations.

Joelle caught Giles's eye on the other side of the clearing where he waited with the children. For that moment, there was only his dear face in all the world, only his gaze holding hers.

As Marie Claude and Thomas came forward, someone jostled Joelle and she became aware of a rumbling in the crowd.

"What kind of slut . . ." she heard. And from someone else, "A jigaboo . . ." "Someone should show him what we do to . . ."

Colonel Blaise stepped forward. "I have a few words to say before the next ceremony." He hardly needed to raise his voice to be heard, his presence commanding everyone's attention.

His steely gaze swept over the crowd. "We are about to see a white woman marry a black man, something we have not seen before. Some of you think this is wrong. Some of you might think you will take action, you will show a black man his place in the world."

His tone grew stern and his gaze hardened. "I am the law in this colony. I will not tolerate violence of any kind against this man and this woman or against their property."

Joelle saw one of the mean-spirited speakers gazing at her shoes. Ashamed, Joelle hoped. Another looked mulish and defiant, but he held his peace.

"We are a new people, in a new world." His tone softened. "We have a chance to build something good here. Let's begin by celebrating Marie Claude's marriage to this man Thomas."

He nodded to Father Xavier, who motioned for the two to come before him.

Catherine and Agnes stood with Marie Claude. Simon, Remy, and Edda stood beside Thomas.

Marie Claude held a bouquet of wildflowers Agnes had gathered for her. She could hardly look at Thomas for fear she would cry. She loved him. She had for a long time, though of course she had not told him, and she thought he cared for her. Had he not walked with her the first time she took the path to Agnes's house and then waited for her in the woods until she was ready to go home? Had he not stitched up her wounds when her husband attacked her and cared for her when she was so badly beaten? Those kindnesses were a kind of love, weren't they?

He stood beside her in his bright white shirt, tall and dignified. He glanced at her and seemed caught for a moment before he turned his gaze back to Father Xavier.

Oh, she had not heard the prayer or the blessing, she realized. She swallowed and resolved to pay attention to every word in this moment. She was marrying Thomas!

When Father Xavier pronounced them man and wife, she turned to Thomas, so happy her breaths came in little pants. Thomas took her by the arms and kissed her sweetly on the forehead.

Valery clapped Thomas on the shoulder. Laroux took Marie Claude in his arms and delivered a smacking great kiss on the mouth. Jean Paul shook Thomas's hand, and Agnes and Catherine both managed to hug her at the same time.

Marie Claude looked at her husband, so serious, honest, and true. He turned to her and in that moment's look, she saw what she hoped for. He loved her.

And she saw what was to come. There would be trouble, now and then, but she would take care no one hurt her Thomas, and together they would take care no one hurt their dark-skinned children. And there would be children, six or ten or even twelve, running in and out of the cabin, laughing and learning and loving.

She closed her eyes and smiled. God was good.

~~~

It was time. Joelle was about to marry Giles Travert, to become a wife and a mother. Butterflies flitted in her chest and her hands trembled. Not because she doubted she had made the right decision. She had God's blessing, she was sure of that.

What had her floating above the ground was the enormity of it. She had never dared to dream of a family of her own. Had never imagined what it might be like to love a man.

Marie Claude thrust her bouquet into Joelle's hands, Seraphina nudged her, and she stepped forward to stand next to Giles. Isabel and Rosalie and Felix stood clustered between them, as much a part of this wedding as she and Giles.

Giles's eyes were on her hair, the green ribbon, the white flowers. He grinned at her, and wonder of wonders, instead of blushing, Joelle grinned back.

As Father Xavier performed the ceremony, Joelle heard Sister Bernadette crying quietly behind her. "Shh," Seraphina was saying to her in a kindly murmur. "It's a happy day, Sister."

Father Xavier pronounced them man and wife. Giles took her face in his hands and kissed her. Isabel held her arms up for Joelle to bend and take her kiss, and then Rosalie and Felix delivered theirs.

Joelle was a married woman. A wife. A mother. She could not feel the ground beneath her feet as her family led her among the well-wishers.

# Chapter Forty-Two

## *Home*

Joelle watched her new husband lift a drowsy Felix from the boat and set him on his feet. Isabel raised her arms. "Spin me," she said, and he gave her a whirl before he set her down. Rosalie reached for him. "Me, too!" Giles whirled her around and gave her a smacking great kiss before he let her go. Then he turned to Joelle.

She bit her lip, the enormity of the moment lifting her as if she were filled with sweet air. This was her husband, holding his hand out to her, his eyes intent on hers. Beyond him, her home. Her children greeting the dogs, running and playing. Her family. Her life.

"Giles," she said, her fingers pressed to her mouth.

He stepped back into the dugout, sat facing her, took her hands and kissed them.

"A little too much?" he asked quietly. She tried to smile, blinking back tears.

"I rushed you, I know," he said. "This isn't the life you expected. You needed more time to get used to the idea."

"No. It's just . . . Giles, I used to look out the window in the convent and watch the wives, the husbands, their children. I didn't realize -- I wanted that life, too. And now . . ."

"And now you have a husband and three children."

She gulped a laugh and felt her face must be beaming sunshine at him. "And now I am a wife, your wife, Giles. And a mother."

"You're not overwhelmed then?"

"Oh yes, absolutely I am."

Giles leaned in and kissed her gently on the cheek.

"Shall I give you a whirl when I lift you out of this dugout, Madame Travert?"

"Yes, please, Monsieur Travert."

He stepped onto the shore, leaned in and lifted her as if she weighed no more than Rosalie. He whirled round once, twice, and then held her close as he set her down.

Wrapped in his arms, Joelle laid her head against his chest. "Thank you, Giles," she murmured.

"For a whirl? Any time, madame."

She tapped his chest. "Thank you for marrying me, for making me part of your family."

He kissed her, open mouthed and fierce. She felt his need and her own began to stir. She felt consumed, and confused.

He broke the kiss and looked into her eyes. "Don't worry, my darling Joelle. I won't rush you in this. Just kisses, maybe more gentle ones for a while, until you are ready."

Joelle gazed into his brown eyes, saw his gentleness, his loving heart. Thank you, God, for this man.

"We better get some supper in our little savages," Giles said.

He had made a rabbit stew in the morning and buried the iron pot among the hot coals. He carefully removed the still-warm coals and brushed away the ashes. The stew was piping hot when he ladled it into five bowls.

Joining hands they said grace, and dinner commenced with all three children trying to talk to Joelle at once. How wonderful, to be needed.

"Did you hear me, Sister Joelle?" Rosalie said.

"You're going to show me where the mulberry tree is. We'll take a basket, shall we?"

"No," Rosalie said sadly. "The mulberries are all gone until next summer."

Giles stretched his arm across the table and took Joelle's hand, smiling as Isabel chattered on.

"What shall the children call you, now you are no longer Sister Joelle?"

"Oh, I had thought . . ." She felt the heat rise in her face. "I mean, I know you remember your real mother, Rosalie, but I thought maybe you would call me maman?"

Rosalie licked her fingers. "All right," she said as if this were a moment of no consequence.

Giles squeezed her hand and again Joelle felt afloat. They didn't understand, the children didn't and maybe Giles either, what this meant to her. She trembled, inside, where it didn't show. On this day, she had been reborn, remade. Finally, on this day, her life had begun.

After supper, Joelle told stories, all three children crowded around her on the steps outside. A Bible story first, and then a made-up story about fire-flies and the secrets they flashed at each other.

"Maman, can you really read the flashes?" Felix asked with a note of skepticism in his voice.

Joelle hugged him. "That was a make-believe story, Felix."

"Magic isn't real, Felix," Rosalie said. "It's just for fun."

"Ah, hear that?" Giles said. "The owls are out. Time for bed."

With a little grumbling from Isabel and a big yawn from Felix, Giles and Joelle put the children to bed, tucking them in against the night's chill and kissing them goodnight.

Giles took the blanket from his own bed and led Joelle back outside.

"Let's watch the stars awhile," he said and wrapped the two of them in the blanket, shoulder to shoulder. They sat quietly, star-gazing and listening to the chorus of the crickets and the chirring of the nighthawk.

"You warm enough?" he asked.

"Hmm." It was hard to relax or to concentrate on the stars with his body touching hers. So unfamiliar, this touching, and so wonderful. He wore a shirt, and she a long-sleeved dress, yet her skin seemed hot and alive where his thigh lay along next to hers, his arm pressed against hers.

"Giles?"

"Hm?"

"Will you kiss me?"

She could see his smile in the star-glimmer. His arm came around her shoulders, his hand cradled her cheek, and he whispered kisses across her mouth, gentle as butterfly wings.

She closed her eyes, and Giles dropped kisses across her face, on her eyes, behind her ear and under her chin.

Giles ran his hand down his bride's back and inhaled her sigh. She liked to be touched, his darling. Mindful of her innocence, he allowed only a little of his hunger into his kisses.

Her breathing became deeper and more rapid. Her arm came around his neck, and Giles felt his heart swell.

They kissed, glorious, mindless kisses until Giles's thumb felt the hard pulsing in Joelle's neck. Her heart raced -- too much, too soon? He didn't want to overwhelm her when there was so much more to teach her.

Slowly he brought them down, calmed their frantic heartbeats, and then pressed Joelle's face to his chest while her breath slowed.

"My precious love," he sighed into her hair.

"I don't know how to be a perfect wife, Giles," she said, her voice muffled in his chest.

"Nor I a perfect husband. We'll have to make do with imperfect happiness and imperfect joy."

Joelle laughed. "Then we are entirely blessed."

"Yes," Giles agreed. "We are blessed."

# ABOUT THE AUTHOR

Gretchen Craig's lush, sweeping tales deliver edgy, compelling characters who test the boundaries of integrity, strength, and love. Told with sensitivity, the novels realistically portray the raw suffering of people in times of great upheaval. Having lived in diverse climates and terrains, Gretchen infuses her novels with a strong sense of place. The best-selling *PLANTATION SERIES* brings to the reader the smell of Louisiana's bayous and of New Orleans' gumbo, but most of all, these novels show the full scope of human suffering and triumph. Visit Gretchen's Amazon Author Page at

**www.amazon.com/author/gretchencraig**

Made in United States
Troutdale, OR
12/12/2023